IN MEMORY OF
PAUL LEE STINE,
18 December 1939–11 October 1969
Husband, 29, English doctoral student, San Francisco State College, Yellow Cab Co taxicab #912 driver, fatally shot at Washington and Cherry Streets, San Francisco, California, Zodiac Victim
Together with David Faraday, Betty Lou Jensen, Darlene Ferrin, Cecelia Shepard and Donna Lass
AND
IN CELEBRATION OF
CLINTON "CLINT" EASTWOOD JR'S
82ND
BIRTHDAY,
31 May 1930
This story, about what might transpire were *DIRTY HARRY* called out of retirement and back into action, is for you!

DISCLAIMER:

All characters appearing in this original creative work are fictitious. Any resemblance to real persons, living or dead, is purely coincidental.

§

ACKNOWLEDGMENT

Inspiration for this work was drawn however from both the exemplary *CHAUNCEY BAILEY PROJECT*, in its dauntlessly courageous exposure of the supremely corrupt Your Black Muslim Bakery, as well as the exhaustive Zodiac books of fellow Pensacolian, *ROBERT GRAYSMITH*— despite the fact that Mr. Graysmith named the wrong suspect as the...*ZODIAC KILLER*

CONTENTS

PROLOGUE:

ZODIAC

IS

BACK!

"THE ZODIAC KILLER IS DEAD!"
the speaker pronounced positively.

HERBST THEATRE
401 Van Ness Avenue
SAN FRANCISCO, CALIFORNIA

§

Directly opposite San Francisco's stately City Hall, the four–story Beaux–Arts War Memorial Veterans Building hovers high and majestically over lively Van Ness Avenue, a noisy north–south thoroughfare constantly astir with restless nocturnal traffic. Greenish lambent light hazily illuminates the lofty archways and fluted columns of the exterior loggia, overlooking the expansive promenade below. Tall, flickering black lanterns throw aslant their greenish light upon the row of shiny brass–lined doorways set at even intervals along the first–floor level. Occupying the first three floors of the building's center is the elegant but intimate Herbst Theater, the historic site where the United Nations Charter was signed onstage in June 1945.

Throughout the theatre's crowded but hushed 916–seat auditorium the speaker's amplified British accent resonated distinctly.

Making that positive pronouncement was the richly successful, best–selling true crime author, Robert Naysmith.

Resolutely rebutting him was the reputable black investigative reporter for the San Francisco Chronicle daily newspaper, Chance Bailey.

"Arthur Leigh Allen—your primed, prime suspect in the Zodiac case—is dead, you mean," Bailey retorted, just as adamant in tone as Naysmith.

"They are indeed one and the same," Naysmith insisted.

"Based on absolutely nothing but some very weak circumstantial coincidences, which are hardly conclusive or convincing as evidence," Bailey answered back again, just as insistent.

These two articulate writers traded their contradictory remarks on the brightly lit theatre stage, where they sat comfortably on Art Deco club chairs, squaring off verbally before a near capacity crowd. Spaced between them sat their lady moderator, noted criminal profiler, Dana Lund.

Behind these three participants, stretching the full length of the stage, was draped a graphic backdrop—depicting the well–recognized, black–hooded figure in executioner's costume, brandishing a sharp glinting bayonet, and displaying in white the infamous crossed–circle symbol—and heralding the special event in great printed letters:

ZODIAC KILLER CONFERENCE:
Robert Naysmith and Chance Bailey, Writers, In Conversation With Criminal Profiler, Dr. Dana Lund

"Recapping your positions, gentlemen," Dr. Lund solicited the two opposing writers, "let's sum up for the audience the chief facts and circumstances indicating whether or not Arthur Leigh Allen actually was, in fact, the Zodiac Killer. First, Mr. Naysmith—"

"Most significant," Naysmith started, "is the fact that Arthur Leigh Allen wore the famous Swiss Zodiac brand wristwatch, displaying the very exact same symbol—the crossed circle—which the Zodiac Killer himself appropriated as the sinister signature he used to sign his taunting letters to the police and press.

"Only in the Zodiac Killer's letters—as with the watch itself—do the Zodiac name and the crossed–circle symbol appear together in the same place!'"

"Mr. Bailey—" Dr. Lund interjected.

"Ah, yes," Bailey scoffed, "that notorious—as well as notoriously expensive—Zodiac Astrographic Automatic, manufactured in Le Locle, Switzerland, by Ariste Calame, a company founded in 1882—the name Zodiac being registered in 1908.

"Manufactured in 1953 was the patented Zodiac Sea Wolf Watch #26894—and later the Super Sea Wolf, boasting a pressure rating of 750 meters.

"Manufactured in 1969 was the Zodiac Clebar Skin-Diver Underwater Chronograph—an aviator and skin-diver's stop watch tested for 20 atmospheres, which is comparable to 660 feet underwater.

"Depending upon whom you believe," Bailey continued, "Allen reputedly owned all three models of the Zodiac watch at different times. Allen himself told police that his sister sent him the Clebar skindiver watch in 1967 and that his mother gave him the Astrographic Automatic on the 4th of August 1969. Allen's own brother, Ron, claimed their mother gave that watch to Arthur Leigh as a Christmas gift two years before in December 1967.

"Whichever the case: how many countless people could purchase and possess a wristwatch of whatever model made and sold by a Swiss company dating back to the late nineteenth century?"

"Mr. Naysmith—" Dr. Lund interjected.

"On September 27, 1969," Robert Naysmith recounted, "the Zodiac Killer, wearing his black hooded executioner's costume, attacked Cecelia Ann Shepard and Bryan Hartnell at Lake Berryessa in Napa Valley, binding and brutally stabbing them both—leaving behind his telltale footprints, size 10-1/2.

"Arthur Leigh Allen's shoe size was of course 10-1/2!"

"Mr. Bailey—"

"Police casts made of those footprints," Chance Bailey elucidated, "showed they were made by a chucker–type boot called the Wing Walker—the uppers of which were manufactured by the Weinbrenner Shoe Company in Merrill Wisconsin; the soles being manufactured by Avon in Avon, Massachusetts.

"Over one million of these shoes were manufactured in 1966 as part of a government contract. In 1969, 103,700 pairs of Wing Walkers were shipped to Ogden, Utah and distributed to Air Force and Navy installations on the West Coast.

"Wing Walker shoes were worn almost exclusively by aircraft maintenance crewmen for walking the wings of jets.

"Such shoes could only be purchased at military base exchanges by active–duty or former active–duty personnel, or their dependents, who were required to present an I.D. card displaying both a photo and thumbprint.

"One million of these shoes were manufactured with well over one hundred thousand being distributed throughout the West Coast alone," Bailey stressed, sneering. "Out of that prodigious number: dare we even speculate how many countless suspects could wear a size 10–1/2 shoe—much less a style of shoe Arthur Leigh Allen has never been shown to wear!"

"Mr. Naysmith—"

"Not one but three reliable informants—all intimately acquainted with Arthur Leigh Allen—have testified as to his direct criminal complicity as the Zodiac Killer," Naysmith asserted, "as admitted to each of them, in turn, by Arthur Leigh Allen himself!"

"Correction: three not–so–reliable–or–credible snitches harboring their own dubious ulterior motives for fingering Arthur Leigh Allen as the Zodiac Killer!" Bailey readily refuted him. "In each case, their so–called testimony amounts to nothing but hearsay, which would no doubt be ruled inadmissible in a court of law."

"Continue, Mr. Naysmith—" prompted Dr. Lund.

"First," Naysmith related, "is Donald Cheney, who was once a regular fishing and hunting companion of Arthur Leigh Allen. In January 1968, according to Cheney, the two had a conversation—couched in the hypothetical context of writing a novel—in which Allen proposed to call himself Zodiac, assuming the Zodiac watch symbol as his own personal symbol.

"Allen conceived that he would stalk and kill people at lovers' lanes, resorting to a weapon with a flashlight attached to it for sighting at night: suggesting that he would write taunting letters to confound and antagonize the police, and sign the letters as the Zodiac, exploiting the Zodiac watch symbol.

"In his letter to the press, dated 7 August 1969, the actual Zodiac Killer alluded to this very device: a flashlight attached to a weapon for sighting victims at night.

"Allen confided to Cheney that he would shoot children disembarking from school buses—as the actual Zodiac Killer threatened to do in his letter to the press, dated 13 October 1969, saying he would 'shoot the little darlings as they came bouncing off the bus.'"

"Mr. Bailey—"

"Donald Cheney broke off his relationship with Arthur Leigh Allen," countered Bailey, "who allegedly became over–friendly with Cheney's daughter and made improper advances towards her—even going so far as touching her inappropriately during a camping trip.

"Conveniently, Cheney put off reporting his allegations against Allen to the police until 1971—some two years after the fourth and last verified Zodiac attack! Out of the obvious animosity and resentment he harbored against Allen, Cheney had plenty of time to concoct this fanciful story to falsely implicate Allen as the Zodiac Killer."

"Mr. Naysmith—"

"Next is Phillip Tucker, another familiar friend and fellow employee of Arthur Leigh Allen," Naysmith related, "who likewise affirmed that Allen discussed shooting with special sights for targeting at night—a special light attached to a gun barrel—and that he spotted the Zodiac symbol at Allen's house as well as some unspecified type of ciphers or cryptograms, which the actual Zodiac Killer sometimes resorted to in writing his taunting letters.

"Tucker also affirmed that Allen discussed the notion of stalking and hunting people for sport, instead of wild game, because they made more cunning prey—again as an idea for a book he intended to write.

"In his first letter to the press, dated 1 August 1969, the actual Zodiac Killer alluded to Man as 'the most dangerous animal of all,' prompting speculation that he was referencing Richard Connell's novella, The Most Dangerous Game, which Arthur Leigh Allen admitted was his favorite book read in high school."

"Mr. Bailey—"

"Phillip Tucker," countered Bailey, "once worked together with Arthur Leigh Allen at the Greater Vallejo Recreation District, which Allen left, once more, allegedly due to inappropriate conduct towards small children—the pretext he used for breaking off his relationship with Allen.

"Tucker made his first allegations against Allen as late as 1969. In 1971 he suffered a most convenient memory loss concerning his accusation that Allen spoke of special sights for shooting at night.

"As late as 1991, Tucker specifically disavowed the book, The Most Dangerous Game, as providing the inspiration for Allen's fantasy concept about hunting people instead of wild game.

"Feeling himself too superior to associate with anyone labeled a sex–deviate, Tucker—in his own words—washed his hands of Arthur Leigh Allen."

"Mr. Naysmith—"

"Then there's Ralph Spinelli," Naysmith related, "whom Arthur Leigh Allen actually confessed in 1969 to being the Zodiac Killer. Allen proclaimed he would carry out a killing in San Francisco to prove he was the Zodiac.

"On 11 October 1969, Paul Lee Stine, a taxicab driver in the City of San Francisco, was indeed shot to death. On 14 October 1969, a letter from the Zodiac Killer took credit for the Stine killing, and contained with it a bloody swatch of Stine's shirt."

"Mr. Bailey—"

"By all means," Bailey snickered, "let's examine close-ly career criminal, Mister Ralph Spinelli: a fifty–year-old, two–time loser, twice convicted of armed robbery, and facing a thirty–year prison sentence with a most con-venient secret to trade with police—in exchange of course for a deal to drop all outstanding charges against him for some nine other stickups committed in San Jose, Califor-nia; either that or a lighter prison sentence.

"Spinelli's startling and stupendous secret: allegedly the true identity of the Zodiac Killer, whom he proclaimed of course was none other than Arthur Leigh Allen!

"Spinelli divulged this supposedly staggering revela-tion in January 1991. Spinelli's association with Arthur Leigh Allen goes way back—at least as far back as 1958 when Allen beat him up in Vallejo, California the first of two times; the second time was after the Stine cabbie kill-ing.

"Spinelli certainly awaited the most opportune mo-ment to start singing that Arthur Leigh Allen's the Zo-diac Killer—just as he was about to be sent up for the long haul! No doubt Spinelli harbored a grudge against

Allen for many years and saw his chance, not only to get even with Allen, but also to get off easy with this bargain–basement bid for leniency. His testimony was rotten fruit from a tainted tree.

"In Arthur Leigh Allen's own words, Spinelli's nothing but a punk and a hood."

"Mr. Naysmith—"

"Most incriminating and damning of all, finally," Naysmith declared, "is the unimpeachable eye–witness testimony by one of only two eye–witnesses who survived an attack by the Zodiac Killer: Michael Mageau.

"On 24 March 1992, at the airport in Los Angeles, California, Mike Mageau was met upon his return from Germany by Vallejo detective, George Bawart, who showed Mageau a blown–up photo spread of six black–and–white driver's license pictures of fat–faced people from 1967 or 1968—roughly the start of the Zodiac killing spree—one of whom was Arthur Leigh Allen.

"Out of that photo lineup, after examining it for about twenty or thirty seconds, Mike Mageau pointed to Arthur Leigh Allen's picture and positively identified him as the man who shot him at Blue Rock Springs Park on July 4th, 1969!"

"Mr. Bailey—"

"Poor Mike Mageau," Bailey sighed, shaking his head. "You have to deeply sympathize and feel sorry for him.

"By his own account of the attack, the Zodiac Killer carried by a handle a large high–powered flashlight when he approached the vehicle Mageau was sitting in to shoot him and Darlene Ferrin multiple times.

"At the time of the shooting all the 19–year–old Mageau could recall of the Zodiac Killer was that he had a large face, which he glimpsed only in profile from a sideways view.

"From the interview he gave Vallejo detective Ed

Rust, Mageau stated the following:

"States he just saw subject's face from the profile, side view, and does not recall seeing a front view. States there was nothing unusual about his face, other than it appeared to be large…He could not recall anything unusual except that he had a large face. Michael reemphasized that he did not really get a good look at subject other than his profile. Also, it was dark out and it was hard to see the subject. Michael states that he could possibly recognize responsible if he had a profile view, as this is the best view he had of the subject.

"Mageau did both alcohol and drugs, and has been medically treated for multiple psychosomatic problems, probably attributable to the psychological scars suffered as a consequence of his horrific encounter with the Zodiac Killer. For a while he was even a street person—the polite politically correct euphemism for a homeless man.

"Twenty–three years after the fact, this drug–addicted gunshot victim, who was wounded multiple times and in excruciating pain, who admittedly and briefly only glimpsed the side–view profile of his assailant—in the dark of night or in the glare of a blinding flashlight—positively identifies said assailant picked out of a photo lineup of extremely dated driver's license pictures!"

"Now I ask you, ladies and gentlemen," Bailey exclaimed incredulously, "how miraculously and incredibly credible an eye–witness is that?"

Abruptly the attending audience erupted into clamorous cheers and applause.

"At the first search of his trailer in Santa Rosa, California in September 1972," Bailey declared, raising his voice above the uproar, "police fingerprinted Arthur Leigh Allen—extensively—and took multiple samples of his handwriting—from both hands in case he was ambidextrous!

"Fingerprint comparisons failed to match Allen's

prints with bloody latent prints found at the scene of cabbie Paul Stine's murder in San Francisco—those believed to belong to the Zodiac Killer.

"Handwriting comparisons failed to match Allen's handwriting to the writing in the Zodiac letters.

"In November 1975, the California state Department of Justice subjected Arthur Leigh Allen not once but twice to a polygraph examination—or lie detector test—which he passed with flying colors both times, and indicated that Allen told the truth when he denied any involvement in the Zodiac killings.

"In October 2002—ten years after Arthur Leigh Allen died of natural causes in August 1992—a DNA comparison of Allen's brain DNA failed to match genetic markers taken from a verified Zodiac letter.

"All put together," Bailey exclaimed emphatically, "a combined total of not one but three police searches, fingerprints, handwriting and DNA comparisons have one and all failed to match Arthur Leigh Allen with any evidence recovered from the Zodiac crimes! There was never any proverbial smoking gun found! Any case against Allen is like a flimsy ball of string—pull on it and it falls completely apart!

"I think it's high past time for Zodiac investigators to home in on a fresh suspect in this celebrated but as yet unsolved mystery!"

Robert Naysmith sat silent and still, looking unexpectedly morose and mortified while the uproarious applause continued unabated.

"Closing comments, gentlemen," Dr. Lund prompted them, holding up her hands to quiet the crowd. "Mr. Naysmith—"

"Another critically incriminating circumstance," Naysmith related, "is the fact that Arthur Leigh Allen was arrested 1 October 1974 by the Sonoma County Sheriff's office for child molestation involving a young boy—a crime for which he was convicted and sent to serve out his sentence at Atascadero State Hospital on 14 March 1975. Allen completed his sentence and left Atascadero on 31 August 1977.

"Breaking a two–and–a–half year silence, the Zodiac Killer previously wrote several of his taunting letters in 1974—the last presumed authentic letter received that year on 7 August 1974. Zodiac waited until 1978 to write next.

"Throughout Allen's entire two–year incarceration at Atascadero, most telling, not a single letter from the Zodiac was received. Nor was any Zodiac–M.O. attack reported."

"Mr. Bailey—"

"Ironic indeed," Bailey conceded, "during 1961–1962, Arthur Leigh Allen, himself a college graduate with a major in elementary education, worked two summers as a psychiatric technician at Atascadero State Hospital where he was subsequently imprisoned.

"I feel very sorry for Arthur Leigh Allen, nevertheless, as he continues to this day to be posthumously tried and convicted—wrongfully and unjustly—in the court of public opinion without the first shred of credible or conclusive evidence.

"As Arthur Leigh Allen put it most poignantly: he was the Zodiac Killer's last victim!'"

"The Zodiac killings are tantamount to sex crimes," the noted criminal profiler moderator, Dr. Dana Lund, declared categorically, interrupting, "during which the killer degrades and dehumanizes his victims into sex–objects—over which he has complete power and control—who cannot escape or spurn him, existing just to give him sexual satisfaction achieved though his murderous acts. Hunting and stalking his prey was his pre–sex. His attacks were his sexual substitute. Zodiac was a sexual sadist, or psychopath, who achieved his sexual satisfaction from tormenting and killing his victims, because killing and sexual pleasure were desperately disordered in his deranged mind. Their pain affords him pleasure.

"Murder is the supreme relationship he can have with a woman. He kills to achieve sexual satisfaction. Killing supplies potent satisfaction and replaces sex.

"Playing cat–and–mouse with the police subsequently becomes the primary motivation for the murders. Baiting and taunting the police becomes part of his substitute satisfaction.

"The irreducible dynamic is the power relationship and the uncontrollable compulsion to be all–powerful and dominant as opposed to the objectified victim. Zodiac feels pleasure by exerting power over his victims.

"A sadistic sociopathic killer like Zodiac targets his victims for the purpose of venting certain deeply rooted sexual and sadistic urges, such as the need to mutilate parts of the victim's body to achieve sexual satisfaction. Though seemingly selected at random, the victims satisfy some psychological or symbolic desire within the killer's system of delusions."

"Where then is this most elusive fugitive serial killer today?" Dr. Lund asked the audience rhetorically. "Is he really dead—as Mr. Naysmith so ardently believes—or has he already been put away someplace, incarcerated in prison or institutionalized in some mental hospital? Has he committed suicide or been killed? Or is he still out there somewhere, laughing, reveling in his infamy, watching and waiting—waiting to write the final postscript as shocking as any of his most atrocious and bloodthirsty crimes?

"Whatever the truth of the matter," Dr. Lund concluded rather dramatically, "this heinous criminal remains still unidentified and still very possibly at–large!"

§

As if in direct response to Dr. Lund's closing statement, the dark figure of a tall, barrel–chested man abruptly got to his feet amongst the audience in a rearward row, his stocky shape momentarily silhouetted against the somber shadows of the rearmost part of the theatre. Hurriedly he lumbered toward the nearest aisle to make his hasty exit as the audience broke out once more into boisterous applause.

At the same time the stage lights grew dim as the house lights brightly irradiated the two–tiered auditorium. Three great ornate chandeliers, suspended high up above, shed their radiant light on Belgian artist Frank Brangwyn's eight magnificent murals, which decorate the facing walls and depict in twin sets of arcade paintings the classical elements of earth, air, fire and water.

On all sides, Brangwyn's animated and colorful canvas inhabitants—fruit pickers, grape dancers, farmworkers, hunters, fishermen, water–bearers, fire–gazers and potters—all looked out indifferently on the crowded spectators bustling noisily below at their inert feet.

None of Brangwyn's resplendent lifelike people could have seen, much less known, that the lone, lumbering man, who so abruptly got up in the rear of the darkened theatre auditorium, was already long since gone and lost to sight.

§

Millennium Tower
301 Mission Street
San Francisco, California

Bounded far off below by Mission, Fremont and Beale Streets and the north end of the Transbay Terminal trans-

21

portation complex, and resembling a lofty translucent crystal, the sleek, luminous, 58–story, blue–gray glass late–modernist highrise condominium soars sky–high above San Francisco's Financial District.

Robert Naysmith carefully unlocked and nudged open the eight–foot–tall Honduran mahogany door to his penthouse apartment, stepping inside the stately entry-way and latching it shut behind him. Underfoot his shoes scuffed the thick solid beech–plank hardwood floor of the otherwise silent foyer. In the faint half–light of night he reached out a hand to touch the overhead light control.

"Don't move, Mr. Naysmith, and don't turn on that light!" rasped the strange voice of some unseen presence from someplace across the living room. "Or you'll be dead!"

Naysmith stopped cold but with a start.

"Who the hell are you?" he demanded with an indig-nant intake of breath. "What the fuck are you doing in my house?"

"I've come to pay you a long overdue visit, Mr. Nay-smith," the stranger drawled, speaking in a low and level monotone, "and to pay my respects."

"What do you want?"

"Just take it easy, there's nothing to worry about. You, Mr. Naysmith, all I want is you."

"Whoever you are," Naysmith snapped, "you have no fucking business being in my house. So get the hell out of here right now!"

Agitated, he stepped slightly forward.

"Stay right where you are, Mr. Naysmith," the strang-er commanded menacingly, "and make no sudden moves! I have a forty–five caliber gun aimed directly at your heart, and I'm an expert shot!"

Naysmith stopped cold again and shuddered.

"Aren't you afraid of the noise it would make if it went

off?"

"It has a silencer," the stranger answered stoically, "so nobody would hear it. Or you getting shot with it."

"Who are you?" Naysmith insisted impatiently. "What do you want?"

Naysmith stood still, squinting and peering intently into the shadowed room, but the taciturn stranger stayed momentarily silent.

Dim lamplight suddenly shone from across the room, illuminating an indistinct but darksome figure quietly reclined in the mocha crème limestone window–seat.

Seated in that window–seat was a dark–garbed figure, wielding calmly a .45–caliber handgun. His hulking shape was outlined in silhouette against the striking cityscape of San Francisco, showing through the floor–to–ceiling UV–coated window rising behind him.

San Francisco's 850–foot Transamerica Pyramid—the city's tallest iconic skyscraper—towers above all others; its angular crushed quartz facade glistens amidst the darksome night's twinkling starlight; atop its tapering and pointed spire brightly shines its beaming light. From afar, sprawled across the shimmering skyline of San Francisco Bay, the twin vermilion towers of the outstretched span of the 746–foot Golden Gate Bridge sparkle.

Looking like some fearsome executioner right out of the Middle Ages, this intruder wore a ceremonial midnight–black hood, stitched perfectly square on top, its four corners like an upside–down paper sack. Draped over his stocky shoulders, the sleeveless hood's front and back flaps reached almost to the waist of his blueblack nylon parka–style windbreaker.

Emblazoned across his chest was stitched–in–white that distinctive three–inch square cross superimposed upon a circle—its tips protruding past its ring. Into the cloth were cut slits for the eyes and mouth over which he wore a pair of clip–on sunglasses.

At his left waist hung a foot–long, bayonet–type knife sheathed in a scabbard with brass rivets. At his right waist hung a black, open–flapped holster. His comfortably crossed legs showed baggy, pleated slacks tucked into half–boots.

In his right hand the intruder brandished a blue–steel single–action, semi–automatic, magazine–fed, recoil–operated, .45–caliber M1911 handgun with silencer!

"There," the stranger said accommodatingly. "Is that better? Don't you know me, Mr. Naysmith?"

"What kind of freak are you to pull a stunt like this?"

"Who do you see? Don't you recognize me?"

"All I see is some pervert of an intruder—dressed up in some scarecrow costume, holding me at gunpoint in my own home!"

"Of all people, I thought you would especially enjoy having some quality face–time to spend with me."

"I don't know you!" Naysmith exclaimed shakily. "You're a fucking freak! And I don't associate with freaks!"

"For someone who has no use for freaks, you certainly have a peculiar penchant for writing quite a number of books about them," the stranger challenged him, gesturing slightly to the room's sumptuous surroundings. "And about me. You've made quite a killing—in a manner of speaking—capitalizing on my name and my fame. I'm an avid reader of all your books about me."

"Wearing that playact costume makes you think you're the Zodiac killer?" Naysmith asked in mock defiance.

"This is the Zodiac speaking."

Naysmith winced at the stranger's ominous tone of voice.

"If you've really read my books," Naysmith disputed, "then you'd know the Zodiac killer was never known to use a gun silencer."

"I've upgraded," the stranger said sedately.

"You're obviously a fake copycat imposter if anything," Naysmith scoffed. "You're not even a decent imitator. You're just a phony pretender. So why don't you go play–pretend someplace else."

"I haven't come here to pretend at anything."

"What have you come for?"

"Who I've come for is the question. I've come for you, Mr. Naysmith, I've come for you."

"What do you think you want with me?"

"I've come to protest! And to express my deep contempt for all the lies you've written about me so spuriously."

"What lies?" Naysmith asked, incredulous.

"Those are far too numerous to mention," the stranger said serenely. "But the most intolerable lie is the most unforgivable and unpardonable one."

"And that is?"

"That I am dead, of course! As you can see, I am very much alive and well. And I intend to prove it to everybody."

"You're speaking in riddles. I don't believe you're the Zodiac killer. And nobody else would either unless you publicly confessed, and could prove who you claim to be. That's the only way anybody would believe it."

"Killer is such a distasteful label," said the stranger with marked nonchalance. "But I believe I have a better and more practical way to prove to the world at large that I am the Zodiac—and that I have indeed returned."

"And just how would you propose to do that?"

"To begin with," the stranger said forebodingly, "by your death."

"My death wouldn't prove you're the Zodiac!" Naysmith exclaimed, taken aback.

"The mode of your death would. My modus operandi would validate me."

"You can't simply be killed," the stranger added emphatically, "you must be sacrificed."

Leisurely the stranger exposed to view a looped coil of white hollow—core plastic clothesline.

"Time's running short. Now the time has come for you to accept the reality," the stranger said threateningly, "that resistance is futile and resignation final: that terrifying moment for every murder victim who knows he is about to die—that you must choose to fight or flee, knowing that whatever you decide, dying is inescapable. You know it's about time for you to die. You know you're going to die. You know I'm going to kill you.

"Are you prepared to capitulate, Mr. Naysmith? It's time...for you to surrender to your fate."

§

"San Francisco Police Department," the non—emergency dispatcher neutrally answered the incoming caller.

"I want to report a murder," drawled the caller's voice in a low and level monotone. "Go to the penthouse suite of Robert Naysmith at the Millennium Tower highrise condominium, where you will find the resident dead of multiple mortal wounds."

"What is your name and number, sir?" asked the dispatcher.

"This is the Zodiac speaking," rasped the caller tauntingly. "I'm the one who did it. Goodbye."

And without another word the caller hung up.

§

Two tall, stalwart uniformed police patrolmen stood

on watch on either side of the wide open entryway to Robert Naysmith's penthouse suite, which was by now an active police crime scene. Alert as they were, the two patrolmen kept their composure, staying silent and still with the unhurried approach of a pair of almost identical looking plainclothes detectives.

Sporting dark suits and fedoras, the two were tall but big, brawny and robustly–built men with swarthy Italian features. Their clothes clung tight to their muscular and powerful looking frames. Despite their stout size, they moved in concert with a languid grace and ease.

Stepping inside the grand foyer, the two imposing detectives stopped in their tracks to survey the situation, taking the full measure of the grand living room beyond.

Already the rooms were astir with busily engaged members of the crime scene investigation team, all wearing protective coveralls and gloves—a sketcher free–drawing diagrams; a photographer taking a progressive series of pictures from all angles; a fingerprint collector dusting and soft–brushing surfaces with powder; a trace evidence collector, pinching a pair of tweezers and looking for blood, fibers, hairs and the like to deposit into plastic bags; an evidence collector and recorder keeping an evidence log.

"Heads up!" a voice from amidst the team called out roguishly. "The Big Foe are here!"

"Good evening, detectives," the team's senior investigating officer came up to greet them with cheerful informality. "I think you're going to find this one especially interesting."

"What have you got?" one of the two asked seriously in a no–nonsense baritone voice.

"A knifing victim—expertly hogtied and stabbed multiple times," answered the officer with a casual gesture of presentation. "If you'll step right this way."

Passing through the partitioned rooms, the officer led the detectives wordlessly to the grand living room's remotest recess—but a step away from the window seat commanding the sweeping view of San Francisco's cityscape.

"We've already photographed some bloody shoe prints," the officer mentioned cursorily as they gingerly picked their way across.

Abruptly the officer turned on his heel to confront the detectives, looking skyward.

Lifting up their eyes, the detectives were taken aback by what they saw: the bloodied body of Robert Naysmith hogtied and hoisted to hang heavily from the topmost part of the ten–foot–high ceiling!

Intently the detectives inspected the blood–spattered corpse—tightly entwined with plastic white clothesline from top to toe—hands tied behind the back, feet tied together, one end of the line looped around the neck. Another end of rope wound multiple times through the mouth as a rope gag. With the neck, back and legs unnaturally arched, the stomach protruding downwards, the sagging corpse was twisted into a grotesquely contorted shape and position. It swayed slightly; and creaked from the weighty strain pulling the line extremely taut.

"Suspension bondage," observed one of the detectives, heaving a sigh of disgust, "teardrop style."

"It looks like he was bound and gagged before being stabbed. There's no outward sign of any sexual mutilation though," the officer qualified.

"Stabbed how many times and where?" dryly asked the other detective.

"From a preliminary examination," answered the officer, "it looks like sixteen times evenly divided front and back, over a broad area, with deep, frenzied thrusts."

"Type of weapon?"

"Most likely a bayonet blade. The killer wasn't considerate enough to leave it behind. Being a psychopath, he's probably kept it as a souvenir."

"And that's not all, by any means," he added forebodingly.

"Oh, yeah?"

"Direct your attention to that," the officer invited them, gesturing to a spacious bare patch of wall obliquely opposite the window seat. "You won't believe it."

"Christ!" rasped the first detective to set eyes on the frighteningly familiar outline as they both turned around together to look aghast.

Painted upon the facing wall—in thick strokes heavily smeared in human blood—was the outrageously ominous crossed–circle symbol!

"The fucking Zodiac?" exclaimed the second detective. "That's a cold case decades old!"

"Forty–four years old to be exact," confirmed the officer.

"What's the current status?"

"It was placed inactive as of April 2004—official excuse: case–load pressures and strapped resources. The department made some noises about re–opening it sometime before March 2007, but I doubt anybody's taking it too seriously."

"It's got to be a copycat! It can't be the original Zodiac after all this time!"

"It wouldn't be the first time," confirmed the officer. "At least three other copycats have been documented over the years."

"Who reported this?"

"Anonymous caller with another Zodiac M.O. match."

"Don't tell me," declared the detective, exasperated.

"The call was traced to a phone box directly across the street from the Hall of Justice."

"I'm almost afraid to ask," grudgingly remarked the

other detective. "Who was the chief investigating officer in charge of the original Zodiac case?"

"The one and only, legendary, infamous Inspector Seventy–Three: Dave Toski!" the officer brashly announced with mock melodrama. "Also affectionately known as... Unsavory Dave!"

At once the two detectives turned to confront one another, scowling and shaking their heads with dread and disbelief. Temporarily speechless, they looked agape before chiming in unison, "Oh, shit!"

PART ONE:

ZODIAC RETURNS

ONE:
UNSAVORY DAVE IS BACK!

One Rincon Hill
Residential Condominiums
425 First Street
San Francisco, California

At the apex of 100–foot–high Rincon Hill, the 60–story South Tower of the late–modernist One Rincon Hill residential complex soars another 641 feet above San Francisco's Financial District south of Market Street. Bounded by Harrison Street to the west, the Fremont Street exit ramp to the north, the approach to Interstate 80 on the east, and the First Street entrance ramp to the south, the hilltop endures as the serpentine rock anchorage and abutment for the double–decked, twin–spanned San Francisco–Oakland Bay Bridge. Three sides of the South Tower face southeast, northeast and northwest, forming a linear glass curtain–wall. Its southwest side is curved and clad in a white glass–and–aluminum panel pattern. A banded weather beacon, consisting of 25 LED floodlights, crowns the tower and beams bright throughout the night.

Lined on either side by rows of petite trees and silver–metal railings, a wide sloping and sectioned, brick–paved ramp ascends from First Street to a circular drive, rounding a ring of grass in a paved loop at the foot of the South Tower's lower–level lobby. Through an overarching tunnel of petite treetops, a rising, paved, railing–lined footpath stretches alongside the drive–ramp to the circular drive above.

A black Lexus LX 570 full–sized sport utility vehicle swerved recklessly off Harrison Street and screeched to a shrill stop at the foot of the drive–ramp. Doors abruptly slid open and a quartet of darksome, shadowy figures nimbly emerged from the vehicle. Together they promptly tramped up the shadowed footpath, carrying in hand some obscure, elongated objects. Up the steep ramp the Lexus bowled along and swerved to a second stop at the westward curve of the circular drive, idling at the curb with doused lights.

In sight of the circular drive, an elevated extension of the lamplit Highway 101 overpass was whizzing with back–and–forth freeway traffic. A thick, fuming fog saturated the circular drive with a lurid murkiness, reeking of some unseen menace.

Inside the South Tower's spacious, high–ceilinged lower–level lobby, a lone security concierge sat in a black, high–backed swivel chair behind a lengthy, crescent–shaped reception counter. An elderly gentleman with a speckled beard and moustache, he wore the typical security uniform: black shoes, grey trousers, white dress shirt, thin black tie, navy blue blazer with brass buttons— but sported incongruously the simple but painstakingly wrapped pavo blue Dhamala Dastar or turban. He was a Punjabi Sikh!

It was around midnight—and about the very same witching hour during which true crime writer, Robert Naysmith, was being killed by some mysterious murderer at the Millennium Tower—at no great distance away from One Rincon Hill!

Suddenly some faint but indistinct movement outside attracted the Sikh's attention. Curiously the Sikh fingered the upturned tips of his curled moustache as he squinted intently, straining to peer out through the tall double–glass doors facing his desk. He abruptly stood aghast at what he saw.

Out of the pitchy black mouth of the tree–tunnel footpath emerged the four dark and shadowy figures carrying their long, club–like objects. Into the murky haze of smoky fog they marched in an angular V–formation with strict military precision. Before long they strode purposefully across the circular drive, bending their steps directly toward the South Tower's lobby entrance, overhung above with a transparent crescent canopy.

Looming ahead of the lobby doorway, the awestruck Sikh could make out the imposing shapes of four tall and burly young black men with neat, short–cropped hair, all wearing identical tailored black suits with white bow ties and sunglasses. Tightly gripped in the right hand of each was a hard–handle, yard–long sledgehammer with a 20–pound flat metal head!

Surreptitiously the Sikh security concierge pressed the push–to–talk intercom microphone button atop his Motorola deskset remote–controller console.

"I'm about to be rolled on out here by four black dudes carrying sledgehammers," he said softly, seemingly muttering to himself.

"Roger that," came back the curt squelched portable two–way radio reply.

Outside the four approached the doorway precipitately.

"Let's put the bum rush on this toy cop!" rallied the apparent ringleader, parting company from the rest of the pack.

He stepped up promptly to the doorway with a malign glare. His three laconic cohorts dispersed to fall in behind him, forming a staggered single–file line.

"Open up this fucking door!" the ringleader demanded, wrenching the locked lobby door violently. "We're the destruction crew!"

"I am sorry," the Sikh called out, holding up his hands appeasingly. "The lobby is closed to non–residents after ten o'clock!"

Savagely the ringleader banged the door with a clenched black–gloved fist, making it clang loudly. Dropping back he unhesitatingly swung his sledgehammer with a wide–arc flourish. Its heavy head pulverized the door explosively, shattering and scattering shivery shards of glass all over the shiny polished lobby floor inside.

"I am sorry," the Sikh repeated helplessly. "There is no admittance to non–residents after ten o'clock!"

"Tear this shit up!" the ringleader ordered his cohorts. "We're going to get buckwild in here tonight!"

They promptly proceeded to ravage the plush lobby and its furnishings. They started smashing to pieces the big bulky potted plants set at even intervals along the lobby's spaced floor–to–ceiling columns. Dirt and mangled plant limbs got strewn everywhere. Letting their sledgehammers fly, they battered the easy chairs and divan set out in the visitor's section.

"Why are you doing this?" the Sikh pleaded excitedly. "The police will come!"

Suddenly the four laconic blacks stopped dead in their tracks. In concert they turned together slowly and fixed their eclipsed eyes on the alarmed and befuddled Sikh.

Ahead of his cohorts, the ringleader directed himself toward the reception counter. He stepped straight up to the Sikh, who looked fidgety but unflinching.

"Do we look like we're afraid of the fucking Po–lice?" the ringleader asked snidely.

Abruptly he drew back, upraised his sledgehammer high above his head, bringing it down with a ferocious crashing blow against the fractured counter top. Springing back, the Sikh threw up his hands to protect himself from the splintered pieces the slam sent flying.

"You want to play some superman shit?" the ringleader taunted the Sikh threateningly, brandishing the sledgehammer against his shoulder. "I'll break your fucking face if you don't keep your fucking mouth shut!"

Timidly the Sikh shrank back against the grid–divided wall behind him.

"Look at this doddering old head!" the ringleader called out to his cohorts scurrilously. "We've got ourselves an over–the–hill A–rab here! Who's standing here looking pretty stupid in the face!"

"I am Punjabi Indian!" the Sikh protested irately.

"I don't give a flying fuck what you are, sand nigger!" the ringleader snapped disparagingly. "Or should I call you diaper head? Yeah, diaper head fits you a whole lot better. You don't mind if I call you diaper head, now do you?"

Unexpectedly a gravelly voice—at once strangely familiar and unfamiliar—answered back in direct reply to the ringleader's contemptuous question.

"I mind," rasped the foreign voice reproachfully with an emphatic pause, "shit head!"

Together the ringleader and his cohorts turned nimbly on their heels and faced the distant direction from which the voice resonated.

From the darkened corner niche flanking the lobby's far northward end the aging, graying man wearing the blue–grey sport coat gradually emerged. Ceiling lamps shed shadowed light across his craggy features, which looked like they were deeply and sharply etched in stony granite.

His tall, gaunt frame stepped lithely into full view. Leisurely he crossed the disheveled visitor's section until he passed by the foot of the single–landing, L–shaped stairway leading upstairs to the lobby's mezzanine level. He positioned himself beside a colossal, circular column, which scaled the lobby's lofty, frontal plate glass. At that spot he stayed and stood silent with a defiant, squinting, taciturn stare—just waiting.

"Who the fuck are you, pops?" the addled ringleader finally challenged the stranger.

"I'm your elder, boy!" answered the stranger sedately.

"So don't let your mouth get your ass into trouble."

"Who the fuck are you calling, boy? You best check yourself, pops, before you get your ass busted! I'll bust your shit to the white meat! You're dealing with grown men here!"

"A boy is always bragging about what a big man he is. A grown man doesn't have to. And a grown man should always know his station in life."

"My station? Are you talking about putting me in my place, master?"

"You have to know your station to play the position, boy."

"What the fuck is your station, pops?"

Deep clefts creased his cheek as the stranger smirked mirthfully.

"His station is to detect, deter, observe and report," he explained facetiously with a discernible nod toward the anxious looking Sikh. "As his immediate supervisor, my station is to make sure he enjoys a pleasant, safe and stress–free work environment!"

"What I look like to you?" the ringleader sniggered maliciously, gesturing to his three laconic cohorts. "You know what this is. This be my crew. They're going to beat the blood out of you, pops!"

Following their ringleader's advance, their upraised sledgehammers held ready, the three cohorts moved slowly toward the stranger, step by step. Suddenly they stopped dead in their tracks.

From overhead they overheard the synchronized sound of a rigidly engaged twin–bolt operating mechanism emitted by a distinct variant of armament!

Together they reluctantly lifted up their startled eyes to pick out three kneeling members of the San Francisco Police Department's Special Weapons and Tactics(SWAT) team—decked out in full black–brown–green–tan camou-

40

flage battle dress fatigues—setting their adjustable iron sights on them from the mezzanine–level balcony above. Accurately aimed at them were the blunt barrels of three German–made Heckler & Koch MP5 9mm submachine guns—their slightly curved steel magazines showing through the transparent balustrade.

"This be my posse!" said the stranger mockingly. "Their station is being damage control experts! And I reckon they're going to arrest you for malicious vandalism and assault with a deadly weapon. That is, if they don't light you up first for not dropping those sledgehammers in a jiffy."

All at once their four weighty sledgehammers clanged loudly to the lobby floor—the rackety clamor echoing off the walls. Hurriedly the police trio scrambled down the stairway to detain the black trio with weapons trained.

Coming up intimidatingly close, the stranger faced down the ringleader, who stood with arms akimbo, his mouth contorted into a grotesque, malicious grimace.

"Your mouth was moving, boy, but it wasn't saying anything," the stranger derided him. "I reckon my guard here has something he wants to say to you."

He gave a knowing nod to the Sikh, who watched expectantly. Prompted by the stranger's signal, the Sikh came out from behind the reception desk and stepped up stoically to the emasculated black ringleader.

Without warning the Sikh deftly thrust the glinting blade of his ceremonial Kirpan dagger to the black's throat—denting his skin with the sharply pointed spike.

"Face down on the floor, boy!" the Sikh brusquely commanded him. "All I want to see is assholes and elbows!"

TWO:
PREACHER DELIVERS HIS SERMON

Star Security
450 Beach Street
Fisherman's Wharf
San Francisco, California

Dave Toski pulled his car into his slanted space and parked at the spiked grill fence behind the drab two–story bay–colored building trimmed in sea green. Everything about the building was emblazoned with dark marine green—from its evenly spaced casement windows, moldings and roof-top merlons to the green–striped canopies overhanging its entrances.

Toski strode straight up to the canopy–covered, green–framed doorway at the building's westward end. He mechanically pressed the keypad on the wall's electronic intercom lockbox multiple times, entering his access control code to admit himself. With a buzzing sound the door budged open, he stepped inside the confined foyer and nimbly climbed the narrow carpeted stairway to the second–floor hallway, extending the length of the building.

Toski punctually entered his cramped security company office. Its sole window opened out on the building's rearward side, overlooking the spacious back parking lot.

Pitching his copy of the daily edition of the San Francisco Chronicle newspaper onto the top of his dingy desk, he ambled in behind it and sat down, grimacing and shaking his head with disbelief. Heaving a heavy sigh of disgust, he muttered under his breath as he re–read the paper's blazoned banner headline:

ZODIAC IS BACK—OR COPYCAT?

Agitated, Toski got to his feet to thoughtfully look out on San Francisco Bay just over roughly a block away and beyond, to the craggy and woodsy 22–acre outcropping of Alcatraz Island, the Rock—overtopped by its towering lighthouse, water tower and crumbling prison edifice—a mile and a half offshore to the north.

Unexpectedly, Toski's deep but brief reflection was rudely interrupted by the clamorous outcry of raised, contentious voices emanating from the adjoining office of his chief operating officer, Albert Powell; the quarrelsome voices were muffled only slightly by the building's thin walls.

He could overhear something of the back–and–forth exchange between two fractious voices:

"What part of no don't you understand? The n part or the o part? I'm not fronting for you!"

"Let me school you on some things before you get into trouble around here. When you play, you have to pay!"

"Pay you? I'll pay you no mind! You can talk your ass off, but I'm not paying you anything!"

"You don't need to get on my shit list, nigga. The last thing you want to do is test me!"

"Don't talk that whooptie–woo shit to me! You're always talking that big willie talk! What makes you think you can come in here and regulate? I'm tired of you coming here trying to rough me off!"

"Because I run this around here!"

"You don't run shit! You ain't running anything around here but your mouth!"

"You best believe I do! If I have to, I'll get it in blood."

"I'm not having it! Your name holds no weight around here!"

"You're never going to have anything because you've got no hustle in you! You've got to be in it to win it!"

"You can just get down or lay down!"

Curious, Toski stepped out into the hallway, directing his eyes to the open doorway of the nearby outer office. He tilted his head slightly, straining to overhear the bellicose altercation taking place; his cheek creased with the intent squint of his eyes behind his dark, reflective shades. He boldly crossed the threshold.

Seated behind the outer office desk, typing at a computer keyboard, was a lusty–looking young black girl with big sparkling eyes, full luscious lips and long black braided hair. Whatever short skirt or flimsy blouse she wore, her supple plump bosom, wide hips and thickset thighs verged on the brink of bursting out of her tight–fitting clothes.

In passing he cursorily greeted the voluptuous black secretary seated behind the outer office desk with a curt nod.

"Isha," he said, heading straight for the closed inter–connecting office door.

"Inspector Toski!" Aisha Taylor protested with an overwrought gesture, half–rising from her seat. "Mr. Powell's in conference!"

"I'm retired!" Toski stated adamantly with just a fleeting glance before bursting into the main office suite.

"Al," Toski sedately greeted his boss with another curt nod as he stepped up to his desk. "I see you're by yourself."

"There's a fungus among us!" snidely cracked one of four tall and burly young black youths, sporting their trademark suits and bow ties, who abruptly linked together and formed a protective human chain around a fifth black man of decidedly shorter stature.

"Dave!" protested Albert Powell, a tall, handsome, imposing black man having short–cropped hair and thick moustache, a high forehead, dark and deeply penetrating but quizzical eyes, a sharply flared nose, uncommonly thin lips and a strong, square jaw, rising from behind his desk. "How many times do I have to tell you not to barge into my office like that unannounced? We're having a private meeting here!"

"To me it sounded like a private shouting match," Toski replied dryly. "Is there some problem here?"

"Look, chief," condescended the midmost black youth, stepping up. "This is an A and B conversation, so you can C your way right out of it!"

"Oh, I can see why you were retained," Toski scoffed, casting his eyes on his boss. "Who's this, Al? The undertaker and his pals?"

"Don't you see grown folk talking?" persisted the black youth with a sardonic grin, exposing two front teeth gaped and capped with gold. He was the very same young black ringleader whom Dave Toski recently encountered vandalizing the lobby at One Rincon Hill. "This is grown folk business. You best stay out of grown folk business."

"That's funny," Toski said stoically. "Except for me and Al here, I don't see any grown folk present."

"Who are you trying to get jazzy with?"

"You're going to have to give me five feet," cautioned Toski, gesturing for the black to move back with the Gargoyles sunglasses he took off, folded and pocketed in his sport jacket.

"That's what's wrong with people nowadays," the black blustered, dropping back a step. "They don't know how to mind their own business. That's why the graveyard's packed now."

"You're just bumping your gums, boy. I hope you don't kiss your mother with a mouth like that."

"Stop faking," growled the black, coming at Toski again. "You don't want none. You ain't ready for this."

"If you had brains," Toski mocked him, "you'd be dangerous. Why don't you act your age and not your brain size?"

"You're acting like you said something."

Toski ogled him with a frigid, squinting glare.

"You have your whole life to act stupid, boy. Why start today?"

Maliciously the black snarled, his quivering face convulsed with rage, his knuckles blanching from tightly clenching his fists at his sides.

"Ease up," advised a voice previously unheard of. "Don't sweat that."

From behind his four youthful cohorts a fifth black man, sporting a pair of Stacy Adams shoes, pushed forward. Older, and of shorter and slighter stature than the others, he wore a zoot suit decked out in garish and gaudy jewelry: most conspicuously diamond–encrusted gold–and–platinum pendants draped on gold–and–platinum rope chains. He stepped right up to Dave Toski, who faced him down with a severely stern, laconic look.

"Dave," introduced Albert Powell, trying to temper the intensifying tension, "this is the Reverend Dr. Joseph Mustapha."

"Doctor of what?" Toski asked skeptically after a crisp pause of bated breath.

"The School of Hard–Knock Life."

"You don't look too disadvantaged or underprivileged."

"I'm a champion of The Struggle."

"What struggle is that?"

"The struggle to survive in the United States Ghetto. The struggle against The System and its racist trappings of oppression. I'm on a mission. These fine young men here are my spiritually adopted sons—Isaiah, Jeremiah, Joshua...and Zechariah."

"Sounds to me like you're the Jackleg of a storefront church."

"I preach to the Believing and the Faithful to pimp the system—and not let the system pimp you! And to respect my game."

"What game are you running here today?"

"The game is meant to be sold—not to be told!"

"He is righteous and sanctified! Tell it! Tell the truth! That ain't nothing but the truth!" chanted his euphoric youthful cohort.

"A two–bit extortion racket and protection scheme if I had to give it a guess," Toski remarked grimly.

"There ain't no shame in my game. There ain't no mystery to my history."

Mustapha stepped up closer and stared Toski point–blank in the face.

"Your jaws is tight now. You got that mean, mad dog mug. And that evil eye. I heard you were once a big, bad cowboy Supercop back in the day," he said soberly.

Toski stood immovably firm.

"Yeah?" came his rasped reply.

"You're the Man," Mustapha chimed. "I'm just a fan. But you better ask about me and check my pedigree."

"Mongrels don't have any pedigree," Toski coldly deadpanned. "But if I have to ask anybody, it won't be your breeder. I'll come straight to you."

"Don't do that, son," Mustapha admonished him, "you bigger than that. God don't like ugly."

"God don't like jive–ass bullshit, either."

Mustapha suddenly cackled out aloud. With a knowing nod he gestured to Albert Powell, who was taken aback.

"We go back like Cadillacs," Mustapha soliloquized, "Al and me. Now let me drop some science. This is some serious business. And we're going to square business."

"We shouldn't even be talking because this is a dead issue," Albert Powell spoke up assertively at last. "I already told you this is a dead issue."

Mustapha turned to directly confront Powell with a hostile stare.

"You know what this is," he muttered menacingly. "You know my style."

"That's what your mouth says," Powell answered back

brazenly. "And your mouth ain't no prayer book."

"You can't talk with dirt and rocks in your mouth, nigga!" Mustapha snapped, his grimacing face flushed with rage.

"Don't start anything," Powell warned him, "there won't be anything."

"So long as you know," Mustapha threatened outright, "if I do start something, we'll take this to another level. We'll be taking it to the streets!"

"I'm right here all day every day," Powell told him defiantly, "whoever wants it!"

Impetuously the headmost black youth—the one called Zechariah—started to charge forward full–tilt. Dave Toski boldly and deliberately stood in his way, blocking him bodily.

"I'll stomp a mudhole in your ass so deep, boy, you won't be able to tell the smut from the shit!" Toski threatened him.

Face fuming, the indignant black youth stopped cold in his tracks once his leader held up a halting hand.

"I think you should get stepping," Powell insisted at last, "because I ain't even trying to hear that slum shit you been talking."

"You better open your eyes and recognize," warned Mustapha, wagging an admonishing finger, his wrist ablaze with a rattling Rolex watch, "or get penalized!"

"It's time to clean house," Powell demanded, fed up. "Tell your story walking. Let me see your head get small."

"Just remember," Mustapha warned ominously once more. "Nothing comes to a dreamer but sleep."

At his beck and call, Mustapha's four disciplined youths falling in around him to dutifully escort him to the building exit, all five black cohorts filed out of the office together in an orderly, regimented manner.

Albert Powell sank down into the seat of his swivel

chair, heaving a wheezing sigh of relief. He lifted up his big dark eyes and raised his long thin brows, looking quizzically at Dave Toski.

"I was in there getting my grown-man on until you showed up," he gloated.

"What's the deal here, Al?" Toski asked exasperatedly. "Where the hell do you know those crudballs from?"

"Dave," Powell grumbled, looking glum, "every time I turn around, you're all up in my business!"

"Put the bullshit aside," Toski persisted, "and give it to me raw and uncut. I can take it. I know a shake—down when I see one."

"Real recognizes real," Powell said, nodding resignedly. "If I don't become one of his legitimate business fronts, he's threatening to kill off my business by trashing my high—profile client sites—like One Rincon Hill. You have to be careful with those cats, Dave. They all have hate in their hearts. It's in their blood."

"It sure didn't take long for those punks to make bail."

"How did you get wind of their hit on the condo?"

"Anonymous tipster."

Dave Toski stepped gingerly through a green—framed glass door opening out onto the white—painted balcony grille overlooking the expansive rear parking lot. Intently he watched, steadying himself against the rail, as Joseph Mustapha and his costumed cohorts bent their steps toward a big—bodied Mercedes Benz. At the same time a battered Buick Electra 225 pulled gradually into an adjoining space to park.

Out of the Buick stepped a portly but courtly young black man who eagerly greeted Mustapha. Exaggeratedly the two executed together a hearty and intricate Soul Shake to demonstrate their supposed solidarity, juxtaposing each other's thumbs and grasping each other's fingers in their palms.

They'll be playing grab–ass next, Toski sniggered to himself. He overheard Mustapha mirthfully mock the younger black's "hoopty Deuce–and–a–Quarter" Buick. In turn he overheard the corpulent young black compliment Mustapha's "tricked out Benzo" Mercedes.

Deliberately Mustapha paused to lift up his eyes to Toski once he caught sight of him staring down from his elevated perch on the building's backside. Glancing around, the chubby young black with the cherubic and cheerful face followed suit, casting his curious eyes on Toski likewise. With a scurrilous smile, Mustapha compressed his right hand into the symbolic shape of a handgun, leveling it at Toski like a gun barrel and squeezing his flinching forefinger as if pulling a trigger!

"I'll be seeing you, Mister Overseer!" Mustapha mouthed to himself.

Mustapha's corpulent black onlooker sidestepped the Mercedes Benz as he slid smoothly through the rear door held open for him and into the back seat. Mustapha's costumed entourage likewise piled into the car which—with a grinding skid across abraded asphalt—started up and screeched off.

Once Mustapha's car was lost to sight in hectic Fisherman's Wharf traffic, the portly but sprightly smiling black bystander left behind crossed the parking lot and stepped up to the foot of the building's backside balcony. Coolly he screwed up his eyes to look on Dave Toski.

"Inspector Toski!" he blithely greeted him.

"I'm retired!" Toski stated adamantly. "What can I do for you?"

"My name's Chance Bailey," he announced, "correspondent for the San Francisco Chronicle. I'm real interested in the Zodiac case and I'd like to discuss it with you."

"Zodiac's a cold case," Toski scowled scornfully, shaking his head, "currently inactive as I am. Nothing happens on that anymore. And I'm not big on talking to reporters out to spin their next sensational story."

"I appreciate that, Inspector—"

"Retired!" Toski snapped.

"Sir!" Bailey relented. "But I'm an investigative journalist. Somebody out there's trying to warm up this case again. And I firmly believe I've come up with a brand—new angle to analyze it with that's totally untried! I believe I've come up with a novel line of inquiry that could ultimately uncover Zodiac's true identity!"

"Another half—baked, half—assed theory, you mean?"

"No, sir!" Bailey asserted with fervent conviction. "A completely fresh and practical approach to examining the available evidence!"

"Approaches are like assholes. And you know what they say about those?"

"I know," Bailey chuckled likably. "Everybody has one! But I'm not talking about mere guesswork or speculation."

"Just what are you talking about then?"

"I'm talking about a fresh outlook and perspective! I'm talking about fresh prospects and possibilities! I'm talking about fresh probabilities!"

"Sounds like fancy semantics for somebody's pet theory to me. I've heard so many theories they all tend to run together. The umpteenth time you pick up the phone on one of these calls, it's just another wacko who's pulling something out of thin air."

"No!" Bailey protested, shaking his head adamantly. "There are special aspects to this case which have never been explored! I'm talking about treading a totally unbeaten path! As a police inspector for the city, you had a reputation of appreciating tips coming from the public, especially concerning how to catch Zodiac."

"If the tips seemed to have some substance and the

sources seemed sincere, I was still appreciative. I could never know when I'd take a tip that could be a positive lead that could make or break the case. I was never going to make this case by pushing tipsters away. But I'm officially off this case. So I'm not accepting tips anymore."

"You're telling me you don't care about this case anymore?"

"Oh, I care. It's the case of a career. But it was also the most baffling and frustrating case of all my cases. And it's not worth getting ulcers over."

"That's why there's probably a Zodiac still out there. And he's just laughing himself to death."

"I've always felt obliged to listen to everyone—no matter how outlandish their story. At least you don't talk ghetto. That's definitely a point in your favor."

"Contrary to Spike Lee, not all black males are ill–bred, illiterate, foul–mouthed, uncouth and vulgar savages. Fortunately my parents taught me better. They gave me a good education."

"Well that was mighty white of them," Toski joked with a wink, suddenly switching the subject. "Do you know those salty dudes who just left here?"

"Sure," Bailey nodded. "Everybody knows the Preacher. He cuts a pretty wide swath through this city."

"Is that so?" Toski mused, creasing his cheek with a cheerful smile. "There's a small park with a statue of Saint Francis at Beach and Taylor Streets...don't meet me there, beat me there...and I'll follow you in a few."

THREE:
ZODIAC'S
ESPRIT
DE
CORPS

Saint Francis of Assisi Statue
Taylor & Beach Streets
San Francisco, California

S aint Francis of Assisi's 18–foot tall, 12.5–ton, granite statue hovers over the corner fenced–in, tree–enshrouded park with outstretched arms in graceful benediction. From the middle of a con-crete, hexagon–shaped hedge it rises high up to the clus-tered treetops. At the foot of its pedestal it's flanked by a twin pair of concrete, bowl–shaped planters. Double–ended PCC—1930s–style Presidents' Conference Commit-tee—streetcars rattled by along nearby Beach Street on San Francisco's Municipal Railway's F Market & Wharves light rail line.

Dave Toski sauntered into the park and directly sat down at one of two green–grooved metal benches facing aslant from each other. Chance Bailey was already sit-ting alone on the opposite bench, gazing at the statue, en-grossed.

"Sculptor, Beniamino Benvenuto Bufano, hand–crafted this statue in Paris in 1928," Bailey mused aloud. "It wasn't brought to San Francisco until 1955. It was the long–time president of the International Longshoremen's and Warehousemen's Union, the late Harry Bridges, who finally arranged to bring it here to Fisherman's Wharf."

"That's all very nice," Toski condescended. "Now about this fresh and practical approach to examining the Zodiac evidence..."

"In particular," Bailey started, "three primary attri-butes point to Zodiac as being possibly of British extrac-tion with drafting or engineering experience—and who's attached in some way to the military."

"None of which is new."

"Let me drop it on you."

Toski nodded drearily.

"On Sunday the 19th of April 1970," Bailey recounted, "a ship's steward named Christopher Edwards stopped to ask directions of a stranger while walking to Fisherman's Wharf. Edwards was from the Peninsular and Oriental Steam Navigation Company liner, Oronsay; the P&O is a British shipping and transport company dating back to the early nineteenth century.

"This stranger identified himself as a British engineer who had lived in San Francisco for ten years. He offered Edwards a ride in a late–model hardtop parked at the corner of Bay Street and the Embarcadero.

"Edwards declined because he was getting 'bad vibrations' from this stranger, who ran on at great length and in great detail about the crime rate and all the murders—thirty–five to date that year—occurring in the city.

"Except those that were on the minds of most people at that time: the Zodiac killings.

"'It's not safe to walk alone,' the stranger proceeded to warn Edwards, 'with all the muggings, murders, rapes, and crime.'

"This stranger's reluctance to discuss Zodiac so impressed Edwards that he couldn't shake the encounter from his mind. So as soon as he reached the Wharf, Edwards called the cops."

"I take it you're on the verge of delivering the punch line."

"At the Central Station, at 766 Vallejo Street, Edwards identified the stranger from a composite sketch of Zodiac!"

"So did Kathleen Johns and a whole lot of other people," Toski scoffed. "And Johns claimed she went on a nighttime joyride with Zodiac."

"Let's take these attributes one at a time," Bailey suggested. "In his letter to tort attorney, Melvin Belli, postmarked the 20th of December 1969—one of the letters

containing a bloody swatch of cabbie, Paul Stine's shirt—
Zodiac made use of the phrase, 'a happy Christmas,' just
as he used the slang term, 'kiddies,' in his fifth letter postmarked the 13th of October 1969, threatening to shoot
children getting off a school bus.

"Both those phrases are in more common usage in
Great Britain, Canada or even Australia than in the United States. Not to mention his use of 'rather' as an adverb,
which he does twice in his letter to the San Francisco
Chronicle dated the 9th of November 1969.

"Most significant was Bryan Hartnell, who survived
Zodiac's attack against him and Cecelia Shepard at Lake
Berryessa in Napa County. Bryan recounted that Zodiac
had a 'unique way of talking' that sounded 'like a song.'
A sing–song accent or drawl, as Bryan described it, could
most definitely be Australian or British."

"And?" Toski prodded him.

"In Zodiac's fifteenth letter—a florid Halloween card
he posted to San Francisco Chronicle reporter, Paul Avery
on the 27th of October 1970—Zodiac resorted to white–
ink lettering on the back of the card such as artists and
draftsmen use. Likewise, the upper and lowercase lettering exhibited in Zodiac's letters used to be standard drafting practice.

"Whoever Zodiac is, he had to have use of a light table, grids to place his symbols, a T–square and triangle,
along with other drafting tools.

"Zodiac accompanied his Z–signature and crossed–
circle with a brand–new symbol, which has been identified by a mass consensus as being an H–beam, I–beam or
Wide–Flange beam, representing a structural steel shape
used in building construction, suggesting Zodiac could be
some kind of civil engineer.

"In fact, it's been observed that the type of mathemat-
ical plotting used in Zodiac's three–part cryptogram—in

which all eighteen characters are numbers with both coordinates followed by numerals after the decimal point—is widely used in mechanical engineering."

"Go on, get to the gist."

"Remember officer, Donald A. Fouke," asked Bailey, "one of two Richmond District patrolmen who first responded to cabbie, Paul Stine's killing in Presidio Heights—on Columbus Day, the 11th of October 1969?"

"I remember him well," Toski said. "Along with officer Eric Zelms they were on the crime scene within three minutes of the call."

"Right," acknowledged Bailey. "A month after the Stine shooting, officer Fouke submitted an inter–departmental memorandum, mentioning a pedestrian they observed walking east on Jackson Street on their way to the scene at Washington and Cherry Streets.

"Officer Fouke described that pedestrian very specifically as appearing to be of Welsh ancestry!

"But most significantly, some years later, officer Fouke recalled that this pedestrian they passed was wearing engineering boots!

"In the 1960s to the 1970s, the Sears company was a major distributor of Chippewa engineer boots—with knee–high, stovepipe legs fashioned over an English Riding Boot last!

"The name, engineer boots, comes from their original use by land surveyors!"

"Field boots are also often worn by motorcycle riders," Toski agreed, "even by police officers riding motorcycles or on horse–mounted patrols."

"In early 1969," Bailey continued, "as American involvement in Southeast Asia escalated, the United States Army constructed a ten–story reinforced concrete hospital to replace the original Letterman Army Hospital— also known as the Letterman Army Medical Center. It was erected to cope with the increased demands being made on the hospital at that time. In 1975 a theater was added to the hospital structure, expanding the medical center further.

"From 1969 to 1974, the Letterman Army Hospital was being modernized and the Letterman Army Institute of Research, a five–story annex, was built in 1976.

"This time period coincides almost exactly concurrent with Zodiac's active years, as documented by the dates of the authenticated cards and letters he sent to individuals and the media, from 31 July 1969 to 8 July 1974.

"At the time, of course, this major construction work on these historic landmark buildings was taking place on the Presidio of San Francisco—then a military installation of the United States Army."

"So?" Toski said.

"On the night of cabbie, Paul Stine's killing," Bailey related urgently, "your probable Zodiac suspect wearing the engineering boots disappeared into the Presidio—via Maple Street and the Julius Kahn Playground—and escaped, despite an extensive search of the area assisted by military police and fire truck searchlights, never to be seen again!"

"I still don't get the point you're trying to make—if there is one," Toski remarked impatiently.

"I'm just putting two and two together. I thought it was easy arithmetic."

"Well, it's not. So why don't you just break it down in baby terms?"

"Engineering plus the United States Army Presidio equals...," Bailey paused for melodramatic effect, but looking and sounding gravely solemn, "the United States Army Corps of Engineers!"

Toski looked stunned as if hit hard between the eyes.

"That's right," Bailey nodded knowingly. "There's

more."

Toski looked expectant.

"Despite plenty of theories put forth about what Zodiac's crossed–circle really meant or represented," Bailey said, reaching into his coat pocket to extract a plain white letter–sized envelope, "Zodiac himself never explained what his symbol signified."

"I suppose you're about to tell what his symbol stood for."

"No," Bailey shook his head with an impish smile, "but I am going to tell you where he most likely derived it from—and it wasn't from that notorious Zodiac wristwatch, either."

"Where from then?"

"In December 1932," Bailey recounted, "the Swedish Silva Company manufactured and sold its famed Silva compass, which was designed for outdoor orienteers and army officers—a precursor to the modern military compass that's frequently integrated with a circular, three hundred and sixty–degree protractor having crosshairs as orienting lines. A protractor's for measuring angles in a vast variety of mechanical and engineering–related applications.

"A specialized surveyor's compass, which accurately measures the headings of landmarks or horizontal angles for map–making, typically has this crosshair protractor.

"Crosshairs are common in optical instruments used in astronomy and surveying. Crosshairs amount to what's called a simple reticle—most commonly represented by intersecting lines in the shape of a cross.

"To engineers this crosshair reticle is known as a bolt circle!"

Obligingly Bailey reached out to hand over the envelope. Inquisitive, Toski peeled open its flap and took out the neatly folded sheet of plain white paper inside; he spread open the piece of paper and gaped, openmouthed, at the simple drawing of the crossed–circle design—a straighter, more rectilinear version though.

At the bottom of the sheet just two emboldened words captioned the design:

BOLT CIRCLE

"Bolt circle?" Toski asked curiously. "What's that?"

Bailey smiled widely, looking supremely triumphant.

"A bolt circle," he explained, "is in engineering a theoretical circle on which the centerpoints of bolt holes lie when the bolt holes are positioned as equally spaced in a circle.

A common example are the bolts on a bolted joint between pipe flanges. It's often abbreviated 'BC' or 'B.C.' on engineering drawings. It's typically treated as a basic or reference dimension, unless true position for the centers is specified using GD&T—or geometric dimensioning and tolerancing."

"In plain and simple English if you please."

"If the Zodiac was any kind of engineer," Bailey said solemnly, "he never had to steal from a popular wristwatch an ordinary rendering he was already well acquainted with employing in the engineering trade!"

FOUR:
ZODIAC
BREAKS
THE
SEAL

Apartments
1501 Leavenworth Street
Unit 11
Russian Hill
San Francisco, California

His daily mail in hand, Dave Toski stepped inside his long–time second–story flat in the four–story apartment building at the corner of Leavenworth Street at Jackson on Russian Hill.

He went straight to his high–performance Dell XPS desktop personal computer, set snug inside of a computer armoire, pressing its on button and waiting for its operating system to turn on. Anxiously he sat down at his desk, overlooking the single–ended, bell–clanging Powell–Hyde Street cable cars rolling along back–and–forth below on Jackson Street—to–and–from the Hyde–Beach streets terminal turntable at the waterfront in sight of Alcatraz Island offshore.

Leafing through a fistful of mail, Toski paused to intently inspect a plain, white, letter–sized envelope addressed with strangely familiar, slanted, hand–printed lettering. He peeled it open, unfolding the piece of plain white bond paper contained inside. Hand–printed on the paper in blue felt–tip pen ink were the foreboding words:

Soon You'll Be Next

Abruptly the telephone set atop his nightstand across the room rang. Toski glanced around, fixing his eyes on the phone, waiting for four rings and his outgoing message to finish. His answering machine began recording an ominous incoming voicemail message—delivered in a soft, raspy whisper:

"This is the Zodiac speaking, Dave. Tell everybody that I am back in San Francisco!"

Toski got to his feet and flung himself at the telephone, snapping up the receiver violently with a snarling, teeth–clenching grimace.

"Listen to me," he growled gutturally, "you perverted sonofabitch!"

Toski swore at the dead telephone line, cut short by the pronounced and prolonged dial tone. Furiously he banged up the phone.

He opened up the nearby closet to expose to view the battered, five–foot–tall, steel–gray, fireproof filing cabinet. Its first drawer is labeled, Concerned Citizens; its second drawer, Suspects. From a third drawer labeled Paul L. Stine, he pulled out a tattered, bulky black folder, which he carried back to his window–facing desk.

Toski deftly typed into the Google search engine box a pair of words: Bolt Circle.

Toski's craggy, sharply chiseled features were aglow from the bright light reflected by his computer monitor's ultra sharp, 24–inch flat panel widescreen. Toski clicked his computer mouse to zoom in and enlarge the vivid image displayed before him.

"Jeezus," Toski muttered under his breath, loosening his necktie.

A spine–chilling sensation made Toski's flesh creep as the perfectly rectilinear outline of Zodiac's crossed–circle symbol stood out before his unbelieving eyes!

Suddenly his flat's doorbell buzzed aloud. Startled, Toski flinched with a start. Hastily he wriggled out of his sport jacket, draping it over the high back of his swivel chair.

Exposed to view now was Toski's black–leather concealment shoulder–strapped handgun holster—out of which Toski deliberately drew his signature Smith & Wesson Model 29 Fiftieth Anniversary .44–Magnum six–shot, double–action revolver!

Resting his revolver across his left chest, Toski gently slid up the window opening out onto the downward sloping street below. Forking the northwest corner of the brick building, tall and wide window panes—fenced in by the same low–lying, black, ornate fretwork for over four decades—exposed to view its hardwood foyer and parlor.

Moving back from the window's sidewise edge, Toski cautiously drew aside the curtain, cracking open just enough space to look out onto the sidewalk and over-arched, twin–step threshold.

At the building's doorsill Toski caught sight of two big, brawny and swarthy Italian men decked out in dark suits and fedoras. They stood, fidgety, in front of the triple–framed doorway adorned by the same ornate black fretwork hemming in the base of the corner windows. Toski took the extra precaution of cursorily surveying the facing facades of the buildings directly opposite—on the other side of the street—looking out for similar silhouettes or outlines in open windows.

"Howdy!" Toski called out to them suddenly but cheerfully.

Taken unawares, the two lifted up their eyes in concert to contemplate Toski, staring down at them from above from behind the curtain he'd drawn across his torso.

"Inspector Toski?"

"I'm retired! What can I do for you two gents?"

"We're San Francisco police inspectors, Moretti and Marino. We were wondering whether you—who are extremely knowledgeable—would be willing to talk with us. We'd really like to consult with you about Zodiac."

"Is that a fact? You know, of course, I'm not actively working on that case anymore—and haven't been for some time. So officially I'm off the case."

"Yeah, we know. We've been authorized to retain you on a contract–type basis to help us follow up any new Zodiac leads that might trickle in. You'd be on reserve to help the PD solve any apparent Zodiac—related homicides."

"Retaining me entails making some token compensation, I trust."

"Most certainly. We'll coordinate the effort. We'll be the chief field investigators while you'll help analyze the data we assemble. We're trying to dig into this somewhat seriously again."

"That's fine and dandy. It doesn't matter to me as long as you do it."

"Fine. Let's get it done."

"Well, gents," Toski retorted wistfully, "I don't consult where I rest at."

Toski ruminated momentarily.

"Pick me up tomorrow afternoon at one—thirty sharp," he instructed them after a crisp pause, "at the Pinecrest Diner."

"Will do," they chimed in unison, "nice meeting you."

"Inspector Toski?" one asked as an afterthought.

"Retired!" he exclaimed, straining his throat.

"We're rather surprised you didn't greet us at the door with your famous forty—four!"

"Yeah, I should've," Toski answered back, letting the curtain fall and exposing his singular revolver to view; lightly tapping its ten—inch barrel against his left shoulder. "You can never be too careful in the hood!"

§

THOMAS J. CAHILL
HALL OF JUSTICE
Homicide Detail
Room 455
850 Bryant Street
San Francisco, California

Embossed in the hard facade of The Hall, or the Southern Station, is the great Seal of the city and county of San Francisco, California, adopted in 1859, and ringed with the municipality's name.

Its shield shows the Golden Gate, bordered by hills, with a paddlewheel steamship entering San Francisco Bay. Above the shield is a crest with a phoenix, the legendary Greek bird rising from the ashes. It's flanked by two supporters, a miner, holding a shovel, in dexter; and a sailor, holding a sextant, in sinister, both in 1850s period clothing. At the feet of the supporters are a plow and anchor, emblems of commerce and navigation. Below the shield is its motto which reads, "Oro en paz, fierro en guerra", which is Spanish for "Gold in peace, iron in war."

Engraved in the wall beneath the Seal are these stirring words:

**HALL OF JUSTICE
TO THE FAITHFUL AND
IMPARTIAL ENFORCEMENT
OF THE LAWS WITH EQUALITY
AND EXACT JUSTICE TO
ALL OF WHATEVER STATE
OR PERSUASION THIS
BUILDING IS DEDICATED
BY THE PEOPLE OF THE
CITY AND COUNTY OF
SAN FRANCISCO
ERECTED
1958–1960**

Homicide Detail is hand–painted in stark black lettering on the frosted–glass door to Room 455. Inside, a stark black clock on the wall marks time. Crowding its spacious polished floor are old wooden desks and gray metal file cabinets.

Lackluster lamplight from outside faintly illuminated

the grimy window overlooking oily Bryant Street below—along which the sporadic traffic slowly crawled. A faded white pedestrian crosswalk leads straight from the Hall's front brass–railed steps to the undistinguished chalky-colored building directly across the street at 835. Its uncommonly blue–and–white neon signs flashed in the dead of night with bright, luminous letters:

ALADDIN BAIL BONDS
OPEN 24 HOURS
WE GET YOU OUT
WE GET YOU THROUGH IT

Detectives Moretti and Marino huddled together in front of the slim LCD monitor set atop their worn wooden desk. Connected to the monitor was an operating digital video recorder device.

"Have you ever met or spoken to Dave Toski before?" one of the detectives asked the other.

"I never heard of the man. I first heard his name when he was quoted all over the place at the police academy. I heard lots of war stories. When it comes to violent crime, he has a bad–ass reputation for being something of a public avenger who isn't big on due process."

"Sounds like my kind of dude. He isn't too big on bureaucracy, red tape and incompetent supervisors, either. There's been some displeasure expressed by the department's upper echelons, who consider him a loose canon."

"And a lot of professional jealousy, I imagine. He was once busted out of homicide to the frigging pawn shop detail for his unconventional methods. But he's worked all four units of crimes against persons: from sex, homicide, aggravated assault to robbery. Now the top brass are a little leery about conferring with him on this case."

"What's their real beef with this guy?"

"In a nutshell, it all boils down to his perceived attitude about justice. That's why he's been called Unsavory

Dave. His idea of clearance rate for violent crime isn't through arrest and conviction—it's to run these hoods out of town or simply blow them away before they can do any more damage to anybody. He has a raspy personality, too, but that's just his way of doing things."

"Translation—he gets results! I can see how that would grate on the incompetents upstairs. What's his current status then?"

"He retired in 1988 after thirty-two years on the force. Now he's with Star Security Services as their operations director. S.F.P.D. marked the cold case inactive as of April 2004, citing caseload pressures and limited resources— the same old song and dance routine."

"I've read all the files and reports on the original Zodiac case. For the longest time Dave Toski was the only one working it. He was handling it out of the pawn detail for Chrissakes! But he was the only one trying to track anything down. Of course he had all his other cases to work within the department at the same time. Nothing ever came up to turn the tables on this thing one way or the other."

"What have we got here?"

"This is the security footage playback from Aladdin's exterior closed circuit television surveillance camera. It coincides with the exact same time the caller claiming to be Zodiac called the police department to report Robert Naysmith's murder at the Millennium Tower—from this pay phone directly across the street from the Hall of Justice! The phone receiver was dusted for prints which yielded no results."

Conspicuously displayed on the glowing monitor screen was the non-enclosed, open-air, receiver-shaped pay telephone placed directly in front of the Aladdin Bail Bonds building.

Into full view abruptly stepped a dark-garbed and

stocky figure of a man, wearing baggy, black woolen, pleated, bellbottom pants and a lightweight, blueblack, hooded, nylon, parka–type windbreaker with a black knit cap, black gloves and dark shoes. His eyes were disguised by a pair of black, thick–rimmed glasses or welding goggles—kept in place by elastic band like a machinist might wear.

Picking up the pay phone receiver and putting it to his ear, he made his brief call and unceremoniously hung up.

Before retiring from sight outright, he paused to lift up his eyes and stare straight into the video lens of the security surveillance camera mounted outside of the Aladdin Bail Bonds building.

Cheerfully he waved with a mirthful flourish of one of his black–gloved hands. Then he was gone.

"A brazen bastard," one of the detectives remarked, "isn't he?"

PART TWO:

KEY
CABBIE
KILLING

FIVE:
PAUL
LEE
STINE
RETRACED

Pinecrest Diner
Open 24 Hours
Theatre District
401 Geary Street
San Francisco, California

P rinting on the drab–colored canopy over-hanging the diner's front double–glass doors reads:

PINECREST
RESTAURANT
Since 1969 Open 24 Hours

"We serve the best breakfast in San Francisco," boasts the banner on a sidelong awning overhanging the diner's checkered storefront. Hedged in by beige walls, rust–colored leatherette booths and faux–wood Formica tables fringe the L–shaped dining area and lengthy counter with its swivel–seats.

Dave Toski emerged from the diner carrying a disposable cup of coffee in one hand and his tattered, bulky black folder in the other.

At the curb outside idled an unmarked full–size Ford Taurus Police Interceptor sedan. Detectives Moretti and Marino sat waiting in front. From his driver's seat, Moretti swung open the car's left rear passenger door. Dave Toski slid into the back seat, flinging his folder in beside him.

"Good afternoon, gents!"

"Hello, Inspector!" one of the detectives greeted him.

"Retired!" Toski snapped, sipping from his coffee cup. "I couldn't start the afternoon without a strong fix of black blood."

"You've been hanging out with too many ex–felons," cracked the other.

"A beautiful Greek waitress named Helen Menicou

served me this coffee for over 20 years," Toski reminisced sullenly, "before this scumbag of a Jordanian cook blew her away one morning with a .380 semi–automatic."

"I remember," the detective commiserated. "July, 1997. He shot her five times the day after she chastised him for taking some hot chick's order for poached eggs, which wasn't on the menu."

"Yeah," chimed in the other, "the petty shit people in this city will kill each other over is frigging unreal some-times."

Toski brooded briefly, sipping more coffee.

"What's on the agenda for today, sir?" Moretti asked finally.

"Paul Lee Stine," Toski related, "a 29–year–old driver of Yellow Cab #912, was Zodiac's fifth fatal victim. It was Saturday, Columbus Day, the 11th of October 1969.

"At roughly nine–thirty that night, Zodiac flagged down Stine's cab out in front of the Curran Theatre at 445 Geary—a stone's throw away on this block.

"Zodiac ordered Stine to drive him to the intersec-tion of Washington and Maple Streets in Presidio Heights. We're going to retrace Stine's exact route to the crime scene at Washington and Cherry Streets. Head west on Geary and hang a right on Van Ness."

"You got it," Moretti acknowledged, gunning its 3.5–litre EcoBoost V–6 engine, putting in gear the SelectShift 6–speed automatic transmission and tearing off into bus-tling Tenderloin traffic.

"Care for some candy?" Marino offered, picking up from the gear stick's center console a little liftable tray heaped with a small pile of button–shaped, multi–colored, filled candy shells—each piece imprinted on one side with the lower–case letter: m!

"Don't mind if I do," Toski assented with an acquies-cent but unsuspecting nod.

"We're not called the M&Ms for nothing," Marino said with a smile.

"Thanks," Toski said, munching a mouthful of the crunchy morsels he scooped out of the tray.

Bowling along the squalid Tenderloin's northernmost, graffiti–and–mural infested thoroughfare, overpopulated with seedy strip joints and liquor stores, Toski resumed rendering his account.

"At roughly nine–forty–five," Toski continued, "Stine was dispatched to pick up another fare at 500 9th Avenue in the inner Richmond District—a destination he never arrived at—so that dispatch was reassigned to another cab at nine–fifty–eight. Stine got shot at roughly the very same time.

"Stine had reported to work at roughly eight–forty–five. So prior to picking up Zodiac, Stine had only one other fare, whom he drove from Pier 64 to the Air Terminal."

Turning north onto Van Ness Avenue, they moved along the auto row dealerships in the stop–and–go traffic.

"Hang a left at California," Toski told Moretti, who turned west.

From Market and Spear Streets in the downtown Financial District, California Street—a major thoroughfare and one of San Francisco's longest streets—extends its four to six lanes for 5.2 miles over fifty–four blocks in a near–straight, east–west line until it dead–ends at 32nd Avenue in Lincoln Park.

"Drive eleven blocks and hang a right at Divisadero," Toski directed. "Hang another left in three blocks at Washington Street. Slow down as you get to Maple, the cross street—in nine blocks."

"There's been some discrepancy in reports about whether Zodiac rode in front or back of the cab as a passenger," Toski pointed out, "but he most likely sat in back."

§

Presidio Heights

Presidio Heights is a smaller–scale neighborhood with snug and breezy tree–lined streets inhabited by majestic mansions.

"Stop here for a minute," Toski directed as they slowly pulled up to the intersection of Washington and Maple Streets, idling at the northeast corner.

"This intersection was Zodiac's stated destination," Toski recounted, "but for some unknown reason Zodiac told Stine to drive ahead one more block to stop at Cherry Street.

"Maple Street here leads more or less to the southwest corner of Julius Kahn Playground, where a possible Zodiac suspect was later sighted disappearing into.

"Zodiac instead tells Stine to drive on one more block to Cherry Street, where he smokes him.

"Go ahead, take us there."

Presently they pulled up to the curb between two stunted trees at the northeast corner of Washington and Cherry Streets in Presidio Heights—directly in front of the grand house across the street at 3898 Washington Street. A lofty street lamp towers high up above the southeast corner. Ironically a police telephone callbox still stands watch at that corner as a silent sentinel.

"From behind," Toski said solemnly, "Zodiac pressed the muzzle of a 9mm semi–automatic weapon tightly against Stine's right cheek just in front of his right ear— and fired point–blank.

"Three youngsters watched from the third–story windows of the house across the street as Zodiac exited the cab's right rear door and entered the right front door.

"These teen–aged witnesses were just fifty feet away

from the crime–in–progress and had a completely unobstructed view of it as it occurred.

"As he cradled Stine's exploded head in his lap, Zodiac picked Stine's pockets and took his car keys, black leather wallet and tore off a sizable portion from the back of Stine's bloody shirt.

"Zodiac took neither Stine's Timex wristwatch nor his class ring. He left the cab with both its engine and meter still running.

"Zodiac wiped the cab clean—both inside and out— with a white cloth, possibly a handkerchief. He paid particular attention to the cab's exterior left door.

"Then he fled north on foot on Cherry Street toward the Army Presidio—a block and a half away. He was in no great hurry. Like Zodiac wrote in his letter sent the 9th of November 1969: 'I disappeared into the park a block + a half away never to be seen again!'

"Responding officers found Stine slumped supine across the cab's front seat, his upper torso on the passenger side, his head facing north and resting on the floorboard.

"An ambulance was summoned, Code Three, and the steward who examined him pronounced Stine dead at the scene at ten–ten.

"The first inspector on the scene—Walter Kracke— summoned both dogs units and a firetruck spotlight to assist in the search for the suspect. We had the whole area flooded with lights.

"As I responded—together with another inspector, a sergeant and a lieutenant—I notified the Sixth Army military police headquarters of the Presidio. I arrived at the scene at eleven–ten—exactly at the same time as the MPs.

"An intensive search of the Julius Kahn Playground area was made by seven dog units, other Richmond Station and California Patrol units—all to no avail. So we had seven police dogs and a great number of patrolmen searching the area tree by tree and bush by bush. The dogs were the best in the country. A mouse couldn't have escaped our scrutiny. Interestingly, I've never read any reports on this case by the Presidio MPs.

"Almost underneath the front seat—close to the cab's center post—we found a single copper–colored 9mm semi–automatic shell casing—9mm Winchester Western ammunition. I suspect it was from a relatively rare new–model Browning.

"Quite honestly," Toski sulked, "I didn't know what the hell was going on! Stine's was the fourth murder since the seventh of October! Christ—four homicides in four days! This poor man bled profusely."

"What about the possible Zodiac suspect who was later sighted?" asked one of the detectives.

"That was the worst and most tragic part of this awful crime," Toski lamented mournfully. "Turn right and drive to the next block."

They rounded the corner and coasted to a stop at the intersection at the end of Cherry Street.

"Within just two to three minutes of the officially dispatched report, a radio unit out of the Richmond Station responded and raced to the scene, reaching the intersection of Jackson and Cherry Streets at ten o'clock straight–up!"

"Patrolmen Donald Fouke and Eric Zelms?" asked the other detective.

"Yes," Toski answered glumly. "Roughly a month later, Officer Don Fouke filed an intra–departmental memo reporting that he'd possibly sighted a suspect fitting the description of the Zodiac killer while en route to the Stine crime scene.

"Fouke observed this suspect walking east on Jackson Street—the parallel street north of Washington Street— toward the very same direction from which Fouke and Zelms were just coming!

"Fouke observed this suspect turn left on the cross street—Maple—and head north toward the Presidio—in the area of the Julius Kahn Playground!

"This suspect—who was white—was not stopped or detained since the description broadcast by dispatch was for a black male.

"What I've never understood is why this Zodiac suspect—if he really was the Zodiac killer—didn't simply continue on Cherry Street just past Jackson Street for another half block—which dead–ends at a small and secluded vehicle turnaround. Beyond the turnaround, some stone steps lead to a ledge and a four–foot drop to the road bordering the Presidio's southward edge. It's just a minute's walk from the Stine crime scene and gives easier and quicker access to the Presidio woods. Had he just kept on going straight—heading north instead of turning off and heading east—he would've been virtually guaranteed of escaping into the Presidio unseen! Turn right and drive to the next block."

They rounded the corner, heading east on Jackson Street and coasting to a stop at the intersection with Maple Street.

"Maybe Zodiac had a definite, pre–arranged game–plan in mind—and a definite reason for taking that particular route," suggested one of the detectives.

"In retrospect," Toski speculated, "my rough guess is: Zodiac intended to take that route as his street of retreat from the start. And the obvious reason why he directed Stine to drive on from Maple to Cherry Streets was so that no witnesses near the crime scene would see the direction of that line of retreat."

"Witnesses like the kids at the house at 3898 Washington Street?"

"Exactly," said Toski, nodding. "What Zodiac didn't figure on was the prompt response of that radio unit on

Jackson Street—or other witnesses in the neighborhood catching sight of him retreating into the Presidio. His escape route was so one–track–minded, he might've had another reason altogether that we haven't yet surmised. Turn left and drive to the end of the block."

They rounded the corner and coasted to a stop at the northward foot of Maple Street.

"There was always this nagging feeling the Zodiac case was a roundneck," Dave Toski confided.

"A trash basket case?"

"Yeah, and wind up in a file labeled, Unsolved.

"Zodiac was the most daunting of all my cases as well as the most frustrating. It was the most baffling murder case in our history.

"I used to stop at the corner of Washington and Cherry Streets to relive old memories. I'd park and observe a few minutes of silent contemplation. And every time I drove away, I couldn't escape the sense that I hadn't been alone on that dark corner among those solemn mansions.

"In 1988, I retired without having the pleasure of reading Zodiac his rights. That's all I wanted to do was close the case—tap Zodiac on the shoulder and say, 'Let me advise you of your Miranda rights.' And then handcuff him."

Dave Toski clutched his black folder and abruptly stepped out of the car.

"This is where I get off, gents," he told the detectives with a definite finality.

"You're not driving back downtown with us?" one or the other detectives asked, surprised.

"No thanks," said Toski, most adamant. "Everything that happened that night's been coming back to me. It's brought back a lot of memories. Forty–four years ago, I never dreamed that I'd be here today talking about this. I didn't know what to expect, how I'd feel. Recollecting some of the things that took place—it makes you feel helpless. Someday down the road we'll meet up again and put our heads together over this."

Dave Toski turned on his heel and the two detectives waited and watched as he stumped along, crossed West Pacific Avenue—and much like the Zodiac Killer over four decades before him—retired from sight along the secluded, frequently unfrequented road bordering the Presidio's southside.

"It's funny," Moretti mused aloud.

"What is?" Marino asked.

"That Toski would be making this pilgrimage back to the Presidio after all this time."

"Why's that?"

"He mentioned the Browning as being the probable murder weapon in the Stine killing."

"So?" said Marino.

"The Browning Hi-Power, single-action, nine–millimeter pistol," Moretti recounted, "is one of the most widely used military pistols of all time, having been used by the armies of over fifty countries. After the second world war, it was adopted as the standard service pistol by over ninety–three nations—including Canada and Great Britain!"

"How about that?"

SIX:
PRESIDIO
REVISITED

Julius Kahn Playground
Presidio Heights
San Francisco, California

anging from the tall olive green post standing at the entrance is the spare, olive green, swivel–sign bordered in black and imprinted with white letters:

Julius Kahn
Playground
San Francisco Recreation & Park Department

This well–known neighborhood playground is named in honor of Julius Kahn, a German–Jewish immigrant and Republican United States Congressman, who was a noted advocate of military preparedness.

Chance Bailey pulled over to the side of the bordering road to park his trim–interior Buick Electra Park Avenue Ultra with burled elm trim on the doors, padded vinyl top and aluminum wheels. His stout, undulating shadow preceded him after he got out to step up to Dave Toski, who sat at a green–painted picnic table close to a trio of tall trees shading the nearby cream–colored clubhouse.

"Inspector Toski?"

"I'm retired!" Toski snapped, looking out on the adjoining playground, where spirited children romped boisterously on an assortment of climbing frames, slides and swingsets.

"Sometimes I think San Francisco owns a franchise on homicidal maniacs," he pondered aloud unexpectedly, "who kill just for the thrill of killing.

"The city's a magnet for kooks, wackos and every crackpot imaginable. It's been plagued by kidnappings, political assassinations, religious cults, urban guerrillas—and serial killers.

"Charles Manson recruited his so–called family from

Haight–Ashbury's dropouts. The SLA kidnapped Patricia Hearst. The New World Liberation Front, the Zebra Killers, Jim Jones' People's Temple, Dan White and Zodiac have all called the city home.

"What is it about San Francisco that draws the dregs of society to seek sanctuary in such a splendid place?"

"Its tolerance for diversity?" Bailey cracked sarcastically.

"Its tolerance for scumbags, you mean," Toski said scornfully, getting to his feet. "And when Zodiac sent a bloody swatch of Paul Stine's shirt to the Chronicle, I knew we had a psychopathic killer on the loose. I knew we were involved in a very heavy case. I knew we were involved with a mass murderer.

"Let me introduce you to a true leading citizen of this magnificent city."

Toski led Bailey along a narrow, shrub–shrouded dirt footpath sidling a battered chain–link fence, hedging in an expansive open space directly behind the playground clubhouse—a sandy space, empty except for a flagpole, a pair of picnic tables and a circular cluster of bushes. In back of the clubhouse a low–lying green–metal fence hemmed in the open space.

Toski tread a path along the fence across clumps of grass until they came to a lone, solitary, green–painted bench perched upon a raised cement platform.

Toski gestured to the small gold–lettered plaque embossed on the back of the bench that read:

JAMES REAM, F.A.I.A.
ARCHITECT OF JK CLUBHOUSE
HE LOVED FAMILY, FRIENDS, THIS CITY, SUNSETS
AND BENCHES TO ENJOY "SWEET NOTHING TO DO"

"Jim Ream not only designed the Julius Kahn recreation building," Toski related, "he also lived just south of here on Clay Street—one block over from Washington

Street and just five blocks east of Cherry Street."

"The designer of a clubhouse at the Julius Kahn play-ground—through which Zodiac escaped into the Presidio never to be seen again—lived roughly just six blocks away from where Zodiac killed cabbie, Paul Stine, at Washington and Cherry Streets!"

"Exactly," Toski confirmed. "Ironic, isn't it?"

Together the two sat down on the bench, commanding a sweeping, panoramic view of the woodsy Presidio spreading far and wide before their eyes.

"So how do you think Zodiac made his getaway after escaping police pursuit into the Presidio?" Bailey reflected.

"Conventional wisdom assumes that Zodiac escaped in a getaway car parked someplace in the vicinity," Toski said skeptically, "but I've never bought the silly scenario that Zodiac parked his getaway car at the Presidio, hiked nearly a mile south to Geary Avenue to ride a crowded 38 Geary MUNI bus all the way back downtown to the theatre district to hail a taxicab to take all the way back to the Presidio—just so he could off the driver and foot it into the military base!

"That theory just makes no sense at all—especially since he didn't have to commute all the way back downtown to hail a cab. If he had hiked over to Geary Avenue—a continuously busy four-lane boulevard—he could've just as easily hailed or even called a cab from there to drive him back to Presidio Heights. Commuting to the theatre district just to catch a cab was totally unnecessary to carry out that scenario."

"Conventional wisdom likewise assumes that Zodiac was a navy man," Bailey reminded Toski with a knowing nod, "because of his crewcut hairstyle, the wing–walker boots and windbreaker he wore, the seaman–style knots he tied in clothesline, and some of the cipher symbols he used in his letters."

"What if Zodiac was instead," Bailey suggested with melodramatic seriousness, "not a navy man, but an army man?"

"What?" Toski rasped apprehensively under his breath.

"Paul Lee Stine's killing is the key to solving this entire mystery," Bailey elucidated. "His is the only authenticated Zodiac crime that deviates and breaks his established pattern of attacking young couples at lovers' lanes or secluded spots, in or around their cars near bodies of water. Being in the Army is the only logical or rational reason to explain the reason why Zodiac would hire a taxicab to take him within easy walking distance of the Army Presidio!"

"Jeezus," Dave Toski mused aloud, suddenly looking aghast as if he had just regained his eyesight after being blind for a long time. "Talk about not seeing the forest for the trees. We've been shopping for surplus in the wrong part of the Army–Navy store. Zodiac could've simply been...going back to base!"

"What's really intriguing is the timeline of coincidental facts linking Zodiac to the Presidio," Bailey elucidated. "Letterman Army Hospital's new building was completed in May 1968 and renamed the Letterman Army Medical Center. Exactly six years later, Zodiac wrote his infamous 'Badlands' card dated the 8th of May 1974. Zodiac's first authenticated attack on David Faraday and Betty Lou Jensen on Lake Herman Road in Benicia, California occurs on the 20th of December 1968.

"Exactly a year later to the day, Zodiac writes a letter to San Francisco tort attorney, Melvin Belli. on the 20th of December 1969.

"Letterman Army Medical Center is officially dedicated on the 14th of February 1969, Valentine's Day. Exactly five years to the day, Zodiac wrote his infamous 'SLA' card, received the 14th of February 1974. Zodiac's second authenticated attack on Darlene Ferrin and Mike Mageau in Blue Rock Springs Park in Vallejo, California occurs on the 4th of July, 1969. Exactly five years later, Zodiac sent his infamous Count Marco Red Phantom letter dated the 8th of July 1974.

"Zodiac's third authenticated attack on Bryan Hartnell and Cecelia Shepherd at Lake Berryessa north of Napa, California occurs on the 27th of September 1969.

"Zodiac's fourth authenticated attack on cabbie, Paul Lee Stine, in San Francisco's Presidio Heights occurs on the 11th of October 1969.

"In 1973, the adjoining Letterman Army Institute of Research occupied a new complex of four inter–connected concrete buildings constructed between 1973 and 1977."

"This period of construction activity relating to the Letterman Army Hospital demarcates Zodiac's scope of operation," Toski concluded, "from beginning to end."

"As good as book ends!" Bailey concurred, nodding. "The new Army Letterman Hospital was erected in May 1968 at the height of the Vietnam war. It was a modern, ten–story, 550–bed, reinforced concrete facility designed by San Francisco architects Milton Pflueger and Douglas Stone.

"Their joint venture architect–engineering firm of Marraccini, Patterson, Stone and Milton T. Pflueger prepared the plans and specifications for the new Letterman.

"Halverson and McLaughlin, under the supervision of the U.S. Army District Engineer, Sacramento, completed the construction in the fall of 1968; it was dedicated in 1969.

"In 1973, it was re–named the Letterman Army Medical Center. The entire Letterman Complex covered 60 acres.

"That old Army Letterman building was ultimately demolished in 2003 to be replaced by the existing Lucasfilm's Letterman Digital Arts Center."

"Why didn't the San Francisco District of the U.S. Army Corps of Engineers supervise Letterman's construction in San Francisco's Presidio?"

"In 1961, the South Pacific Division of the U.S. Army Corps of Engineers formally transferred the San Francisco District's military design and construction work to the Sacramento District! Under OCE General Order No. 9, dated 7 April 1961, the Sacramento District assumed responsibility for military design and construction for San Francisco District projects. Even San Francisco's civil and military real estate activities were transferred to Sacramento.

"In 1970, the Division assigned to the Sacramento District the design and construction work for the Seattle District, which had held centralized responsibility over military and design construction for the entire Pacific Northwest prior to this re–assignment. This meant that the Sacramento District then oversaw the design work not only for California but also for Arizona, Idaho, Nevada, Oregon, Utah, Washington—and Montana—from which Zodiac claimed he had escaped from Deer Lodge state prison during the Lake Berryessa attack.

"This official transfer meant that the Sacramento District's engineers took over a considerable number of military design and construction projects—including the construction of veterans' hospitals in general, and the new Letterman General Hospital in particular!

"Not to mention military work at bases in the neighborhood of verified Zodiac kill–sites: the Benicia Arsenal—the Lake Herman Road shootings occurred in Solano County within the Benicia city limits; Travis Air Force Base in Fairfield in Solano County—in which resides Vallejo, where the Blue Rock Springs shootings occurred; Hamilton Air Force Base in Novato, which is roughly ten miles north–northwest of San Rafael—from which Zodiac posted his last confirmed Count Marco Red Phantom letter dated 8 July 1974; Almaden Air Force Station on the peninsula in Santa Clara County—from which Zodiac likely sent his last disputed letter in 1978; and Castle Air Force Base, northeast of Atwater and northwest of Merced, along with Sharpe General Depot in Stockton, both located within San Joaquin Valley—where Kathleen Johns claimed Zodiac abducted her and her ten–month–old infant daughter on the 22nd of March 1970.

"By 1967—roughly a year before the first verified Zodiac attack on Lake Herman Road—the Defense Contract Administration Office was established and assumed full authority for all contracts assigned to manufacturers in the San Francisco Bay Area. With that transfer of responsibility, the San Francisco District's association with military projects ended!

"During this time period the Sacramento District of the U.S. Army Corps of Engineers became western America's hub for military design and construction work—including its new wartime role of constructing veterans' hospitals."

"So?" Toski asked.

"So your Zodiac killer could've easily operated out of the Sacramento District. And if you're looking for engineers occupying the Presidio," Bailey answered, "the Sixth Army was overrun with engineers—not to mention engineer battalions, engineer companies, engineer detachments and engineer groups! In 1957 alone the Presidio's Topographical Survey included the 1000–man 30th Engineer Group, an active army unit, all of whom took up quarters at the fort, where it remained the Presidio reservation's single largest troop unit for several years!"

"Was?" Toski asked.

"Following the transfer of the Presidio from the Army to the National Park Service," Bailey clarified, "both the hospital and the research institute were de—activated in 1995."

"Transfer?" Toski asked.

"The Presidio's current role as a public urban park was first written into law in 1972 when Congress established the Golden Gate National Recreation Area," Bailey explained. "The National Park Service assumed stewardship of the Presidio from the U.S. Army in October 1994.

"Once the Army post was closed, the 1972 law required the Presidio's conversion to National Park status.

"On the 30th of September 1994 the Sixth Army and Presidio Garrison held an Inactivation—Retreat Ceremony.

"On the 1st of October 1994 the official ceremony was held transferring the Presidio to the National Park Service. Once the Sixth Army vacated, the Presidio officially became part of the National Park Service."

"What are you driving at?"

"Let's take a stroll down Lover's Lane," Bailey suggested, holding out his hand with an inviting gesture.

SEVEN:
PROMENADING
LOVER'S
LANE

Lover's Lane
The Presidio
San Francisco, California

Lover's Lane is a narrow and steep footpath cutting a tilted, slanted and stony swath through the Presidio's scenic southeast sector—a forest of live oak, palms, redwood and eucalyptus trees—its westward edge sidled by wooden fence posts. It's likewise flanked by tall lamp posts set at regularly spaced intervals. It originates at the Presidio Boulevard entrance crossed by Pacific Avenue in Presidio Heights. From that starting point it threads a lengthy but straight path in a steeply downhill direction to the northwest. It terminates at its outlet at the foot of winding Presidio Boulevard. At its bottom a commemorative sign chronicles its history:

This trail has witnessed the passing of Spanish soldiers, Franciscan missionaries and American soldiers of two centuries. It is perhaps the oldest travel corridor in San Francisco.

In 1776 this path connected the Spanish Presidio with the mission, three miles to the southeast. During the 1860s it became the main route used by off–duty soldiers to walk into San Francisco. Many of those men made the trip into town to meet their sweethearts, and the trail became known as Lover's Lane.

"Physical evidence—such as the Wing Walker shoes and the Zodiac letters themselves—appears to substantiate the irreducible proposition that Zodiac was a military man having engineering knowledge and experience; and who was stationed—at least for a while—in the San Francisco Bay Area," Bailey continued. "Military transfers could account for those gaps in his murderous activities."

"It's highly unlikely Zodiac could keep on arranging to return to a Bay Area post even if we assume he was a military man," Toski suggested.

"Improbable maybe but not impossible," Bailey smilingly corrected him. "Impossible were he a regular military man. Not so improbable were he a military–affiliated engineer assigned to work on a number of different and various and sundry engineering projects throughout the Bay Area."

"All this conjecture is pretty tenuous."

"Not so tenuous as basements," Bailey proposed surprisingly, "which are rare in San Francisco buildings as a rule—but not at the Presidio!"

"Oh," Toski said stoically, "now you've lost me. What have basements got to do with Zodiac?"

"Think back upon Zodiac's letter of November 9, 1969," Bailey reminded him, "which alluded to the bomb he threatened to detonate—the so–called 'death machine' he threatened to explode."

"I recall it well."

"'What you do not know,'" Bailey quoted directly from a copy of Zodiac's letter, "'is whether the death machine is at the sight(sic)or whether it is being stored in my basement for future use.'"

"I don't follow you," Toski admitted.

"One of the numerous architectural characteristics of the Letterman Complex," Bailey divulged gravely, "and I quote directly from its lengthy list of final planning and design guidelines: 'A basement story is often clearly visible. Because of the slope of the site, the basement story is often fully above ground, at least on one side of the building...Basement stories that are visible and at grade on the down–slope side of most buildings!'"

"Naturally," Bailey expounded further, "a military post like the Presidio required the construction of all kinds of housing units or apartments to accommodate its personnel—enlisted soldiers' barracks, bachelor officers' and pilots' quarters, enlisted family housing, officer family housing, singles, duplexes, triplexes—for both commissioned and non–commissioned officers—and even guest houses. Presidio housing included even navy as well as army units in case you ever thought intuitively that Zodiac was a navy man—to say nothing of possibly being one of the Presidio's hundreds of civilian personnel.

"In the early 1960s, the Presidio even had an Indoor Small Bore Range for .22–caliber target shooting—Zodiac's caliber of choice for his first Lake Herman Road attack. It's been speculated that Zodiac was a cop–turned–killer—on account of his driving cutoff techniques, his cop I.D. techniques, his outstretched flashlight—not to mention his shooting skill. For all we know, Zodiac could've honed his shooting skills at that very range!"

"Are you inferring Zodiac resided in Presidio housing having a basement?"

"I'm not inferring anything," Bailey refuted him. "I'm affirming the fact of the matter: a great many of the Presidio's housing units are indeed endowed with sub–story basements! Whether Zodiac himself ever occupied one is still an open question left to be determined.

"'Hey blue pig I was in the park—you were useing(sic) fire trucks to mask the sound of your cruzeing(sic)prowl cars,'" Zodiac wrote in his letter of November 9, 1969. "'The dogs never came with in 2 blocks of me & they were to(sic)groups of parking about 10 min apart then the motor cicles(sic)went by about 150 ft away going from south to north west.' From the southward borders of the Presidio, Arguello and Presidio Boulevards both wind from the southerly to the northwestly direction—and both boulevards pass by Presidio housing complexes. For all we know, Zodiac was watching the entire search from one of those basement windows!"

"Look around, Inspector," Bailey invited him, "and

inspect any number of the Presidio's duplexes or triplexes—and see for yourself."

"I'm re–...," Toski cut himself short as he surveyed the military duplexes and triplexes situated nearest the footpath they were traversing, He shuddered as a bitter sensation chilled his spine.

"When I first saw these basements," Bailey confided, "my heart was going pitter–pat!"

Here, there, everywhere he looked—all around Dave Toski nervously ran his eyes over the numerous small, rectangular windows of sub–story duplex and triplex basements exposed to view just above ground–level!

"Are you familiar with the John Stewart Company—the property management company operating the Presidio Residences for the Presidio Trust?"

"Oh, yeah," Toski said with a knowing nod, "I've had some run–ins with that shyster outfit. They've got a corporate office over on Sutter Street. Why?"

"Serial killers like Zodiac have been known to keep articles from their victims as souvenirs and trophies of their crimes. So I considered contacting the company about conducting a painstaking basement–to–basement search of all Presidio buildings to look for artifacts of Zodiac's cabbie killing—like Paul Stine's keys, shirt swatches or even the contents of his stolen wallet. But I seriously doubt they could be trusted to undertake something that important—being the incompetent morons they're reputed to be."

"What would you expect of a company founded by a graduate of Stanford University?" Toski said facetiously.

"There's one other coincidental fact that might interest you," Bailey suggested.

"What might that be?" Toski asked, curious.

"The Paul Lee Stine killing marked a morbid Presidio anniversary," Bailey elaborated. "Pvt. Richard 'Rusty' J.

Bunch, a 19–year–old prisoner at the Fort Scott stockade, attempted to escape a work detail and was shot and killed by a 22–year–old Mexican–American guard. Three days later, twenty–seven prisoners refused to work in protest and staged a sit–down strike—precipitating the so–called Presidio Mutiny! That shooting incident occurred on the 11th of October 1968—exactly a year to the day before Zodiac shot and killed cabbie, Paul Stine! Killed ten years later, Stine was ten years older than Bunch when he died."

§

Detectives Moretti and Marino pulled up in their Ford Taurus, parking behind Chance Bailey's Buick Electra on West Pacific Avenue's southward roadside.

Glancing around discreetly, Marino got out to hastily step up to Bailey's car to surreptitiously place upon its undercarriage a GPS tracking unit—a Global Positioning System device module to report and record the car's precise position at regular intervals.

"I take it we're not getting a warrant for that," Moretti said once Marino settled back into his seat.

"Welcome to Unsavory Dave's world!" Marino sniggered with a slight sneer.

EIGHT:
A
LOVELY
LASS
NAMED
DONNA

Apartments
225 Mallorca Way
Marina District
San Francisco, California

Chance Bailey pulled up his Buick Electra to a gentle stop at the curb across the street from the brightly–lit, four–story, white apartment building, hovering high from its perch at the corner of Mallorca Way and Capra Streets in San Francisco's Marina neighborhood. Twin lanterns shed lambent light on either side of the building's arched entryway. A shining ceiling globe threw beamy light upon its ornate foyer and grated front door and dual, elongated windows.

"Why have you brought me here?"

"I wanted you to see—and sense—where she once lived."

"Who?" Toski asked.

"Donna Lass," Bailey answered, "a pretty young nurse who's a suspected but unconfirmed Zodiac victim."

"On the 22nd of March 1971," Bailey recounted, "Zodiac sent the San Francisco Chronicle his infamous postcard plastered with newspaper cutouts and phrases—like 'around in the snow,' 'peek through the pines,' 'Sierra Club' and 'Sought Victim 12.' It bore Zodiac's cross–and–circle symbol.

"Zodiac decorated the card's edges with circular cuts made by a paper punch. Pasted to the back of the card was an artist's rendering of an ad for Forest Pines, a condominium complex under development near Incline Village on Lake Tahoe's north shore.

"The ad for the condos had run in the Chronicle just two days before.

"This particular postcard directly links Zodiac with the Presidio."

"How's that?" Toski asked curiously.

"Six months earlier," Bailey explained, "a 25–year–old casino first–aid nurse named Donna Lass went missing on the 6th of September 1970 after she left work at the Sahara Hotel in Stateline, Nevada.

"Her car was found parked near her Monte Verdi apartment. There was no sign of any struggle. Her purse and the clothes she was wearing was all that was missing.

"On the day she disappeared, an unidentified male caller told both her employer and her landlord that she would not be returning due to an illness in her family.

"The call was a ruse. Police were advised by Lass' family that there had been no such illness. Lake Tahoe police believed Donna Lass had been abducted and killed. She's never been found or seen since."

"I still don't see the connection to the Presidio."

"From February to June of 1970," Bailey said gravely, "Donna Lass worked as a nurse at Letterman General Hospital on the Presidio—close to where she also lived here at 225 Mallorca Way in the Marina! She relocated to Lake Tahoe three months later and vanished without a trace—and, like Zodiac, never to be seen again.

"According to a girlfriend of Donna's—a dialysis nurse named Jo Anne Goesttsche—Donna had dated somebody from Sacramento. Sometime in early October 1970—after Donna's disappearance—South Lake Tahoe police received a phone call from a male in Sacramento, but he never called back.

"Donna was last seen on the 7th of September 1970 walking with a young blonde man near the Monte Verdi apartment she'd rented just the day before—but never lived in. She left behind a new car, bank account and considerable wardrobe."

"Leading you to draw what conclusion?"

"I think Zodiac was closely connected to the Presidio,"

Bailey asserted excitedly. "I think he was tied directly to the Letterman Army Hospital—most likely in some engineering–related capacity. For all we know, Zodiac—who's been described with a blonde crewcut—could've been a temporary patient of Donna's at the hospital! The date of Donna's disappearance coincides with authenticated Zodiac correspondence during a time period in which he claimed victims ten through thirteen.

"Coincidentally, construction for the new Letterman Army Hospital at the Presidio had been supervised not by the San Francisco District but rather by the Sacramento District of the United States Army Corps of Engineers!"

"You know," Toski brooded, "after you investigate so many cases, you get to be jaded to the degree that you discover so many coincidences—you just don't believe in coincidences after awhile. The only thing I put any stock in is something that I know for a fact. I handle any investigation like the limbs on a tree. I methodically follow each lead as it branches from the facts."

"I've nailed down some pretty interesting facts for making out a case for further investigation—for the sake of Zodiac's victims if nothing else. In February 1971 Donna's family offered a five hundred dollar reward for information leading to the discovery of their daughter, who disappeared without a trace. For that time five hundred dollars was a lot of money. Forty years later, nobody gives a damn about the victim much less the reward."

"In homicide," Toski confided, "you spend a lot of your time dealing with relations of the victim and relations of the suspect. You have to sympathize with one and be extremely sensitive with the other.

"Of course, I'm not actively working on the Zodiac case anymore. Nobody's pounding on my door. Paul Lee Stine's family isn't there every day asking what are you doing about the death of my husband, or whatever. It's the age–old adage—the squeaky wheel gets the oil.

"So I completely understand the demands of current cases—and the current victims from more recent homicide cases. But Zodiac's always stood to me as symbolic of S.F.P.D's commitment not to give up on unsolved homicides. Homicide cases generally get worked only if the heat for them's turned up under the boss' butt!

"Once I retired I put it all behind me. When I quit, I really quit. Since then it's been like I've been living in a cave. I wish we could've followed up further back then. Outside of Zodiac's letters, what evidence did we have? We were grasping at straws."

"That was then, Dave, this is now," Bailey audaciously volunteered. "Maybe it's time you came out of your cave."

"Obviously," Toski conceded with a careless shrug, "you've uncovered a lot of fascinating—even startling—information. I'm really amazed at your background information on Zodiac. Some of the information you have on him really grabbed my attention. I think it's terrific. You could be on the right track and onto something really big—or then again, you could be going down a blind alley. What do you want me to do about it?"

"I'd like to see it all come together," Bailey pleaded imploringly, "but I figure I need your help to bring it all together—and crack this case wide open once and for all.

"I'm convinced of one thing: if you could compile a comprehensive list of all personnel residing at the Presidio reservation on the 11th of October 1969—the night of Paul Lee Stine's murder—and narrow down that list to draftsmen or engineers who were either British, Canadian or even Australian—then I firmly believe you would at last find and unmask your Zodiac killer!"

"That means going through official channels to contact the Sixth Army and request dated and possibly non-existent records," Toski cautioned, "which could prove to be pretty complicated."

"Not to mention politically inexpedient?" Bailey cracked.

"No more inconvenient than the favor I'll be asking of you in return," said Toski, creasing his cheek with an ironical smile.

"What's that?"

"I want the full lowdown on this Joseph Mustapha and these Black Muslim pals of yours," Toski stated flatly.

"I don't really know the dudes," Bailey disavowed. "I'm acquainted with them mostly by reputation. But I could do a little digging."

"Yeah, you do that."

PART THREE: *MUSLIM BLAME*

NINE:
MOHAMMED'S MOSQUE

"We have always been taught to respect the laws of the land. We are taught never to carry arms, to make war or to be the aggressor, for this is against the nature of the righteous."—**Nation of Islam(NOI)**

MOSQUE MOHAMMED
5048 3rd Street
Bayview–Hunters Point
Southeast San Francisco, California

Running along newly constructed light–rail tracks, gunmetal gray, red–streaked cars of San Francisco's T–Third Street Muni Metro Line cross north–south Third Street for most of its dreary, interminable route through the blighted Bayview–Hunters Point district. Pairs of light–rail tracks extend in both directions on either side of the roadway, which is divided in the middle by a shrub–covered, asphalt island lined with five lofty palm trees.

Two green street lamp posts—one tall, one short—stand over the smutty sidewalk in front of the faded, three–story, brownstone, block–like building hovering high above. Between the two street lamps stands a single, scraggly, threadbare tree. Beneath the eaves overhead a twin–tier pair of ornate, fire–escape balconies protrude midway from the front facade.

Chance Bailey's Buick Electra was parked at the green–metered curb space directly in front of the facing black–grill doorway, opening out at the building's northward, street–level corner.

Inside his corner third–floor office, Joseph Mustapha sat behind his grand desk next to a simple, white–draped, four–panel window overlooking Third Street below. His favorite four young adopted sons—Isaiah, Jeremiah, Joshua and Zechariah—stood as silent sentinels in suits, arms akimbo, in the rear of the room.

"I'm a man who has great respect for the press," Mustapha spouted, gesticulating grandiosely, "but I also have respect for myself, my mission and my message. I've never tried to manipulate the press for my own advantage. So I rarely grant interviews."

He poured out malt liquor into tumblers from a forty ounce bottle of Olde English 800; the two took drinks while talking together.

"What is it exactly that Black Muslims want?"

"We want freedom, justice and equality!"

"Freedom from what? Freedom to do what?"

"We want full and complete freedom from our former white slave masters! We want every black man and every black woman to have the freedom to accept or reject living completely separate and apart from the descendants of their former white slave masters!"

"So you consider all white people alive today to be your former slave masters by virtue of their white ancestry?"

"Absolutely correct!"

"What else? Or is that all you want?"

"We want freedom from police brutality and racial profiling! We want freedom from mob attacks against black people in these United States! We want freedom for all black men and women now being wrongly incarcerated in American prisons! We want freedom for all black men and women in prison awaiting executions under unjust death sentences! We want equal justice and equal education and employment opportunity under the laws of these United States! We want equal protection under those laws! And we rightly demand these things now—not later!"

"How do you propose to get all those things? It sounds like you expect the more charitable descendants of your former white slave masters to give you a lot of handouts—and more entitlement!"

"Payback—not handouts—which is our fair and just due! Entitlement? You're fucking right we're entitled to some fucking payback!"

"Payback for what?"

"Payback for giving our former white slave masters four hundred years of blood, sweat and tears—and receiving in return some of the worst and most atrocious treatment human beings have ever been subjected to! Four hundred years of free black slave labor which made our former white slave masters rich and powerful! In return for which so many thousands of black people starve and live a hand–to–mouth existence in ghettos and projects—or barely subsist on the magnanimous charity begrudgingly provided by their former white slave masters! What we're entitled to we're owed by our former white slave masters! We only demand what we deserve and have coming to us!

"We've paid our dues for four hundred years. So now we come demanding—instead of begging and pleading. You can't put no price on slavery."

"How do you rate payback from whites who've never enslaved anybody—especially when you yourself have never experienced oppression at the hands of any white slave masters? You're condemning wholesale the entire white race of descendants for the evil and wrong done by their ancestors!"

"You're fucking right I am! Because the descendants of our former white slave masters remain responsible for perpetuating to this day all the atrocities and outrages inflicted on black people by their ancestors! And each and every existing generation of our former white slave masters is as wicked as the last in that respect!"

"Then you believe that contemporary black people are still victims of white enslavement?"

"You're fucking right I do! The current status of black people in this country is that of being freed slaves who are still not equal with their slave masters—not even after suffering four hundred years of slavery! The inequality and injustice against black people is perpetuated by our former white slave masters everyplace you look! Do I really have to spell this shit out for you—an educated fool of a black man sitting there asking me these dumb–ass questions?"

"Holding such generic beliefs and making such sweep-ing statements smacks of being extreme fanaticism. How can you blame wholesale the entire white race and all its descendants for all the injury and wrong suffered by black people?"

"Because we've never been properly compensated—neither for the contributions we've made to this country many times over, nor for all the suffering that's been forced upon us by white America! So you're absolutely fucking correct: I'm extremely fanatical when it comes to that!"

"Have you suffered at the hands of white America?"

"I was raised in Viz Valley! In the Geneva Towers—before they were razed by the city in 1998. What do you think?"

"Visitacion Valley? The notorious Sunnydale Projects are still one of the city's most violent hoods."

"Hey, where'd you get your ghetto pass? They call the Dale projects The Swamp! When I was younger I used to rep my hood to the fullest. The pain I've seen black people suffer there is more than enough to make me plenty angry with this city and with this country!"

"So you blame white America for all the drug dealers and gangbangers overrunning the area?"

"I blame four centuries of black dehumanization. I blame the injustice of white America. I blame the hostil-ity of white society. Justice is what balances the human mind. Whenever any human being is deprived of justice, the mind becomes imbalanced. The greater the injustice, the greater the imbalance."

"Yet your parents were hardworking, legit black peo-ple. Your own father labored in the shipyards just to send you to Howard University in Washington, D.C., from which you graduated with honors. Before that, they even sent you to the San Francisco Conservatory of Music as a child to receive rigorous training in the violin, which I understand you play quite skillfully. So your own youth wasn't totally wanting in opportunities."

"Dummy up, gumby, and leave my family out of this fucking conversation," Mustapha scolded Bailey sternly. "Let's switch gears."

"Fair enough. Your detractors claim that yours is a distorted branch—a deformed version—of Islam utterly lacking in any core Islamic doctrine or dogma. They claim yours is not an orthodox religion, but rather an un–orthodox cult, which adheres to aberrant ideology and practices. And that although you purport to be motivated by Islamic principles, services conducted at Black Muslim temples are absolutely bereft of any resemblance to any religious rites or rituals."

"So say our haters!" Mustapha exclaimed, chuckling. "Local temples are permitted personal interpretation of Islam's basic precepts. Our common denominator is that we're all black and that we all have the same problems. And that we need to unite to get out of hell!"

"They also say yours is a violent, anti–American cult, dedicated to propagating hatred and hostility against the white race—with a view to overthrowing America's constitutional government as an ill–used instrument of the white race of white devils."

"We learned one great lesson from the white man," Mustapha asserted bitterly. "He's successful. But he makes no apologies or excuses for his failures. He schemes and maneuvers in a collective manner. We concluded that it was in our best collective interests to imitate that strategy. So we're not looking to the white man—not for jobs, not for justice, not for liberty. If that's anti–American then so be it!"

"Then you advocate complete segregation from, rather than integration with the white race?"

"Integration is a hypocritical sham intended to deceive black people into believing that our 400–year–old open enemies are all of a sudden our bosom friends. If our former white slave masters were truly sincere about their professed friendship toward the downtrodden negro, then they'd prove it by dividing up America equally with their slaves!"

"Can we all get along?" Bailey hissed resignedly, shaking his head, echoing Rodney King, famous for being a victim of police brutality at the hands of sadistic police officers from the Los Angeles Police Department on the 3rd of March 1991.

"No," snapped Mustapha, "we can't fucking get along—and we believe that our rightful demand for complete separation from the white man is more than justified! We're white people with black skin. It's all a mentality. We believe not only in the physical liberation of the black man, but also the mental liberation from mental murder! There's no real revolution so long as we remain mentally enslaved by our former white slave masters! We're righteous—and we believe in the liberation of the righteous!"

"You parrot the Nation of Islam's precepts," Bailey challenged him, "but you're not even directly affiliated with the Nation. After all, the Nation openly professes to recognize and respect American citizens as independent peoples—and respects the rule of law which governs them."

"We're down with the Nation in spirit but not necessarily in method! We adapt the Nation's precepts to fit our own special needs and wants. We can't—and won't—ever recognize or respect the laws written by our former white slave masters!"

"Then you do advocate violence as a method of attaining your aims?"

"Let's take this back to the essence: we're down with our martyred brother, Malcolm X, who left the Nation."

"Roughly a year after he left," Bailey said sullenly, "members of the Nation assassinated Malcolm X with 21 gunshots—ten of those coming from a sawed–off shotgun."

"By any means necessary, brother, by any means necessary!"

"That pretty much sums up everything."

"It doesn't explain what you were doing at Star Security the other day when I was leaving," Mustapha said unexpectedly.

"I was looking up former police inspector, Dave Toski."

"What the fuck did you want with that white beast?"

"I wanted to discuss Zodiac with him. He was the chief investigating officer in charge of the case. He wasn't much interested in talking about it."

"What motivated you to hit me up then? I've got no connection to Zodiac."

"Since we happened to cross paths, it crossed my mind to propose doing a profile on you and your temple. You're living large and in charge in this city. I think you'd make a great human interest story."

"Story or exposé?" Mustapha asked skeptically.

"I'm not here to scandalize your name. I could help get your message out."

"Respect the game and I'll think about it. Just don't put me in any of that talk show shit."

Pausing for emphasis Mustapha admonished Bailey ominously.

"And never, ever dis the program."

§

"Joshua—" Mustapha summoned to his side the youngest of his spiritually adopted sons, who broke formation from the regimented quartet of black men in black suits and bow ties, stepping up obediently to his leader.

Together they stared down at Chance Bailey below, watching from Mustapha's third—story window as the reporter got into his Buick Electra and promptly pulled away from the curb, merging smoothly into Third Street traffic.

"I think this brother's an off—brand Oreo who's perpetrating something. He could be working with those peoples. I have a strange feeling the man's a C.I. who might try and dime on us," Mustapha mused aloud.

"Confidential informant, huh?" Joshua snarled. "Do you want me to give that chump the mumps?"

"No," Mustapha said slyly. "First, I want you to play him close and spin him for a while. He thinks he's jive slick. But it's going to be your job to keep him in the blind—even though you may have to rock him to sleep later."

§

Just a short time later, Chance Bailey reappeared at the doorstep of Mosque Mohammed, ringing the door buzzer and waiting patiently for the front door to reopen. He strained slightly to hold up the thing he was carrying.

As the corner door opened out, the tall and burly suited silhouettes of Joseph Mustapha's four main men—Isaiah, Jeremiah, Joshua and Zechariah—filled the foyer doorway. Mustapha parted the middle of the black cordon, pressing forward and stepping up to Bailey. Mustapha abruptly shrank back, standing aghast at the unexpected sight directly in front of him.

"Special delivery!" Chance Bailey remarked mockingly. "I believe this belongs to you! As I was leaving I caught sight of a young woman laying this at your doorstep."

Bailey exerted himself to hold up slightly higher for Mustapha to inspect: a light, sturdy, woven wicker baby bassinet, containing a wiggly, softly whiffling black infant, blanket–wrapped atop a miniature cot and pillow.

Atop the baby's body rested a plain and simple piece of loose–leaf paper with hand–printed letters scrawled in black felt–tip ink:

"I want my paternity rights!"

Wincing, Chance Bailey flinched and abruptly sprang back from the doorstep in mortal fear. Without warning another quartet of young black men sporting dark suits and bow ties, their gun muzzles pointed east toward San Francisco Bay, repeatedly fired off multiple rounds from their AK–47 selective–fire, gas–operated assault rifles! From the rooftop above they suddenly discharged their weapons in unison, shooting into the air.

"What the hell's that all about?" Bailey asked, aghast.

"From time to time," Joseph Mustapha told him seriously, "we like to remind the residents of the hood who's in charge. And make no mistake: around here I'm the head boss nigga in charge!"

TEN:
AT
THE
DEVIL'S
BACKBONE

Alta Plaza Park
San Francisco, California

Alta Plaza Park, surrounded by stately painted Victorians, Mission Revival, Edwardian and châteaux–style mansions, crowns the westward border of San Francisco's wealthy Pacific Heights neighborhood. Bordered by Jackson Street on the north, Clay Street to the south, with Steiner and Scott Streets on its eastern and western edges, the park embraces six city blocks, which interrupt the east–west continuation of Washington Street and the north–south continuation of Pierce Street. Overlooking much of the city's Cow Hollow and Marina districts, the park commands breezy, panoramic views of The Presidio, Fort Mason and Alcatraz island offshore in San Francisco Bay. Its northward half consists of a spacious grassy expanse. Sloping, terraced lawns gently cascade across its southward half. A thick cluster of trees separates the park's northward and southward halves.

Sauntering along a protracted, low–lying hedge, Chance Bailey and Joshua approached each other from opposite ends of an asphalt, east–west footpath. They met atop the wide, central, sectioned steps, descending the sloping grassy terrace to Clay Street far off below. Together they sat down on a green–painted wooden bench, commanding a panoramic view of the sprawling, southward cityscape. Hovering over the hills and far away was the triple–pronged, 981–foot antenna tower close to Clarendon Heights: Sutro Tower.

"Pacific Heights is known in the city as the devil's backbone," Chance Bailey mused whimsically. "It's a made–to–order place for dissing the white devils!"

"Joseph Mustapha much prefers killing to trash talking white devils," Joshua scoffed.

133

"Really? Tell me more."

"Joseph Mustapha's the head of the temple by title only. He's a fake—a fraud who just pretends to be a spiritual minister. He's greedy and power–hungry.

"He's a con man who preys upon the emotions and pocketbooks of ignorant black people. His goal is to appeal to the so–called marginalized and disenfranchised black masses for followers.

"That's why his temple's located in an indigent black neighborhood. He likes to cleanse the area around the temple headquarters of undesirables."

"Undesirables?" Bailey asked apprehensively. "Blue–eyed white devils?"

"Brown, red, yellow—anybody who's not black. He says a lot of vicious things against all groups, gays being the most graphic. He mocks Christians, berates the Jews, calls caucasians devils and teaches his followers that blacks are the world's master race."

"Traditional Islam permits people of all races to follow the teachings of the Koran," Bailey pointed out.

"Mustapha's a fraud—a religious faker who pushes concocted religious teachings—which are in direct opposition to orthodox Muslim teachings. He just pretends to boost the morals of his members by his strong condemnation of adultery, drinking, fornication, lying, smoking, stealing, and so on and so forth."

"What was that kid left on the doorstep in a bassinet all about?"

"Mustapha's had at least forty–two kids with fourteen different chicks!" Joshua snickered. "Getting knocked up is an occupational hazard of serving as a secretary to the Reverend Mustapha!"

"I really don't care about his love life."

"You should care: he's raped no end of underaged black girls."

"What's this about him killing people?"

"Mustapha's Islam is a homemade brand of religion with its own strict rules and regulations. Any criticism or opposition is silenced. His temple's organized like an army. Weapons are commonplace everywhere.

"His word's the law. Basically, it's what he says goes. Everybody knows that nobody does nothing unless he tells them to."

"Then he must have a pretty devoted following."

"He likes having a crew of strong people around him he can depend on. He likes them to do whatever he tells them. He likes them not to be afraid to employ violence to acquire cash.

"Anybody who wants to stay a member has to follow his strict discipline. Its members just follow along trying to obey the strict discipline he demands. Nonconformist members get disciplined by beatings given by the temple's goon squad."

"Who runs this goon squad?"

"The temple captain. The temple captain's an aggressive, domineering dude who gets off on any opportunity to command the temple members. He maintains strict military–style discipline over them. He leads this strong–arm group that beats members who get disciplined."

"Who's that?"

"Zechariah! He's the temple's disciplinarian, second–in–command and the real leader of the men. He leads this special elite paramilitary group that enforces the temple rules—the very repressive and undemocratic rules of the house—with violence if necessary. His group's the black man's army. He's its commander.

"His enforcement's organized and governed by a system with general orders similar to the system in any regular military–like structure. They regularly participate in close–order military drills, engage in group physical exercises and receive judo and karate training. The purpose of this training program is to indoctrinate the minds and bodies of the faithful followers. They act as Mustapha's bodyguards and escorts."

"I've seen news video of that drilling. There's an implied threat of intimidation that gets you viscerally when you watch it."

"Many of his members are felons and ex–cons: gangstas, pimps, murderers—the dregs of society. Hoping that some good might come to them from joining, they've got this what–have–I–got–to–lose attitude.

"Drilling's an integral part of Doctor Mustapha's campaign to save young black men from mental murder."

"Sounds like one big happy dysfunctional family."

"At any given time members there are in various stages of disenchantment and disillusionment. Members leave the temple as fast as new ones join up."

"You make him out to be like some black dictator."

"Joseph Mustapha's been called a black Hitler. He's a master at creating mood, myth and mystery. He's a forceful motivator. His Muslim temple is something like a black Ku Klux Klan."

"These are some pretty strong allegations."

"These allegations are not only true, they're mild. They're allegations you should pursue."

"The temple's supposed to represent black empowerment, self–reliance and self–sufficiency," Bailey reminded him. "It's supposed to be a model of black pride. It's supposed to better the lives of young black men. It's supposed to better the well–being of struggling black families."

"Mustapha knows how to play the angles and plays them well," Joshua sneered. "The temple's his pulpit and his profit center. It's like a collection agency for criminals—or anybody else who'll incur a debt to it.

"He's expanded his operations by using several commercial ventures as legitimate business fronts—bakery outlets, a barber shop, beauty store, dress shop, dry cleaner and laundry, grocery store, apartment properties, security companies."

"And you're claiming that Mustapha is absolutely willing to employ force and violence as debt collection tactics?"

"Bad things happen to people who cross Mustapha. Such people have a way of turning up dead. His immediate predecessor wound up with his bones sticking out of a shallow grave on Bernal Heights Hill."

"I hate to state the obvious but: criminal conduct is totally contrary to the tenets of Muslim belief."

"Mustapha thinks himself untouchable by the law. In his extreme arrogance, he believes he's above the law, So far he has been."

"How does he get away with acting like a law unto himself?"

"Mustapha trades on the help and goodwill of prominent politicians.

"Mustapha represents a bloc of votes certain politicians can't ignore. If you want those votes that you might otherwise discount, you can get those votes, but you have to go through Doctor Mustapha.

"There's blame across the board of politicians in San Francisco who are more than eager to pose for photo–ops with temple members."

"The news media can share some of the blame," Bailey allowed with a nod. "The Chronicle's written plenty of puff pieces about the temple."

"Mustapha's a clown, man, a huckster! He's just bizarre. He's so patently opportunistic. He's just this great big charismatic personality. It's all about him and his own assumed theology. I'm surprised anybody could follow it."

"But people do follow it. You follow it."

"At first, I thought, I better study this cat. This is a throwback to the Black Muslim movement of yesteryear.

"That religion was a way of life. It taught how to resurrect us from the dead state of being American negro men. We're white people with black skin. It's all a mentality."

"Why are you confiding all this to me?"

"It's the younger temple members like me I'm worried about. They have a sick, warped way because of Mustapha. He's very physical to them. He goes around hurting people. This is where they get this violent stuff from. They want to be like him. He runs around like he's a god. I do believe they think he is a god."

"And you don't think he's a god?"

"I'm looking at the lives of the temple people. Mustapha's leading them down the wrong road—when their lives don't have to go down that road.

"These are kids from tough neighborhoods in San Francisco. Mustapha makes a seductive pitch that some street kids from the city can't refuse."

"Aren't you afraid of the consequences of getting caught breaking ranks with the temple?"

"I've grown more realistic about Mustapha. And I just really don't give a damn anymore."

"Don't you feel like you're betraying your brothers?"

"I don't know if I was thinking of any of that."

"What do you expect me to do with these allegations?"

"It's hard for these kids to resist such dead—end temptations, unless somebody convinces them of a better, safer alternative. There needs to be a recognition that people can lose their moral focus and resort to things that are contrary to their high ideals and principles. If you wrote the right kind of story, you could contribute to that recognition."

"What would be the right kind of story?"

"References to white devils come up a lot around the

temple in Mustapha's sermons," Joshua clarified. "Mustapha talked about the devil mentality. All whites are devils by nature. Blacks are not devils by nature. But a black man can be a devil if he's against his own people. Black non–believers are tools and enablers of the white devils. The right kind of story could show that blacks can become devils through their actions."

"You're pretty articulate for a street kid from San Francisco."

"I grew up in the streets of the Western Addition," Joshua confided, nodding knowingly to the pallid blue–gray and green row houses sidling Clay Street at the foot of the northward slope of the park below. "In high school I was enrolled in a mentorship program though the Haas School of Business at the University of California in Berkeley. We from the hood. But that don't mean we have to be dumb."

"Where do you suggest I should start with this?" Bailey asked warily.

"If anything's gonna happen it's in Mustapha's inner circle," Joshua declared unequivocally. "Mustapha's women know a lot but you'll likely never get them to talk because they fear for their lives."

"Except maybe for a woman brash enough to leave a baby on Mustapha's doorstep?" Bailey ventured.

"Tiffany Mustapha," Joshua stated flatly. "Find Tiffany Mustapha. She tell you everything you need to know."

ELEVEN: ZODIAC STRIKES ONCE

One Hawthorne Condominium Tower
1 Hawthorne Street
San Francisco, California

One Hawthorne's 24–story condominium tower—with its twin stacks of bunched balconies—hovers high up above the corner of Howard & Hawthorne Streets in San Francisco's bourgeoning Yerba Buena district. Its solid eight–story base, bordering Howard Street, is composed of sandy concrete punched with steeple–tall windows. Clad in precast concrete panels, the tower's tall, eastward–facing, rectangular panels are aligned in a rippling, herringbone–patterned procession—fringed by a buoyant, 16–story piece of abstract porcelain artwork.

Sculptor Robert Hudson's porcelain–on–steel mural, soaring 144 feet tall, is composed of ninety 43–by–57 half–inch steel panels stacked in rows of three and attached to an eleven–foot–wide aluminum grid bolted onto the tower's eastward wall.

Surfaced in trendier glass, the tower's westward wedged slab consists of ultra–clear windows set in a systematic black–aluminum grid—the sharp, sky–high lines of its flat roof surmounting all the surrounding, older masonry buildings far off below.

At the tower's street–level entrance, an opaque glass canopy caps its limestone paved facade—overtopped by the exalted metallic letters:

One Hawthorne

Directly across the narrow, one–way, single–lane, tree–lined street stands the more modest, robust red brick, two–story building housing Crown Point Press and 871 Fine Arts.

Past midnight the familiar black Lexus LX 570 full–sized sport utility vehicle pulled up slowly to the right curb, braking to a halt with doused lights in a metered parking space next to a tilted tree. Doors loudly slid open and the quartet of tall and burly young black men—Isaiah, Jeremiah, Joshua and Zechariah—all sporting dark suits, bowties and sunglasses, nimbly exited the vehicle. Together they directly crossed the narrow street and stepped up to the double–glass lobby doors, brandishing their long–handled, metal–headed sledgehammers.

"Let's do this!" Zechariah exhorted them.

Their ringleader violently wrenched the locked metal door handle with his black–gloved grip, rattling the glass. Without reluctance he swung his sledgehammer in a wide arc, pulverized the front double–doors and sent flying sharp shards of shattered glass all over the polished inner lobby floor. Splintered pieces of glass crunching underfoot, the four black vandals stomped inside and were lost to sight as they fell to wrecking havoc on the lobby interior.

Outside, the destructive quartet's black getaway driver and a black partner, riding shotgun in the parked SUV's passenger seat, anxiously awaited the return of the four black vandals.

"We'll be chilling like villains while they stir shit up in there!" muttered the driver.

Four parking spaces behind the parked vehicle, a dark and stocky figure, having on a long, dirty and tattered overcoat, and hunched heavily over a black, tarp–draped shopping cart, shuffled along the sidewalk. Lumbering, the shadowy shape passed by the rear double–glass doorway overhung by a slanted awning imprinted with the white words:

ROE Restaurant & Lounge

Passing on, the homeless–looking hulk trudged past the single glass–door rear entrance to 20 Hawthorne Street, where a gnarly tree sprouted from the sidewalk bricks two stories high. Going along with the dark hulk, the cumbersome, creaky–wheeled, tarp–covered shopping cart was being gradually pushed forward. Step by step, by sluggishly slow degrees, the shadowed silhouette of the plodding hulk–and–shopping cart lumbered into full view—reflected unexpectedly in the SUV passenger's right rear–view mirror! Two parking spaces away, the dark hulk–and–cart in back of the vehicle crept closer and closer from behind.

"I got your back!" declared the black passenger. "Some street person pushing a cart's coming up on our right rear."

"Maybe he's laying in the cut to waste your black ass!" snidely cracked the driver.

Before they could stop sniggering together the sight of the metallic, tarp–wrapped shopping cart caught their eye—rolling slowly by on the sidewalk with nobody behind pushing it!

As the muzzle was placed in direct contact with the black passenger's head—just behind his right ear—the small–caliber handgun was cursorily fired at point–blank range.

"What the fuck!" the black driver cried out aloud, startled at the shocking sight of his passenger's head snapping and spurting blood before his dead body banged into the dashboard, toppling over onto the blood–spattered front seat!

A bright penlight attached to the attacker's pistol barrel flashed in the black driver's face. Frozen, he looked aghast, squinting, as the dark hulk's barrel–chested torso filled the entire frame of the SUV's passenger window.

Underneath his tattered overcoat, the gun–wielding attacker wore a ceremonial midnight–black executioner's hood, stitched perfectly square on top, its four corners like an upside–down paper sack. Draped over his stocky shoulders, the sleeveless hood's front and back flaps reached almost to the waist of his blueblack nylon, parka–type windbreaker.

Emblazoned across his chest was stitched–in–white that distinctive three–inch square cross superimposed upon a circle—its tips protruding past its ring. Into the cloth were cut slits for the eyes and mouth over which he wore a pair of clip–on sunglasses.

He had on baggy, pleated pants tucked into half–boots. At his left waist hung a foot–long, bayonet–type knife sheathed in a scabbard with brass rivets. At his right waist hung a black, open–flapped holster.

"Okay, porch monkey!" rasped the attacker. "Don't reach for anything! Get out and run for it before I blast your black ass! I'm giving you only one chance!"

After an instant's hesitation the black driver broke open his door and bolted—making a run for it! Directly he dashed across the street, making a desperate beeline for the condominium's fractured front double–glass doors!

Calmly but quickly, the hulking attacker sprawled across the SUV's hood, taking careful aim with a two–handed, shoulder–point position and firing his handgun six times in rapid but smooth succession.

On the other side of the slick street, the black driver slipped, stumbled and fell headlong across the sidewalk pavement, collapsing prostrate onto the countless shivery shards of glass scattered all over the condominium's dis-integrated threshold. He lay dead in an ever swelling pool of blood.

Stoically, the dark, hooded hulk himself crossed over and stalked southward along the narrow, tree–lined side-walk of Hawthorne Street, passing by a parking garage entrance amid other soaring and solid–looking build-ings—proceeding patiently until he reached the corner intersection at Folsom Street.

Before doing so, he stood aside from the vehicle, taking a nonchalant, single–action, target–shooting position, aiming straight at the front windshield with one out-stretched arm. Firing just two indiscriminate shots, the glass fell to splintery pieces.

At the street corner at the end of the block, parked in the last metered space between two gnarly trees, was a shiny black Holden WM Chevrolet Caprice full–size luxury car. Calmly, the dark hooded hulk opened up the driver's door, settled into the driver's seat, ignited the car's 6–litre, L98 V–8 engine, put in gear its six–speed, auto-matic transmission, turned left, and promptly but gradu-ally rounded the corner until lost to sight from the hind end of the block.

§

"San Francisco Police Department," the non–emer-gency dispatcher neutrally answered the incoming caller.

"I want to report a murder—no, a double murder," drawled the caller's voice in a low and level monotone. "Go to One Hawthorne Tower, where you will find two Black Muslim hoodlums dead of multiple gunshot wounds."

"What is your name and number, sir?" asked the dis-patcher.

"This is the Zodiac speaking," rasped the caller taunt-ingly. "I'm the one who did it. Goodbye."

And without another word the caller hung up.

§

That narrow block of Hawthorne Street—ablaze with the daylight brilliance of beaming firetruck floodlights—was cordoned off by the recognized black–lettered yellow tape that read:

Police Line Do Not Cross

An emergency medical services passenger cargo van—type ambulance idled at the street curb, already aswarm with patrolmen and traffic officers preserving the barricaded crime scene for the field forensics criminalists collecting, photographing and processing evidence; and keeping bystanders at bay.

At the fringe of the crime scene, a gleaming silver, black—trimmed Chrysler KK Jeep Liberty compact, four—door SUV abruptly pulled up and parked at Howard Street.

Out of the unmarked jeep stepped a tall, burly and bald black man sporting shiny C. & J. Clark Wallabee shoes and a dark, long overcoat. He was immediately recognized by the crime scenes officer, who stepped up to greet him.

"Detective Derwin! What brings you out on such a nice night as this?"

"I'm just a black man working," the inspector replied drearily. "What have you got?"

"Two black male gunshot victims," the officer related, leading the inspector to the black Lexus SUV with the disintegrated windshield—its passenger door hung wide open—and nodding to the dead body spun around and supine in the passenger seat, the head steeped in blood behind the right ear, singed by powder burn; the corpse's right cheek bulged with a swollen lump; its closely cropped hair was matted with blood.

"This one got it right in the back of the skull—contact range. We picked up one expended .22—caliber, copper—coated casing off the floorboard. We picked up seven others off the ground right here in front of the vehicle."

"Lukewarm," Inspector Derwin Quagmire murmured to himself, placing his palm upon the SUV's engine hood.

A long trail of blood led to the second dead body, lying prostrate across the street in a prodigious pool of blood; it was outlined in chalk on the sidewalk at the condominium's shattered doorsill.

"This one got it five times in the right side of the back—probably while running," said the officer, gesturing to the blood–bespattered torso; blood oozed from the corpse's mouth and nose. "The remarkable thing is, the entry wounds form a very tight pattern. Your shooter's got plenty of target practice at the shooting range. He left no weapon behind we could find."

"No signs of any struggle? No obvious motives?"

"No evidence of robbery. No witnesses. No motive other than the most obvious: stretch these suckers out!"

"A double–execution?"

The crime scenes officer shrugged.

"Evidently they were drivers," he said soberly. "They were waiting to chauffeur those tourists sitting in there, I think you're already acquainted."

Inspector Quagmire leaned to one side, peering through the condominium's fractured front doorway to catch a glimpse of the regimented quartet of young attired black men, sitting stiffly erect on facing benches inside the lobby—several patrolmen standing over them.

"They surrendered themselves peaceably. They came running when they heard gunshots, but say they didn't see anybody."

"They packing any heat?"

"None that we could find."

"Cite them out," he suddenly ordered the officer. "We'll talk to them later."

"No arrest for malicious mischief or vandalism? Just citations?" asked the officer incredulously. "They trashed the whole lobby big–time."

"You heard me. Just do it."

TWELVE:
ZODIAC
CONFERENCE

**THOMAS J. CAHILL
HALL OF JUSTICE
Homicide Detail
Room 455
850 Bryant Street
San Francisco, California**

Dave Toski stepped inside the roomy homicide detail office, shutting the frosted–glass door behind him and pausing at the threshold to pensively contemplate and survey the spacious surroundings, taking the full measure of all the old wooden desks and gray metal filing cabinets still crowding the polished floor after all these decades since he was last on duty there—except that numerous desks were now enclosed by dimly–lit, armpit–high cubicles and furnished with desktop computers.

"Inspector Toski!"

Across the room, Toski caught sight of detectives Moretti and Marino, sitting in swivel chairs across from each other at the same cluttered desk overlooking Bryant Street; he strode straight over to accost them.

"I'm retired!" Toski snapped sternly.

"Semi–retired!" Moretti cheerfully corrected him. "You're consulting with us now about Zodiac, remember? Welcome back to your old stamping ground!"

"Yeah, thanks," said Toski with a knowing nod. "So what are we consulting about today?"

From an upright row of file folders lining their street–facing window sill, Moretti plucked out one and opened its flap, extracting some sheets of paper he slapped down onto the desktop.

"The autoposy and ballistics reports for the One Hawthorne Tower killings," Moretti announced matter–of–factly, "plus another letter from our suspect taking the credit for it. This time he mentions you by name."

Toski snapped up the papers, inspecting them intently.

"The dude riding shotgun in the passenger seat was hit first with one shot to the back of the skull at contact range," Moretti stated.

"Right side of the head?"

"The dude face–down in the street," Moretti went on with a nod, "got hit five times in the upper right back in a remarkably tight pattern at a distance—in the dark—of at least ten feet or more!"

"Total shots fired?"

"Ten. One hit the passenger inside the vehicle. Five hit the pedestrian in the street. Two took out the vehicle's front windshield. Two strays hit the front glass of the condominium lobby. All expended slugs and cartridges were recovered in the immediate vicinity of the crime scene. All bullets were fired from the same weapon."

"Type of weapon and ammunition?"

"Antique!" Moretti exclaimed scrupulously. "Super X brand .22–caliber cartridges.

"We've got the ballistics match—a .22–caliber— which is like Zodiac, who used a .22 in his first northern California murder.

"All bullets were Western copper–coated .22 long–rifle—even though the probable weapon was a J.C. Higgins, Model 80 automatic pistol.

"So we've confirmed we've got one ballistics match—a .22–caliber, which was what Zodiac used.

"Does any of this have a familiar ring to it?"

"Yeah," Toski conceded. "Except for attacking the vehicle's passenger from the right side—instead of the driver from the left—and except for shooting through the front of the vehicle—instead of through the rear—the shooting mimics the original Zodiac killing of David Faraday and Betty Lou Jensen at Lake Herman Road, Benicia, California, Solano County, the 20th of December 1968. So our copycat killer—if he is a copycat—is aping the original Zodiac killer by roughly replicating his crimes."

"Right down to the gun and ammo used!" Moretti corroborated at length. "Western produced billions of rounds of ammunition during World War II. Its subsidiary—the Winchester Repeating Arms Company—developed both the M1 carbine and the M1 rifle for the military, mostly to United States Army and Marine troops for use lasting through the Vietnam War.

"The J.C. Higgins, Model 88 revolver was produced for the Sears, Roebuck & Company by High Standard Arms, a major firearms manufacturer—at least through 1961."

"So the ammunition is a dead certainty," Toski pointed out, "but the probable weapon is still just a possibility."

"WCC–stamped cartridges were most definitely manufactured for military arms and munitions. J.C. Higgins made mostly sporting and recreation guns for working–class rednecks. So the tragic truth is: identifying the responsible weapon positively and conclusively—even if recovered—will prove to be extremely difficult if not outright impossible."

"All I see for certain," Toski asserted, "is that for a culprit who's long been supposed to be navy–affiliated, he sure shows a marked preference for army–affiliated ammunition!"

"Where's that letter?" Toski asked, shuffling the report papers in hand.

Moretti slipped the familiar plastic evidence envelope containing the blue felt–tip printed letter across the edge of the desktop for Toski to snap up and read aloud:

"This is the Zodiac speaking. I am back with you. Tell Toski I am here. I have always been here. I told you that city pig Toski was a no–good good–for–nothing. I told you I was smarter and better and that he would get tired, give it up and leave me alone. I told you I am crackproof and in control of all things. Now I am back to prove it all over again."

"What do you think?" asked Moretti. "I'd say your Zodiac's back."

"Where did he call it in from?" Toski anticipated.

"Another pay phone traced to the Greyhound Bus Lines station on Folsom Street south of Market," Inspector Moretti answered.

"We've noticed something else that you've been pretty tight–lipped about," Marino interjected.

"What might that be?" Toski asked.

"The killings claimed by this supposed Zodiac copycat are starting to conform to a particular pattern."

"Yeah," Moretti chimed in. "Every crime so far has occurred at a high–rise condominium complex: Robert Naysmith at The Millennium, the vandalism at One Rincon Hill and now this hit outside One Hawthorne—the site of a second vandalism. An anonymous tipster tipped you off about the first but not the second vandalism, suggesting an insider's involved. The conciergé security for every condominium involved is provided by none other than Star Security—which, by curious coincidence, happens to be the very same outfit you're employed by these days."

"Is that a fact?"

"Which begs the question why you should be so reticent about that?"

"I figured you boys are pretty sharp and would work it out on your own," Toski remarked, grinning satirically. He pulled a piece of folded paper from his sport jacket pocket and slapped it down onto their desktop. "You came to me to consult. Do you need me to lead you by the hand too?"

"What's this?"

"The complete list of all high–rise client sites Star Security provides service for," Toski confided, pausing for emphasis, "just in case you cared to put them under surveillance in hopes of a repeat performance.

"He's following the same M.O. We're looking at an individual who's thinking the same things. With this kind of conduct it wouldn't be uncommon for the crimes to escalate—and with shorter time between incidents."

§

Conference Room
Hall of Justice

In front of the room, extending along the wall, was a big blackboard. Etched onto its black surface in white chalk was a sizable crossed circle: the Zodiac symbol!

Dave Toski caught a glimpse of two Zodiac killer wanted posters—together with their attendant composite sketches—tacked onto a big bulletin board posted on the wall just inside the open doorway. Right ahead, the two brawny Italian detectives led the way to a row of high–backed, black–leather chairs set at spaced intervals behind an elongated, low–lying, polished conference table. Discreetly, they took their empty places at the foot of the table among several other plain–clothes investigators already seated.

At the slant–topped lectern equipped with a microphone stand, placed at the head of the table, stood criminal profiler, Dr. Dana Lund, who addressed her modest but regardful audience in her clearly audible and articulate voice.

"Zodiac was the prototype terrorist in terms of holding a sizable population captive by manipulating the mass media.

"Your Zodiac killer of old was one of the first early

157

serial killers to gain notoriety through publicity. His use of a logo and encrypted letters made him a highly marketable news commodity—of great interest and fascination to hordes of news hounds who would love to solve this mystery!

"Zodiac was somebody who felt completely powerless but who seized power through publicity. Because he's powerless to control his own life, his fantasy is to rule the world—to be in control of it.

"He's a nobody who aspires to be somebody by the infamy he incurs—from the crimes he commits.

"Had Zodiac been caught, the whodunit would've been solved. So publicity is often a fringe benefit to serial killers. They feel superior, un–catchable, un–stoppable. They'll play the game, reveling in the celebrity they receive.

"That's why no serial killer wants to get caught—otherwise he loses the power and control that he's achieved through publicity.

"To all those around him, Zodiac may very well appear to be a calm, reasonable and well–controlled individual—even if he does get stereotyped as being a loner having few outside contacts with others.

"Technically, Zodiac's an organized, non–social offender. Organized serial killers like Zodiac are called non–social because they elect to be socially isolated—by choice. Although they may very well be personally charming and charismatic, they may believe nobody else is quite good enough for them.

"They are frequently quite clever. More confident and self–assured than the disorganized a–social offender, these organized killers are ready and willing to prowl far and wide in search of their victims.

"Zodiac fits the pattern rather well of what's called pseudo–reactive schizophrenia. Such an individual engages in his bizarre behavior as a kind of cover–up for an underlying and more deeply concealed psychosis.

"Police officers, in particular, know all about cover–ups—do they not?"

Dr. Lund paused briefly to let her quip elicit some simpering from among the policemen in attendance.

"Zodiac's particular type of psychosis provokes a deepening sense of powerlessness," she continued, unabashed.

"For some psychotics, the act of killing is a denial of powerlessness. Zodiac craves power out of feeling powerless.

"Psychosis is the slow but sure eradication of the ego—a terrifying loss of one's own self–image. Zodiac commits his crimes because he's overpowered by terror. He spreads terror because the life he leads is controlled and dominated by terror.

"Among psychotics, schizophrenics of the paranoid type are very guarded and secretive in their dealings with the outside world. They can deal relatively well with the outside world and, at the same time, harbor their private but warped vision of what they believe the world is really like."

"Is calling the Zodiac psychotic the same thing as calling him crazy?" asked an investigator with a reluctantly raised hand.

"In the media," answered Dr. Lund, "Zodiac's been portrayed to be some insane madman. I think the man's legally sane. In fact, I think he'll prove to be a genius who got so far out—and so far gone—that he just went over the edge. He's certainly demonstrated his shrewdness and cunning by methodically hiding and evading the police.

"He doesn't manifest the obvious aberrations, but instead takes great pains to appear normal and evade capture. Of all killers, he's most likely to repeat his crimes. After the first murder, these cunning killers become amazingly adept at concealing themselves, yet frequently—and perversely—cast suspicion on themselves."

"What creates a Zodiac killer?" asked another investigator.

"Nobody really knows what creates a compulsive killer like Zodiac," answered Dr. Lund. "Maybe a more compelling question is what's created your current Zodiac killer? A missing sex chromosome? A traumatic event in early childhood? Cruel acts of rejection by parents, peers or objects of affection?...Bed–wetting?"

Once more there was some simpering among the policemen.

"Whatever the cause or causes," Dr. Lund concluded in deathly earnest, "the condition is completely incurable."

"Oh, there's a cure all right," emphatically rasped a familiar voice from the rearward rows of the room. "And a permanent cure at that."

Conspicuously perturbed, Unsavory Dave Toski had spoken up vocally at last.

"Do you have a contribution to make to this discussion, Inspector Toski?" Dr. Lund asked, pausing to lift up her eyes and look down her nose at him.

"I'm retired," Toski corrected her. "I reckon I just might, ma'am."

"By all means then, Mister Toski," Dr. Lund said with a mannered smirk, "do tell."

"In my experience," Toski continued, undaunted, "the psychopath doesn't play by society's rules. He acts like a spoilt brat—intent only on doing and getting what he wants. He doesn't care anything about the rules. If society stands in his way, he's openly defiant. He gets his jollies from the excitement he cooks up for himself in the situation. He gives in to all his desires—whatever they may be, however perverted they may be. He has no self–restraint or control. Aggression dominates his personality. When he tries to sate those desires, he runs head—on into society's rules. In the ensuing clash, there's an eruption of violence. Even murder."

"So you're saying what?"

"A certain amount of violent and unsolved murders are randomly committed by psychopaths who don't even know their victims. The murders are casual ones. So I'm saying that any investigation of the psychopath has to go beyond society's rules and accepted conventions. And the investigator has to adopt un—conventional methods of conducting the investigation."

"Meaning...if you get the chance, blow him away?"

"The psychopath sees himself as a survivor in a savage and violent jungle. He never benefits from experience— even if it's positive. So he'll keep on striking out at the society he thinks has wronged him until he's caught or killed."

"Has this approach generally worked well for you in the past, Mister Toski?" Dr. Lund asked scurrilously.

"Homicide investigation's an aggressive business—a lot like warfare—so you have to be ready to use tactics and strategy called for by the situation."

"Could this approach possibly explain why the San Francisco Police Department consistently ranks last among this country's biggest city police forces in solving violent crime—and has one of the lowest clearance rates in solving violent crime?"

"I wouldn't know about the department's clearance rates—I only know about my own."

"Your homicide track record's quite exemplary, Mister Toski—except of course...for Zodiac. It would seem Zodiac's committed and gotten away with the perfect crime in San Francisco."

"Any crime's perfect if it's unsolved—and if the culprit hasn't been caught and convicted. But cops know something that most criminals don't—until it's too late, Ms. Lund."

"What's that, Mister Toski?"

"It's no great secret: but a criminal like Zodiac has to get away with every crime he commits every time."

"So far he has gotten away with it—five dead victims in at least four incidents firmly confirmed to date."

"So far he has gotten away with it," Toski conceded, adding gravely. "But a crime can be considered solved—or cleared—with or without an arrest, such as when an offender dies. To get Zodiac off the streets, cops have to catch—or kill—him only once."

PART FOUR:

MUSLIM SHAME

THIRTEEN:
ZODIAC STRIKES TWICE

The Infinity
300 Spear Street
San Francisco, California

Over a massive, mixed–used, 650–unit residential condominium complex encompassing two city blocks hovers a quartet of distinctive but simple concrete structures having curving walls of blue–green glass curtainwall and metal—two eight–and–nine–story mid–rise buildings and two 37–and–42–story high–rise towers—bounded by Main Street to the southwest, Folsom Street to the northwest and Spear Street to the northeast. Into the clouds aloft, the 37–floor Infinity I tower soars 350 feet; its adjacent 42–floor Infinity II tower soars 450 feet.

Past midnight the familiar black Lexus LX 570 full–sized sport utility vehicle pulled up slowly to the right curb at 301 Main Street, braking to a halt with doused lights at the last metered parking space crossed by Folsom Street at the southeast corner of the intersection. Doors loudly slid open and the quartet of tall and burly young black men—Isaiah, Jeremiah, Joshua and Zechariah—all sporting dark suits, bowties and sunglasses, nimbly exited the vehicle. Together they double–backed along Main Street in sight of a southward elevated section of the truss spans of the Oakland–San Francisco Bay Bridge. Striding briskly along the sidewalk, brandishing their long–handled, metal–headed sledgehammers, they stepped up to the double–glass lobby doors nestled beneath the wedge–like canopy propped by a trio of cylindrical columns. Shining circles hollowed in the ceiling overhead shed bright light on the checkered pavestone their soles scuffed across.

"Let's get busy and get it on!" Zechariah exhorted them.

Their ringleader violently wrenched the locked metal

door handle with his black–gloved grip, rattling the glass. Without reluctance he swung his sledgehammer in a wide arc, pulverized the front double–doors and sent flying sharp shards of shattered glass all over the polished inner lobby floor. Splintered pieces of glass crunching underfoot, the four black vandals stomped inside and were lost to sight as they fell to wrecking havoc on the interior lobby of yet another towering high–rise.

Outside, the destructive quartet's black getaway driver and a black partner, riding shotgun in the parked SUV's passenger seat, anxiously awaited the return of the four black vandals—again.

Directly across the narrow two–way street, the entrance to an expansive parking lot—brightly illuminated by lamplight, closely packed with cars and penned in by a chain–link fence—opened out just opposite the high–rise tower. At the gate a luminous sign hung from a tall post, displaying a familiar commercial logo with dark lettering that read:

Public Parking
Priority Parking

At the rearward end of the parking lot's middle asphalt driveway idled a a shiny black Holden WM Chevrolet Caprice full–size luxury car. Abruptly, its headlights flashed, its 6–litre, L98 V–8 engine ignited, its six–speed, automatic transmission got in gear. Tires pealing, it screeched down the driveway and swerved left into Main Street, braking to a jerky halt to the left rear of the parked black Lexus SUV—in a classic police cut–off position.

Surprisingly, a blazing spotlight mounted on the arriving Chevrolet's rightward side flashed, throwing its brilliant light upon the rear of the parked Lexus SUV—temporarily blinding the two black occupants seated in its front seats.

"The fucking Five–O!" the black driver swore irately,

squinting at the radiant light reflected from the rear–view mirrors. "They're already on us like stink on shit!"

Expeditiously emerging from the Chevrolet was a dark, hulking figure, holding out at arm's length to the left side a shining handle–grip flashlight. Blinding glare from the beaming flashlight dazzled the grimacing faces of the shocked black pair occupying the SUV.

Without a word of warning, the dark hulk—suddenly and squarely facing the driver's window—squatted into a point–shoulder shooting position and repeatedly discharged from the extended right hand a rapid–firing pistol!

With less than no time to react, screaming and squirming in pain from being riddled with bullets, the two young blacks thrashed about violently in the SUV's front seat until at the last they both lay deathly still—spurting and splattered with blood.

Before dying they caught only a fleeting glimpse of the dark hulk's barrel–chested torso filling the entire frame of the driver's window: the ceremonial midnight–black executioner's hood, stitched perfectly square on top, its four corners like an upside–down paper sack; the sleeveless hood's front and back flaps draped over the stocky shoulders and reaching almost to the waist of the blueblack nylon, parka–type windbreaker; that distinctive three–inch square cross superimposed upon a circle—its tips protruding past its ring—stitched in white and emblazoned across the chest; those slits cut into the cloth for the eyes and mouth over which were wore a pair of clip–on sunglasses.

That attacker had on baggy, pleated pants tucked into half–boots. At the left waist hung a foot–long, bayonet–type knife sheathed in a scabbard with brass rivets. At the right waist hung a black, open–flapped holster.

Dousing his hand–held flashlight and holstering his

smoldering handgun, the dark hulk settled back into the driver's seat of the idling Holden WM Chevrolet Caprice. Its beamy spotlight doused and its six–speed, automatic transmission put in gear, the car pulled forward, turned right, and promptly but gradually rounded the corner until lost to sight from the middle of the block.

As quickly and murderously as he had come—in just a matter of fatal heartbeats—the homicidal killer was gone!

§

"San Francisco Police Department," the non–emergency dispatcher neutrally answered the incoming caller.

"I want to report a murder—no, a double murder," drawled the caller's voice in a low and level monotone. "Go to Infinity Towers at 301 Main Street, where you will find two Black Muslim hoodlums dead of multiple gunshot wounds. They were shot with a nine–millimeter luger."

"What is your name and number, sir?" asked the dispatcher.

"This is the Zodiac speaking," rasped the caller tauntingly. "I'm the one who did it. I also killed those Black Muslim hoodlums at One Hawthorne Tower. Goodbye."

And without another word the caller hung up.

§

That narrow block of Main Street—ablaze with the daylight brilliance of beaming firetruck floodlights—was cordoned off by the recognized black–lettered yellow tape that read:

Police Line Do Not Cross

An emergency medical services passenger cargo van–type ambulance idled at the street curb, already aswarm with patrolmen and traffic officers preserving the barricaded crime scene for the field forensics criminalists collecting, photographing and processing evidence; and keeping bystanders at bay.

At the fringe of the crime scene, a gleaming silver, black–trimmed Chrysler KK Jeep Liberty compact, four–door SUV abruptly pulled up to the curb and parked in a bike lane at the corner of Folsom Street—directly in front of the curved face of the towering structure.

Out of the unmarked jeep sprightly stepped a tall, burly and bald black man sporting shiny C. & J. Clark Wallabee shoes and a dark, long overcoat. Once more he was immediately recognized by the crime scenes officer, who stepped up to greet him.

"Detective Derwin. He's done it again. Another double hit."

"What have you got?" drearily asked the inspector.

"Two black male gunshot victims," the officer related, leading the inspector to the driver's side of the black Lexus SUV for a preliminary inspection of the front cab and its two bloodied black bodies.

Inspector Quagmire stooped slightly to look in and run his trained eyes over the SUV's front seat, so profusely splattered with blood. Against the inside passenger door were slumped together the bullet–perforated corpses of two young black men. Blood flowed freely from their gaping mouths as well as from numerous bodily orifices—all oozing blood.

"It looks like all shots—ten in total, we think—were fired from the driver's side of the vehicle," the officer volunteered. "So far we've found nine empty shell casings which look to be ejected from an automatic pistol."

"Caliber?" asked the inspector.

"Nine millimeter. Your shooter's changed up his gun. All torso shots too. Your shooter likes sticking to the center mass—except for a couple strays that hit the inside of the passenger door."

Inspector Quagmire directed his eyes to a triad of bullet holes—conspicuous in the passenger door panel—the officer pointed to.

"They look like copper jacketed slugs," the officer stated flatly.

"Looks look like they were packing heat this time," the inspector observed, looking closely at the high–strength nylon–based polymer handgun frames exposed to view at the belted waistbands.

"Glock subcompacts—26 or 27 model," the officer confirmed. "They came prepared, all right. They just never had the chance to pull them out."

Inspector Quagmire stood up straight and curiously tilted his head to one side, peering over to the double–glass door tower entrance.

"Your four favorite tourists are inside sitting quietly," the officer volunteered with a smug smirk, "if that's who you're looking for. This time you've got them with guns."

"Cite them out," Inspector Quagmire sighed resignedly, nodding.

"Again," he added with quiet but emphatic insistence.

FOURTEEN: CONSCIENTIOUS COPS

**THOMAS J. CAHILL
HALL OF JUSTICE
Homicide Detail
Room 455
850 Bryant Street
San Francisco, California**

Atop the battered wooden desk overlooking Bryant Street below the plastic evidence envelope was abruptly slapped down. Detectives Moretti and Marino waited and watched attentively as Dave Toski snapped up the envelope to pluck out the latest letter printed in blue felt–tip ink. Toski read it out aloud:

"This is the Zodiac speaking. I am still out here. I am still killing. I am still collecting slaves for my afterlife. I am still playing the game for keeps. I am still crack proof. The blue meanies can never catch me. That city pig, Toski, can never catch me. Tell Toski to give it up and leave me alone. Tell Toski I am still in control of all things. Tell Toski I will prove it over and over again until he's gone for good."

"His refrain's about as regular as a bowel movement," Toski cracked with a wry crease in his cheek. "What've you got on the Infinity Tower killings?"

"Two black males dead in their vehicle from multiple gunshot wounds inflicted at close range," Marino replied. "Ten empty shell casings were recovered, all bearing a nine–millimeter caliber, and believed to have been ejected from an automatic or semi–automatic pistol—very likely a luger."

"How do you figure the gun was a luger?"

"The bullet shell casings were brass and marked on the base as nine–millimeter luger with the letters W–W. The ammunition's nine–millimeter Winchester Western."

"Slugs removed from the victims' bodies were copper–jacketed," Moretti chimed in. "It appears that all the shots were fired from the left driver's side of the vehicle."

"Conveniently then," Toski volunteered, "these copy-cat killings mimic the shooting attack of Darlene E. Ferrin and Micheal R. Mageau at Blue Rock Springs Park, Vallejo, California, on the 4th of July 1969, except that Darlene died and Michael survived after being fired at from the right passenger side of their vehicle."

"And when the original Zodiac called in to report the crime to the radio dispatcher for the Vallejo Police Department, Nancy L. Slover, he claimed he shot the victims with a nine–millimeter luger," Marino added forebodingly. "When this copycat Zodiac called in the Infinity Tower attack—from yet another pay phone traced to the Greyhound Bus Lines station again—he's getting sloppy—he likewise alluded to the luger."

"Yeah," Toski agreed. "The Luger P08 pistol—or pistol parabellum—was highly prized by allied soldiers during both world wars even though it was a German–made handgun. It was still a sought–after sidearm during even the Vietnam war.

"The German–manufactured 9×19–millimeter parabellum cartridge was specifically designed for the semi–automatic luger pistol. Worldwide, it's by far the most popular pistol cartridge in use among law enforcement agencies and military branches—in particular the United States Army.

"The German weapons manufacturer that introduced it had a memorable motto:

"If you seek peace, prepare for war!"

"We lost badly another battle in this war," Moretti admitted ashamedly, hanging his head. "We just didn't have enough time to stake out that list of security client sites you gave us."

"You mean you didn't act fast enough to set up the stakeouts," Toski contradicted him with a slightly sarcastic tone.

"This Zodiac struck again before we could even think about putting surveillance teams into place,"

Marino interjected, shaking his head. "We're drastically under–staffed as it is. The department's resources are already spread extremely thin."

"And cops fight for over–time at the expense of case–work," Toski said dismissively. "Yeah, I've heard all those excuses before."

Toski raised his hands defensively to cut short the detectives before they could speak up in protest.

"I know you guys work your asses off with heavy case–loads in homicide," Toski commended them. "You have to triagé, pick up the hottest thing going and run with it. But Ms. Lund has a point: when you're prancing from crime scene to crime scene, what suffers is solving—and clearing cases. That's when detectives start relying too much on interrogating as a substitute for investigating. The second cops get a suspect in their sights, they investigate the suspect instead of investigating the case. When that happens, you're not deploying resources where and when you should be, you're not using strategies you should be. And limited staffing negatively impacts your ability to do comprehensive follow–up investigations.

"All I'm saying is: cops are in the business of solving cases. So there's no substitute for good old–fashioned gumshoe detective work."

"This is S.F.P.D.!" Moretti cracked with a big unburdening grin. "Don't give us too much credit for being hard workers or deep thinkers. The laziest cops around here are mostly in the business of framing people."

"How's that?"

"When they feel that when they make an arrest they're

not going to get the support they need, or the investigation resources aren't there to follow up and make the case,
that impacts the quality of their work. That's part of the
reason we have such a problem in this city."

"Sometimes it makes you embarrassed to say you're
a San Francisco cop," Marino concurred stoically. "They
just show up to work to pick up their paycheck—and then
they go home. Officers say it over and over, they can't wait
to turn 50 when they can retire."

"Well," Toski hissed a resigned sigh, "I think it's safe
to say this supposed Zodiac copycat has at this point established a pretty positive and definite pattern that can-
cels out any chance of mere coincidence."

"How's that, chief?" asked one of the detectives.

Toski's expression turned ominously solemn.

"He's become a serial killer who's taken to stalking
some other pretty ruthless serial criminals!"

"Question is," Moretti suggested, "why are these black
muslim hoods targeting these security client sites with
vandalism? And why is this Zodiac copycat killer targeting the hoods? It seems fairly clear these shootings are
connected."

"A more important question," Toski stressed, "is how
this Zodiac even knows to target the black vandals without having some inside information about when and where
the hoods would strike.

"I've only recently gathered from my boss at Star Security, Al Powell, that this black muslim bunch is trying
a shakedown to make him join their protection racket.
I think Al's been holding out against them but so far he
hasn't come clean to me about it. So now these hoods are at
that stage where they're demonstrating—with these van-
dalisms—what happens next if he doesn't buy in to their
extortion scheme. What I can't figure is why I was tipped
off about the first vandalism but not the other two."

"This damned department doesn't even have an extortion division. But we could report it to fraud."

Toski shook his head dubiously.

"I doubt that Al would even file a formal complaint much less cooperate with an investigation. I know he's afraid that these muslims are threatening him."

"Then we'll re–tool and start looking for more evidence."

"So what's the spin on this Joseph Mustapha character?" Toski asked, deftly changing the subject.

"Joseph Mustapha and his cohorts are a bunch of bums and hooligans," Moretti scoffed with a dismissive wave of his hand. "Mustapha himself is nothing more than a vicious little street thug. And the cronies who follow him are nothing more than a group of street–gang thugs."

"He acts like he's this sinister, Mafia boss–like character who resorts to violence—or threats of violence—to get his way," Marino affirmed. "He aspires to be perceived as this big–shot criminal kingpin who thinks he runs and terrorizes San Francisco. But there are a lot of other hoods over here who are way more serious bad guys than he is— or is ever likely to be."

"So you're saying Mustapha's a poser?" Toski asked.

"There've been plenty of rumors of racist violence related to Mustapha and his organization of young black men," Marino confirmed. "And that he's allegedly led members of his temple on a string of violent crime sprees that've included assault, kidnapping, robbery, torture. But all we've seen for sure are these most recent episodes of vandalism. We've never crossed swords with him in homicide—so far."

"What about this so–called mosque of his?"

"They simply call it the temple. At the core of the mosque is a business enterprise with a quasi–military operation. It's the nucleus of the black muslim movement in San Francisco. It' a place where suspects come from. There've been shootings and rumors of murders associated with the mosque."

"Mustapha's like this dirty little secret in town that nobody wants to admit to," Moretti elucidated. "A lot of people cozy up—or suck up—to him because of this perception of power he pretends to project—including some prominent politicians. He hides behind this aura built up by that phony temple of his."

"So you doubt that Mustapha poses much of a menace to polite society?"

"It's my impression that Mustapha's temple's like a chicken with its head cut off," Moretti said scornfully. "It doesn't know it's dead yet, but keeps running around anyway."

"Now that this Zodiac is doing some of the head–cutting," Toski suggested, "it might be a good idea for you guys to pay Mustapha an official visit."

"There's only one small problem with that," Moretti objected.

"What might that be?"

"Robert Naysmith's killing is our case—not the black muslims—even if they do look strongly connected."

"Who's in charge of the black muslim killings?"

"One Inspector Derwin Quagmire," Marino interjected knowingly. "Quagmire's been tight with Mustapha for several years."

"Just how tight?"

"There's no doubt about it. There's clearly an association between them."

"How so?"

"They're pretty buddy–buddy. Quagmire seems to be like a conduit to Mustapha's temple—like he has some type of partisan pipeline with them."

"Has Quagmire something to hide there?"

"He's pretty open about being a supporter who patronizes the temple—and who professes to be a true believer in the temple's ostensible philosophy of black empowerment."

"It looks like you'll be obliged to confer with Quagmire about these cases at some point."

"We'd be worried about Quagmire," Moretti protested.

"Why's that?"

"Briefing Quagmire could be more harmful than helpful," Marino clarified. "We wonder whether Quagmire's able to separate his relationship with the temple and do his job. We're not so sure about that right now. We don't trust him. But that's on us."

"Besides that," Moretti added disdainfully, "Quagmire's not the sharpest tool in the shack. His homicide work's shoddy and inept. His thoroughness leaves a lot to be desired. This job's way over his head."

"San Francisco's a relatively small city," Toski seriously reminded the two detectives. "The networks, the people involved in criminal activity, are all associated. Because it is a small community, word travels fast. The trick in this business is—travel faster."

FIFTEEN:
LOVE'S SLAVE

Stow Lake
Golden Gate Park
San Francisco, California

San Francisco's late afternoon sunshine irradiated Stow Lake's lofty treetops, swished and swayed to one side by gusty sea breezes from the Pacific Ocean. Long, slanting rays of hazy sunlight sliced gently through the towering trees to brightly illuminate the lake's olive–green, wind–whipped surface, ablaze with perennially sparkling and rolling ripples.

All around the lake's grassy banks winds a slender, sandy footpath, turning and twisting through the sometimes shadowed thickets and rustled foliage girdling the lake's irregular, elongated loop.

Chance Bailey sat together with Tiffany Mustapha at a secluded spot on a lone, wooden, green–painted bench—one of numerous such benches set at spaced intervals all along the lakeshore—overlooking the lake's perennially rippling and shimmering surface. Silently, they looked out on the lake's lustrous waters, alive with no end of endlessly floating and flying birds.

Tiffany Mustapha slouched at one end of the park bench, her head bowed, her face pressed deep into her palms, cowering from nightmarish memories; Chance Bailey sat prudently at her elbow, waiting expectantly but patiently for her to speak.

"Joseph Mustapha thinks he's God's gift to women," she blurted out bitterly once she finally raised her chin. "To him women are just sexual beings and slaves."

"How do you mean?" Bailey asked her with care.

"The woman is to obey, Mustapha preaches!" she said, a snarl curling her quivering lip. "The woman is the floor that we men walk upon!"

"Has he abused women at the mosque?"

"He's fathered forty–two children—most of them born to victims of molestation!" she scoffed contemptuously.

"He's had about nine so–called spiritual wives. He started having sex with most of them when they were still minor children!"

"How did you become acquainted with Mustapha?"

"I first met with Mustapha when I was but eight years old," she recounted, thinking back upon terrible times past. "When I was ten years old, I went to live with Mustapha as a foster child with another of his wives in his temple compound. Mustapha started sexually assaulting me at about that time. He threatened to kill me if I told anybody. He also beat me with his fists and other objects. When I was thirteen years old, I gave birth to a child fathered by Mustapha—the first of three children. The violence and threats of physical harm persisted, as did the repeated rapes. I didn't tell anyone for fear of my life and the life of my child. I had no family other than Mustapha's wife, who was aware of the rapes but did nothing to stop them."

"Can you describe what happened?" Bailey asked gingerly. "How the assaults started?"

"Do you want me to draw you a graphic picture, Mister Bailey?" she sneered scornfully at him.

She swallowed hard for the words with a great gulp.

"He walked me toward the recreation room area," she related painstakingly, afflicted with severe unseen suffering, "picked me up and started rubbing himself on me. I was just shocked.

"'Come with me, sister,' he told me. 'It's okay, it's okay. I'm not going to hurt you. This is our secret. Don't mention this to anyone. You better not tell anyone. No one will believe you. We have to keep what we're doing between us. I will be your daddy.' He promised to make me one of his wives someday.

"He told me that I better not tell anybody. And if I did tell them they wouldn't believe me," she repeated in conspicuous pain. "And he was right. So sometimes he felt free to assault two of us at a time."

"Two at a time?" Bailey exclaimed, taken aback.

"He'd tell me to stand in the closet while he assaulted my sister. Then he'd tell my sister to stand in the closet while he assaulted me. Or he'd come into my room and get with me sexually. And then he'd leave my room and he'd go to her room."

"Did he ever even try to justify or explain away his behavior?"

"He told me that he wasn't going to do anything to me that he didn't do to everyone else. That was his exact words to me. Whatever was, was the will of God, he told me."

"Nobody tried to prevent or stop these things from happening?"

"Nobody could help me because Brother Mustapha did the same thing to all of us. He was messing with everybody who was there.

"Once I tried to interfere between him and two minors he was raping," she ruefully recalled.

"What happened?" Bailey asked anxiously.

"I came to knock on the door and he sent both of them out of the room and pulled me in and beat me. He just beat the crap out of me and kept on yelling at me—over and over again: 'None of your fucking business! None of your fucking business!' He beat me more than any other woman he ever had. He beat other women to a pulp too."

"Tiffany," Bailey started to commiserate, "I'm so sorry—"

"He told me never to tell anybody anything!" she repeated deplorably. "He just did real cruel things, you know. Just real malicious things to me, you know. Having sex any kind of way he wanted to have it. Hitting me with a whip in a little, you know, them little horse things that you hit horses with—with the little tassels on the end?"

"A horse whip," Bailey sighed with a closed–eyed nod of disgust, "otherwise known as a riding crop."

"He would do that," she whimpered, her eyes welling out with glistening tears, streaming freely across her flushed cheeks and full lips. "Just all kinds of things. Oral sex. Anal sex. It was so shameful and disgusting and embarrassing. Just being a slave. That's what we were. Slaves. We were just slaves.

"He even made us let him," she went on, retching convulsively, "ejaculate, urinate and defecate in our mouths! He would force us to swallow all his filth! I blanked it out, blocked it out of my mind—or tried."

"I just can't imagine what you went through," Bailey sympathized, gently laying hold of her trembling hands clutched tight atop her knees. "But nobody deserves what happened to you."

"People who was there, grown people, was letting all this stuff happen. All of them who lived there was letting him molest their kids. He molested his own daughters. I'm not going to put my life in jeopardy and my family's life in jeopardy over something that the authorities won't even do something about. Put yourself in my shoes. All you know is this is a man who has people killed."

"It never occurred to you to report these atrocities to the authorities—the police or social services?" Bailey asked.

"We were little and we had a lot of fear in us." she said with a panicky shake of her head. "When we were little, there was people missing. People were killed, you know, who used to be at the temple. And Mustapha used to always preach in his sermons about people who would be floating in San Francisco Bay and all that."

"Did you think that Mustapha would actually kill you?"

"At the time, really, honestly, I believed that he would have." she said, nodding adamantly. "You hear all that when you're a little kid, you know, you'd be afraid to tell anyone. You didn't question it. I didn't question it so that I can breathe like I'm breathing today.

"What I've told you so far only scratches the surface," Tiffany confided, heaving a sigh of discomfort after a disconcerting pause.

"How so?" Bailey asked.

"Every temple female raped and impregnated by Mustapha was coerced to go on public assistance and collect welfare benefits," she answered deliberately.

"Say again?" he asked, aghast.

"It's part of his business plan," she explained. "It's like an organized, systematic exploitation of the system to inflate the temple's clout. Every temple female is forced under duress to participate in his welfare fraud scheme.

"If you come to the temple, you have to apply for something to bring some kind of money in."

"Is there any woman who was living in the temple compound who had one of Mustapha's children that you're aware of who did not apply for welfare?"

"Not a single one."

"Is there any woman that you're aware of who lived in the temple compound who told the truth in their applications for public assistance about who the fathers of their children were?"

"Not that I know of. Even his daughters, all of them were beating the system. Every single last one of them.

"Mustapha gave me instructions," she clarified. "All the women, the wives, didn't put his name on the birth certificates."

"Did these women receive aid?"

"Every last one of them."

"Did their checks go to Mustapha?"

"Every last one of them."

"I know that the money went to Brother Mustapha," she elaborated. "All I remember is them having me to sign the check because my name was on it.

"Every penny was turned over to him. He took every last cent that came in there."

"How did he ever get away with that?"

"I guess you just have money–hungry people who will do anything to get it.

"Then one day, Mustapha started trying to get my youngest daughter to take rides with him. I felt stuck. 'O my God!' I said to myself, 'How am I ever going to get out of here?' I was depressed because I was pregnant with another kid and I knew that I could not leave. Now where am I going with three children?

"I had absolutely no money or means of support, because Mustapha forced me to lie about the father of the children to get on welfare. Then he took those checks for his own personal use. I managed to escape from Mustapha after he beat me during my third pregnancy. After I left, Mustapha threatened to have me floating in the Bay if I ever divulged any of his crimes.

"This threat has made me and my children fear for our lives. I have kept my whereabouts concealed from Mustapha and his supporters. I have witnessed several people physically harmed by Mustapha. So, I take Mustapha's threats very seriously.

"Mustapha's dangerous. He's proven above and beyond that he intends to harm me any way possible because of his hatred towards me."

"How could he get everyone involved to willingly go along with these schemes?"

"To me people looked like they were brainwashed to

190

follow him, that's how I've known cults to be. They follow everything that the leader wants them to do. And they don't have—they don't get a chance to be themselves or live their own lives.

"Besides, his reputation as a powerful political figure in San Francisco protects him. When I finally tried and tried to get help, I couldn't get help. Social workers told me Mustapha was too powerful to go up against."

§

Abruptly a familiar gleaming silver, black–trimmed Chrysler KK Jeep Liberty compact, four–door SUV pulled up, grinding to a screeching halt at the curb of winding road directly behind them. From the unmarked jeep emerged the tall, imposing figure of Inspector Derwin Quagmire. Aggressively he strode and stepped straight up to Chance Bailey and Tiffany Mustapha, hovering over them menacingly.

"Get in the fucking car!" he barked at the woman, ignoring the newsman as if he were invisible.

"I'm not going anywhere with you!" she defied him.

"The fuck you're not!"

"What is this?" Bailey objected, getting gradually to his feet. "What's going on?"

"You shut the fuck up and stay out of this!" Quagmire snapped, wagging a threatening finger in Bailey's face. "Or I'll haul your black ass in too!"

Quagmire stooped to lay hold of the woman, wrenching her violently by the arm.

"You're hurting me!" she protested.

"You're lucky to still have your teeth!" Quagmire mocked her. "I haven't slapped a young black bitch in a long time! Now move it!"

Uselessly she resisted, struggling to yank her arm free;

but the cop's grip was an uncompromising clamp.

"Do you know what an eye for an eye means?" Quagmire bellowed into her ear, jerking her toward the jeep. "Do you want a swarm of muslims set loose on you and your family? Do you know what they'll do to you if it gets out that you're snitching on him? They'll come after your bitch–ass!"

"This is what Mustapha is, Mister Bailey!" she squalled, straining to look back fearfully over her shoulder. "You can put a bow tie on a pig—but he's still a pig!"

Quagmire threw open the jeep's passenger door, shoved her into the seat and slammed the door shut. He jumped into the driver's seat and with a gravel–grinding skid of tires, the jeep pealed off.

Staggering slightly and looking stunned, Chance Bailey stood aghast—struck dumb with disbelief.

SIXTEEN:
DEATH ROW

Stow Lake
Golden Gate Park
San Francisco, California

"**F**ix your face, dawg," a familiar voice crowed sarcastically out of nowhere. "Better luck next time."

Chance Bailey whirled around with a start to see Joshua standing but a step away, grinning scurrilously.

"You have a big cheese smile on your face," the newsman wryly observed. "Why does it feel like you been trying to sucker stroke me about this?"

"About what?"

"About the girl."

"What about her?"

"I feel like you been trying to work me."

"I'm not understanding."

"You wanted me to find her—for Mustapha. You played me for a sucker. What's Mustapha's agenda?"

"I can't find the words to answer that question."

"Don't play me like that, son, I thought we too cool for that."

"Maybe you thought wrong."

"You've done a switch–up with your attitude too. You've been trying to spin me," Bailey said disgustedly. "I'm tired of you spinning me."

"Mustapha told me to go sit on you—to go baby–sit you."

"I already told you, don't play me like that."

"It was my job to keep you in the blind."

"In the blind? About what?"

"Everything. I been told that you was rotten."

"What are you talking about?"

"Mustapha said you was out here playing police. All

this time you was working with them peoples."

"I'm a newspaper man," Bailey said, adamant. "I write news stories for the San Francisco Chronicle. I was considering writing a piece about Mustapha and the mosque. I don't nark for the fucking cops."

"Doctor Mustapha sent me to admonish you," Joshua said seriously, "that cooperating with the cops gets you labeled as something real bad."

"I feel like I've been beat with a sucker stick," Bailey said resignedly.

"We got to stick up for our brothers and sisters. That's what we do."

"Just don't get up in here and start acting funny on me."

Chance Bailey looked down his nose at Joshua, who was grinning ironically as he suggested, "Let's go take a row on the lake and have a talk!"

§

Joshua led the way to Stow Lake's brown–shingle boat house trimmed in baby blue with scarlet–and–white–painted doors, gates and hatches. After paying the cash–only rental fee, a young Asian attendant guided the two to the narrow, angular and level landing directly in front of the boat house, where a short, jostling string of small wooden rowboats gently bumped ends in the placid water; the attendant braced the boat at the head of the line.

"You row," Joshua bid Bailey, gesturing to the boat's gunwale. "I'll talk."

Looking befuddled, Bailey begrudgingly but gingerly stepped into the rowboat, taking the aft–facing seat at the fulcrum; Joshua sat down in the stern. Bailey had a firm hold on the wooden oars, rattling the metal rowlocks as the attendant heaved with a sturdy shove to launch the rowboat from the flat wooden landing.

"Make a single circuit of the lake," Joshua directed, pointing eastward, "and we'll be done."

Conspicuously perplexed, Bailey started sculling with stout and smooth strokes of the oars—until they first passed by the elevated, faded red, floating platform crowded with teeming, squawking sea gulls.

"I think the temple's a good thing because it helps a lot of brothers become good men," Joshua mused aloud. "The muslims are for black people. They're militant. They pushing a line. They don't be playing. They don't take no shit from nobody. I've been influenced by all that."

"How so?" Bailey prompted him, panting slightly.

"A few years ago I was homeless in the Western Addition," Joshua recalled. "I had only the clothes on my back. At the temple they said, 'Brother, are you looking for work?' They gave me a job, they paid me, they fed me, they got me back on my feet. I stayed there ever since."

"How were you referred to the temple?"

"You may have to be more direct."

"How were you recruited?"

"Through a friend of a friend. Doctor Mustapha wooed me with a promise of more than a job. Doctor Mustapha defines working at the temple as more than a job. You got to know it's more than a job. It's a cause."

"Could you be more specific?"

"Mustapha needs people he can depend on. He needs people who aren't scared. He needs soldiers. Mustapha will order his followers to do stuff you can't ask other people to do. Whatever will come to his mind."

"Commit crimes?"

"I don't say the word crimes. That's not the way I talk."

"How could you let yourself get caught up in all that?"

"Brother Mustapha did for me and thousands like me

by putting out a helping hand when I needed it most and giving me a spiritual foundation."

"A foundation of hate?"

"The foundation's built off of people that the community and society have given up on—the people at the bottom."

Drifting sluggishly along the woodsy, northward side of the lake's island, the rowboat passed through the shadowed arches of an asphalt pedestrian bridge.

"Doctor Mustapha's just another good brother," Joshua declared, shaking his head. "He's a kind dude. He's generous. If it weren't for brother Mustapha I'd probably be going back and hanging out in the streets."

"We are people who found a belief system at the temple," Joshua asserted emphatically.

"Just what is it that you believe?" Bailey questioned him, puffing lustily.

"I would credit Doctor Mustapha with helping me to gain a true love for black people. If you don't love your own people, then you must be sick. That means you don't love your mother, your father, your wife, or yourself. So number one, I would credit him with giving me the knowledge of self and others."

"Others? What others?"

"The ones we're at war with."

"The white devils?"

"Doctor Mustapha tells his followers that we are at war. We've been at war for four hundred years. He preaches that the only criteria for success is to be as rich as or even richer than the white devils—regardless of means."

"Waging war by any means necessary simply means making money—that lowest and most tedious of common denominators."

"We from the hood. We don't do what we do in the streets for the sake of righteousness. We do it because we're greedy. We do it because we ain't got shit—because we trying to get something. People who never had nothing, show them something, just show them something and they going to be ready for whatever. Fuck the white man before the white man fucks you is Doctor Mustapha's motto."

"I can't believe you trying to hit me with that bullshit," Bailey berated him. "You got a lot of bullshit with you. You need to get that bullshit out of your life. Hit me with the really real."

Rounding the island's eastward end the rowboat drifted in sight of Sutro Tower's 977–foot, triple–pronged antenna soaring far off from a hill near Clarendon Heights.

"Have you got a wife and kids, Mister Bailey?" Joshua abruptly asked.

"I'm divorced. My son lives with his mother."

"My mother's a crackhead. My father's long gone. I ain't got no family. Brother Mustapha and the temple's my family."

"You just trying to sugar–coat this shit. The truth is the truth, so don't try and sugar–coat it," Bailey scolded him. "You ain't your parents and they ain't you. So stop blaming them for what you are. Step up to the plate, take some personal responsibility and learn how to be real man."

"What's a real man, Mister Bailey?" Joshua scoffed with a mocking smirk.

"A real man is somebody who's responsible. A man's responsibility is to provide, maintain, and protect your woman and your children. So you got to learn a trade, you got to learn to work. Because you're going to always have to work to take care of that family—even if it's only your crackhead mother."

"She ain't been responsible for me. So why should I be responsible for her?"

"Because she be your blood. You been running with lames who aren't your blood. You be trying to act like them but that's not you. I know that ain't you."

"What do you mean, 'lames?'"

"Mustapha's a punk. He's a little wimp. He won't do any fucking thing on his own at all. His followers are little errand boys. That's how all of them are. That's how come many of them end up dead or in jail. If you're so big and bad, you go do those fucking things yourself."

"You got Brother Mustapha fucked up with one of your females."

"You got life fucked up. I knew they was selling you a bad dream."

"Don't mess with me like that. You worrying about the wrong thing. That'll get your head split."

"Just stop fronting. There ain't no future in fronting for Mustapha."

"You keep it up, I'm going to bust a cap in your ass."

"All I can tell you, do you. You always do you so this time is no different. That's what Mustapha preaches."

"Look, I got hella flaws," Joshua relented momentarily. "I'm not the most intelligent person but I do pride myself with the intellect to learn quickly. If I put my fate in my own hands I might get a better outcome."

"If you do it responsibly—not irresponsibly."

"You're just a wanksta, man" Joshua hissed with a dismissive wave of his hand. "I'm a serious gangsta who takes what he wants from people."

As they went on, going the round of the island, the rowboat drifted in sight of the octagonal, green–roofed Chinese pavilion with crimson columns and alabaster balustrade.

"What's Mustapha making you take from people these days?"

"Look dawg, it don't pay to be that nosy, let's get out

of here."

"What's up with Mustapha and Star Security? And who do you think's smoking your brothers—and why?"

"You don't hear me though. Everything ain't for everybody. So you need to find you some other business."

"What better business could there be besides Brother Mustapha?"

As they made the round of the darkened, shadowed and more somber southward side of the island their rowboat drifted in sight of the flagstone pedestrian bridge arching over glimmering, murky water reflecting muzzy light and woodsy shapes. Carved in stone on the side of the bridge are the chiseled words:

ERECTED

A.D.

1893

"You don't have to violate like that," Joshua muttered menacingly. "Keep my name out of your mouth. Keep Brother Mustapha's name out of your mouth. Quiet is kept. Next time you violate dawg, it's on."

"What's that supposed to mean?"

"It means you in everything but a hearse. All you can do is take it for what it is."

"And just what is it supposed to be?"

Trickling water echoed and reflected ripples flitted against the hard curved undersides of the bridge's double arches.

Joshua abruptly produced the Intratec TEC–9, a blowback–operated semi–automatic firearm, chambered in 9X19mm Parabellum.

Chance Bailey sprang back in the rowboat and froze in mortal fear as Joshua leveled the firearm at him.

"I like the TEC–9 assault weapon because the bullets spew out real fast!" Joshua muttered ominously, brandishing the handgun. "Bbbbrrrrrttttt!"

Chance Bailey cringed, flinching at Joshua's thundery utterance.

"You're going to get a free pass on this one," Joshua admonished Bailey, "but next time you on your own. The game is meant to be sold—not told."

Directly the rowboat drifted to the westward bank of the lake, bumping to an abrupt halt.

Hurriedly and wordlessly, Joshua disembarked from the rowboat, crossed a threadlike, bark–scattered footpath through the underbrush to the access road beyond, where a gleaming black high–performance BMW M5 saloon idled. Once Joshua wriggled into the rearward seat the car sped off with a sand–spurting screech of tires.

§

Severely shaken, Chance Bailey rowed alone back to the boat house. After returning the rowboat to the landing he trudged to the curb space along the northward lakeshore where he'd parked his battered Buick Electra 225. He shuddered with fear and disbelief at the startling sight he saw: scattered all over the car's interior, and strewn all around the immediate roadside, were the shivery shards of glass from the car's shattered windshield and windows—now gaping and jagged holes—completely pulverized by gunfire!

PART FIVE:

STAYING STRONG IN THE STORM

SEVENTEEN: ZEBRAS REVISITED

The Original
TOMMY'S JOYNT
1101 Geary Boulevard
San Francisco, California

Situated on U.S. Route 101 at Van Ness Avenue and Geary Boulevard—the city's crossroads—is San Francisco's original cafeteria–style hof–brau, established in 1947 by Great Depression–era founders whose generations of offspring still own and operate it to this day: Tommy's Joynt.

Its logo is an olive floating in a tilted martini glass.

Its motto is:

There's no place
Any place
Quite like this place
So this must be
The place

"Welcome Stranger" decals above its front doors invite patrons into the eatery "Where Turkey is King"—together with savory corned beef, roast beef, pastrami and ham. To Unsavory Dave Toski, though, the Joynt's barbecue brisket of beef was possessed of the noblest and most exalted and princely pedigree.

Tommy's Joynt was the only unfailingly warm and welcoming eatery he knew of in all of San Francisco, where you could still get the biggest bang for your buck by picking up an incredible daily dinner platter of barbecue beef brisket(or other meat dish), freshly carved and piping–hot, with choices of mashed potatoes or vegetables, beans or salad, along with bread and butter—all for less than ten dollars! Toski typically opted to pay just a little extra for a side aluminum–wrapped baked potato, plus both hickory baked beans and a salad dressed with blue cheese, to go along with his sliced beef soused in delicious barbeque

sauce, which he'd wash down with gingerale. Another side
treat Toski thought it well worth paying extra for were the
Joynt's delectable singly–served meat balls and sausages!

Toski sat alone at the corner of the banquet table,
draped with the classic red–and–white checkered table-
cloth, adjacent to the far end of the long wooden bar and
tall barstools extending the length of the Joynt's southward wall. He was scarfing down his favorite hearty
feast—the Joynt's succulent barbeque beef brisket!

Countless, inexplicable mementos, relics and souvenirs—a bewildering and jumbled mishmash the propri-
etors endearingly refer to as "memorabilia"—clutter the
perpetually busy and noisy Joynt throughout, decorating
the walls and hanging from the ceiling, balustrades, columns and walls.

Toski got up from his battered wooden seat and called
out to his longtime, familiar Mexican friend, sporting the
thick black moustache and chef's cap, who'd cooked and
cashiered at the lengthy, metallic and glass–encased food
bar, extended opposite the booze bar along the Joynt's
northward wall, for as long as he could remember.

"Hey, mi amigo!" he greeted him, bidding him goodbye, "gracias and buenas noches!"

"Adiós, Dave!" he answered him back. "Come back
soon! Don't stay away so long the next time! After all,
we're a San Francisco classic you ought to frequent more
regularly!"

"You can't get much more classic than you, Señor Dia-
blo!" Toski cracked with a cheerful crease of his cheek. "Or
more venerable!"

"Like our ads say," he answered him back with a wry
smile, "we're one of the city's longest living institutions—
just like you, Mister Toski!"

"I'm still aiming to outlast this Joynt!"

"I'm sure you'll survive forever, Dave, you always do!

You always will!'"

§

Dave Toski headed out of the front of the Joynt's florid blue–and–red, mural–emblazoned, corner building and slid into his 2008, forest green, full–size, five–door, rear–wheel drive, police–version, Dodge MAGNUM station wagon parked on Geary Avenue. He promptly ignited its V6 engine, put its five–speed transmission into gear and sped away from the metered curb space, drove two blocks west to make a U–turn onto steeply curved King Way, wheeling around to merge onto O'Farrell Street and doubling back to head downtown toward Union Square.

§

Hilton San Francisco Union Square
333 O'Farrell Street
San Francisco, California

San Francisco Hilton and Towers is a skyscraper hotel with two towers—the 46–story, 493–foot Tower I and the 23–story, 348–foot Tower II soaring south–west of Union Square between Ellis and Mason Streets. Currently the west coast's largest hotel complex with 1911 rooms, it's one of the tallest structures representing the blockish, fortress–like, linear and concrete–predominant Brutalist style of architecture and construction.

At street level, Chance Bailey emerged from the Downtown Center Self–Parking Garage, a nine–story, coiled, corner concrete hulk at 325 Mason Street, where he'd parked his battered–and–shattered Buick Electra 225.

Directly he crossed O'Farrell Street, approaching the Hilton hotel's elongated, glowing, plum–colored awning overhanging the building's front facade, but passing

through the street–level entrance of the hotel's rustic–
looking, city–country decorated Urban Tavern Restaurant and Lounge—deliberately bypassing entry through
the expansive main chandelier–lit lobby.

Passing by the restaurant's marble–topped bar, com-
munal tree–made table and intimate dining booths, astir
with patrons and surrounded by reclaimed wood beams,
claddings, exposed concrete–and–plaster walls, Bailey ca-
sually exited by way of the restaurant's inner receptionist
station.

Parked directly across the street facing the hotel facade was the familiar gleaming black Lexus LX 570
full–sized service utility vehicle, idling in a metered curb
space. From the somber interior its four tall and burly
black occupants directed their watchful eyes in concert to
the portly but gainly black man, whom they'd been scop-
ing out, sauntering through the restaurant's olive–green,
orange canopy–covered doors.

"Got you, motherfucker!" snarled Isaiah, pointing a
scornful finger from the driver's seat. "That's the motherfucker right there! Chance Bailey, the fucking reporter!"

"Yeah," Jeremiah, beside him in the front passenger
seat, chimed in, "that motherfucker wants to write stuff
that slanders the temple!"

"Man, as a matter of fact, that motherfucker's writing against us right now!" Isaiah spouted bitterly, "He's
against us, talking shit against us!"

"That fucker's up there talking to that decrepit cop,
Toski, right now! That motherfucker up there right now
talking to him!"

"We should whack that motherfucker too!"

"Disrespectful–ass devils," Joshua, sitting next to
Zechariah in the back seats, sneered more scrupulously.

Zechariah fixed his probing eyes on Joshua with a still
but suspicious stare.

Stepping inside the hotel's glittering, gold–irradiated lobby, Bailey crossed the plush cobalt carpet until he stepped up to a pair of tall, shining gold elevator doors, reflecting his misshapen image as he awaited the doors to fly open with a hushed hiss. Before long he was scaling the heights of the hotel's highest tower as the elevator crept up slowly and smoothly to the forty–sixth floor.

§

Cityscape Bar & Restaurant
Tower I
46th Floor
Hilton Hotel
San Francisco, California

Chance Bailey exited the elevator, setting foot on the blue–and–gold mottled carpet, and passed through the narrow entrance hall with glass–encased wine bottle displays. Lofty foursquare floor–to–ceiling mirrored columns reflected his approach as he stepped up to the central, blue–and–white marbled bar overarched with its hefty, rectangular, gleaming gold canopy. He went round to the eastward section of the room buttressed with shiny brass posts. Round cocktail tables covered with plum–colored cloths were set at spaced intervals from end to end. Tall, sectioned window panes festooned at the ceiling with plum–colored drapes looked out on San Francisco's singular skyline—overspread with a fuming, fleeting, nomadic fog.

Chance Bailey passed by a shiny brass baluster to drop down a step to a sunken floor and sit down across from Dave Toski at a small square table commanding a panoramic view of San Francisco's characteristic cityscape, sky and fog. Except for the two of them the expansive room was empty of people.

"Hang loose," Toski invited Bailey, gesturing to a brown wooden chair. "The Cityscape room's closed to the public these days except for private events. I know Damian, the hotel security director, he'll ensure we have undisturbed privacy here."

"A spectacular spot for a meeting," Bailey commended him.

Toski dispensed Heineken's Newcastle Summer Ale from a five–liter aluminum mini–keg with a pressurized tap, pouring the English beer into two twelve fluid ounce Wellington glasses. Both men sipped the frothy head of their beers with seeable satisfaction.

"Nice choice!" Bailey heartily approved.

"Let's get down to cases," Toski prompted him. "Now what's the lowdown on Joseph Mustapha and this Mosque Mohammed of his?"

"Joseph Mustapha's practicing a sinister type of worship propagated to the gullible and highly emotional," Chance Bailey expounded at length. "His constituency's been the bottom rung, people living through the crack epidemic, committing crimes, and becoming casualties of the streets.

"His followers are confined mostly to the ignorant and superstitious. Previously the mosque was known for employing the unemployable. What was once a positive force in the black community has become a sad situation.

"And then you have this criminal element over there that's racked up this whole laundry list of crimes and criminal charges. Unfortunately, the whole thing's run off the track. Now these hoods are out of control and greedy. They've gotten involved in some real bad things.

"Whatever were the positive elements of Mustapha's organization have become overshadowed by this current atmosphere of crime and violence."

"By all accounts," Toski suggested, "everybody's known for years that these people are mad dogs biting people out on the street."

"These are demonstrably dangerous people that I'd be writing about who've been associated with many acts of violence," Bailey affirmed. "I'd rather be plying my trade than ducking some crazy hoods fronting for that mosque."

"You better know what you want before you wish for it."

"I think it's more dangerous for you, not me."

"No, it's not going to get any better for you either. Informants often get killed."

"Are these really dangerous people?"

"They are. You ought to be convinced after they shot up your car"

"Well, why would they kill people they didn't like?"

"They'd kill anybody for the hell of it."

"I don't understand the relevance to this copycat Zodiac case."

"You don't understand the gravity," Toski said seriously. "These dudes are killers. I'm telling you, from now on—leave these muslims alone."

"Some of these people have been hoodlums for twenty years and members of the mosque for two years. When they want something they revert to what they know best.

"Mustapha promised to kill Tiffany if she spoke to anyone about his sexual proclivities. He told her, if you tell anybody, you'll be floating in the bay, you and your family."

"This all harks back to the so–called Zebra Killers, a group of San Francisco black muslims who killed random whites, whom they called devils, in the early 1970s.

"The killing of a white was required for initiation into the innermost circles of the black sect. The victims of these ritual slayings were always white, usually male and customarily attacked when they were alone at night on the street.

"The attacks all seemed to come on their victims suddenly, wantonly, viciously and only because the victims happened to be in the right place to be attacked."

"I recollect that," Bailey asserted. "The Zebra Killers were supposed to give whites a dose of their own medicine in the name of justice. White devils, so—called, had no value. It was supposed to be righteous revenge for blacks getting lynched and stuff like that from way back."

"So the slaughter of whites by cult—motivated blacks in a series of random attacks were christened the Zebra killings," Toski recalled. "These had set off an around—the—clock manhunt involving the entire homicide crew. Members of the fanatical cult hacked and shot twenty—three victims in what was to be a one hundred seventy—nine—day reign of terror. Fifteen were killed; only eight of the victims survived. Five of the killers were eventually convicted and sentenced to life imprisonment.

"I was gratified that I was part of the team that brought that terrible case to a successful conclusion," Toski said solemnly.

"I had been forced out of a sick bed to work on the Zebra attacks; and then, on top of that, I had Zodiac back," Toski concluded ironically. "His timing was lousy!"

"I have a simple proverb I live by, Dave."

"What's that?"

"Never give up. And stay strong in the storms."

EIGHTEEN: *AFTERLIFE SLAVES*

Cityscape Bar & Restaurant
Tower I
46th Floor
Hilton Hotel
San Francisco, California

"You're just very enthusiastic," Dave Toski complimented Chance Bailey, continuing their private conversation. "Some of your ideas are very good—such as paring the case down to its essentials."

"Do you think the original Zodiac is still alive?" Bailey asked attentively.

"I believe that Zodiac's probably still alive," Toski reflected. "If he'd died there would be evidence found in a place where he lived. The coroner would have come into it. So I think he's still alive. I think he's still out there.

"It's almost a gut feeling. But if he'd been killed in an accident or committed suicide or been murdered, I believe someone would've gone into his room. And I think he would've left something for us to find. He got his thrills by telling us about the murders. My guess is that he hasn't been killing. Ego's what forced him to kill and write letters, knowing the media would broadcast and print it. I think he's in a period of remission and that some symptoms subsided. Perhaps during this time he had no desire to kill. I sense that Zodiac's still alive and waiting."

"But I can't believe the supreme braggart could go away without leaving behind one last taunting message or some incriminating piece of evidence—a gun, knife, cipher table, or at least the remaining portion of Paul Stine's blood–blackened shirt," Bailey declared.

"Somewhere Zodiac could still have bombs. One day he's going to die and the cops will go through his basement and find guns and bombs—maybe in the Presidio as you

217

suspect—and the case will be solved."

"Zodiac sure refuses to die, living on in gossip, rumor and speculation—in every dark shadow along any lake like Berryessa—and in all our suspicions. The old Zodiac—that thing will never die."

"He's lurking somewhere, and it used to scare the hell out of the public. Of all the cases I've handled, this one's really a personal one. He played the ego game, baiting and taunting us. I tried not to let that bother me but it was frustrating. I haven't given up."

"For sure?"

"It's quite a challenge. I never let a day go by without remembering Zodiac. Ever since I was the only one working on it, it's got to be more personal. I don't know if I'll ever get the case solved, but I'm sure as hell still trying. I feel he's out there. I feel he's going to surface—if he hasn't already."

"How hopeful are you?"

"Did I think we'd ever catch the sonofabitch? Naturally I did. I'd have to feel that way or I'd have given up long ago. To me it's still a major case, a major challenge.

"Once I was the only one working on the case, I never let a day go by without remembering Zodiac. It became more personal. Every day I wondered what became of him—until it reached the point that I just didn't want to do it anymore."

"I agree, Zodiac's definitely alive. I don't think he's doing any more killings. I think when he saw the cops getting closer he stopped."

"That's my theory too. I got real close and he said, 'Uh, oh, I better not do anything.'

"There were long delays in those murders and letters. I always chalked it up to the fact that I got real close and Zodiac backed off.

"Many of the leads I was originally handed have become so old and deteriorated to the point where they don't have much value anymore. I still think Zodiac's out there someplace. I sometimes look out the window and wonder how close I've come to him at times. I rattled so many cages and kicked so many bushes along the way, I must have been near him at least once."

"Especially after the updated composite sketch based on patrolman Donald Fouke's eye–witness description?"

"I thought we were pretty close at that point. Sometimes you get a feeling in the pit of your stomach."

"Maybe Zodiac's worked out his hostility and will kill no more," Bailey speculated. "He may've burned out and stopped killing."

"There's any number reasons why the killings stopped, why he quit," Toski concurred. "'It's not interesting to me anymore.' That explanation's really simplistic, but that's probably the explanation for him if he were Zodiac: losing interest—like me. But I don't think Zodiac's gone. I think psychopaths are capable of stopping their madness and then covering their tracks."

"And where's Zodiac now? Don't serial killers usually want notoriety? That's what puzzles me."

"I'm just hoping this copycat's all a hoax, but maybe if Zodiac surfaces, he might leave a new track that could lead to him getting caught. I can't imagine somebody keeping quiet and staying back all the time if he were as whacked out as Zodiac was. A guy as cocky and conceited as him would've let it be known he was busy again."

"You appear uncomfortable dredging up details of Zodiac."

"Zodiac's continued to prey on my mind," Toski confided. "I was the only San Francisco detective working on one of the most baffling cases in the history of American crime. Then I was the only S.F. cop working on the Zodiac case.

"It's not something that goes away over time. It's the kind of thing that sticks with you. That case just eats at you. It just doesn't let go. I'll smoke him out again."

"It took its toll on you?"

"The case definitely took its toll on me. It was a vivid time that marked us all. It was all adrenaline—very draining. After a time I was becoming increasingly haunted by the case.

"I felt he would keep killing until he was caught. I was going to think about this a whole lot. I've done a lot of walking and thinking about the unsolved case."

"What was the worst part about it?"

"There seemed to be no motive to the brutal slayings—outside of killing for the sheer thrill of it. I could find no attempt at robbery or sexual molestation of the victims. Perhaps Dr. Lund's right—the killing itself had served as a sexual release.

"There were no witnesses, no motives, and no suspects. Everyone was suspect and no one was safe."

"Yet police from at least four different jurisdictions were actively investigating the case."

"The case was just too big, the pool of suspects too numerous, and manpower spread far too thin for constant surveillance to be feasible. There were hundreds—an avalanche—of suspects. Friends, neighbors, relatives, ex-spouses—whoever people wanted to pin the Zodiac murders on became a suspect.

"Who knows? Maybe one of them was right. I was frustrated from the years of false leads and dashed hopes. No real major suspect had ever been developed. S.F.P.D. still hadn't developed a major suspect in the case."

"What was the ultimate upshot?"

"The years of frustration finally caught up with me. Yet when I finally retired, I couldn't stop working on the case in my mind.

"I wondered: with the wealth of information I had had about Zodiac, where was I going wrong? What was the mistake in perception that prevented me from seeing who he truly was?

"There's enough here we ought to be able to break this case. Either that, or he's just running us around in circles."

"The Zodiac case is like the tide—hopes raised only to be dashed against the rocks," Bailey ruminated. "And yet beneath the surface, you always feel strong currents—another unsolvable mystery, a trace of a deeper crime as you wade through the murky water."

"Everybody loves a good mystery." Toski considered. "Has there ever been a greater mystery?

"It's a mystery—because of the letters, the ciphers, the codes, the symbols. It's taunting, it's 'Catch me if you can,' and 'I'm crack–proof.'"

"In reality," Bailey conjectured, "all this business about all these cryptograms didn't have to do with anything. It was a way for Zodiac to play with people's minds for his own perverse satisfaction. Those cryptograms, as it turned out, had no meaning."

"When he'd appeared," Toski confirmed, nodding, "there really hadn't been anything like Zodiac before. This character put a fresh brush stroke on what were really some pretty run–of–the–mill serial murders. He'd captured the people's enduring interest.

"Zodiac was one of the early serial killers to acquire publicity. He used the cryptograms to use the media. The use of a logo and encrypted messages made him both well–marketed and of interest to great numbers of people who'd like to solve the goddamned mystery.

"What fascinates me is that it's still a mystery—that the case is still active and that so many people are still aware of it. All over the world people are so mesmerized by the Zodiac mystery that it's taken on a cult–like fascination. So many other people have killed more people than Zodiac. Why is there so much interest all these years later?"

"Personally," Bailey said seriously, "I find it difficult to believe that such a horrifying murderer as Zodiac hasn't yet been caught. The fact that Zodiac's never been caught—his ability to stay at large—is what makes the mystery so durable.

"Do you think you're closer to getting the case solved any more than you were forty–four years ago?"

"Honestly, I don't think so," Toski conceded. "That kinda saddens me a bit because for me it's the case of a career. You have to want to solve the goddamned thing! You have to! I truly believe it's a solvable case."

"I'm all for you solving it. That's why I tracked you down in the first place."

"As time's gone by, I've had my doubts that Zodiac's still alive. But I still think the case can be solved. After all this time, I want to close this case and I still think I can. I wish I could've closed it already. This is what's preoccupied my mind constantly.

"Until Zodiac's caught, this fear will always be hanging over the survivors—over everybody in fact. Every time I get a crank call, Zodiac crosses my mind.

"It would put closure on the goddamned thing. It would bring relief to those who survived. And make a lot of peace officers happy.

"I've hoped for a resolution to the mystery. That'll happen only when somebody remembers something and comes forward. I really wanted to solve this case before I retired. It would dispel half the nightmare. I'll never give up hope."

"For a great many," Bailey pondered aloud, "Zodiac's history, he's all in the past, Dave.

"We don't create these situations. The Zodiac had shot

two or three people before story one appeared. So, it's not as if it's a chicken–and–egg thing. Sometimes these crimes have been unspooling for a while before we ever get notified of them or even get into them."

"I'll get Zodiac someday," Toski predicted. "And I'll bring him to justice. That's my motivation—justice. I'm not a vigilante type, but when a life's taken, there must be justice. He's taken five lives, who knows how many more? I work with death, sorrow, and tragedy. Yet I liked my job because it was a useful one. I brought in killers for society's judgment. Ringing bells and knocking on doors, good old–fashioned police work. What you really need is a lot of hard work—and luck. That's what does it. I just have to work the case and if it gets solved—it gets solved.

"You want to know who he is. I want to know why he is."

"Now this copycat killer's on the loose."

"After Zodiac, no one ever expected Zodiac's murders to be emulated again."

"But now the killer's undying persona's reached out to dole out death."

"I really didn't think this copycat of the San Francisco Zodiac killer would stir up this much interest."

"This Zodiac's anxious to convince everyone that he's the same Zodiac who killed people here years before. He wants us to think he's from San Francisco."

"Or does he actually believe that he's the California Zodiac reincarnated? This gunman claims to be the Zodiac killer of San Francisco fame in the late sixties, but I don't believe it. Another or the old one back again? Another Zodiac—a copycat of a copycat? What do you think?"

"It's happening again. He's shot people. Remember decades ago? This Zodiac claims to be the original guy who killed all."

"Do you think it's possible he's taken on the persona—

might just think he's the real Zodiac?"

"Who knows, maybe he really believes he's the San Francisco Zodiac."

"For you, this is like twice—what we don't know is if it's the same guy or not. Which is scarier—the same guy who came back or if it's two different ones?"

"Confidentially, I believe it still may be the guy from years ago. There are enough similarities that it could be the same man.

"We get calls saying Zodiac's shot people. He's writing letters. It checks out. He's out there again."

"What I've done is I've developed profiles on the victims that we have. What do they have in common? Any common thread that we can develop. And do you know what? Except for Robert Naysmith, the crime writer, so far all the victims are black muslims employed by Joseph Mustapha."

"But this guy here's shooting people in parked cars, which is a lot more indicative of the guy out there from the past than from the present. That's what gives me the creeps about this. I think the one guy and the other guy is one and the same. Now it's starting to lean that way."

"What are the odds?"

"I think it's a good chance it's the Zodiac, a better than fifty–fifty chance. I've been chasing the S.O.B. for years now, and the M.O. seems to fit him to a T.

"I'm taking a long hard look at these cases. I kind of hope it's him. If it is, it lets us know he's still around."

"At the same time my gut feeling tells me it's not the same guy you investigated then. Hey, this guy looks interesting. But more bells should go off."

"Zodiac claims he's in control," Toski said grimly. "I'd like him to prove it by sending another message before he kills anybody else, because I think it's time for this to move on to the next level. He's not fooling anybody—no matter what his game is."

"This seems to be a very important time," Bailey encouraged him. "Everything coming together."

"Right," said Toski, reassured. "It took a hell of a long time. It's not like this case is going to fall off the face of the earth for us."

"Well, what do you have missing?"

"Let's kick the ballistics of this U.S. Army Corps of Engineers–Philippines connection," Toski said, unflinching.

§

"In his report dated 10 August 1969," Bailey began, "George Bawart, Vallejo Police Department, noted a telephone call received from a source at the Stanford Research Center in Menlo Park, who stated that Zodiac's concept that persons killed would be the killer's slaves in the life hereafter originates in South East Asia, and particularly in Mindanao in the Southern Phillipines.

"So Bawart felt that possibly the responsible party would be either of South East Asian extraction or have knowledge of the area."

"Knowledge of the area is more likely," Toski accepted, "since the stocky blonde caucasian described by eye–witnesses just doesn't tally with a southeast Asian suspect."

"In 1898," Bailey related, "during the Spanish–American War, United States Army Corps of Engineers built bridges and roads, erected landing piers, repaired and operated railroads from Cuba and Puerto Rico to the Philippines.

"That same year, the United States went to war with Spain and the engineers provided extensive combat support.

"In the widespread theaters of the war from Cuba and Puerto Rico to the Philippines, the engineers aided the

Army with the same activities—building and maintaining roads, constructing bridges, erecting landing piers, repairing and operating railroads."

"That was then, this is now," Toski remarked impatiently. "Just hit me with the actual factual."

"Historical background's crucial to the now!" Bailey insisted, continuing.

"Following the Spanish–American War, an insurrection broke out in the Philippines.

"Companies A and B of the Engineer Battalion served in the initial stages of the conflict. The insurrectionists' guerrilla warfare tactics demanded rapid Army movements.

"So, engineer detachments had to build bridges, repair roads and perform reconnaissance rapidly over difficult jungle and mountain terrain.

"Frequently the engineer troops, who carried rifles as well as picks and axes, joined the infantry in fighting off an attack before completing work on a bridge or road."

"Accounting for Zodiac's expert engineering plus marksmanship skills since engineers are also soldiers?"

"The requirements of combat, especially in the Philippines, influenced the 1901 reorganization of the engineers into three battalions of four companies each," Bailey agreed with a nod of accord. "Although the fighting subsided in the Philippines in the early 20th century, it didn't cease, and engineer troops served in the islands, often in combat, for many years afterwards."

"Lay the rest down for me."

"When the Japanese bombed military bases in Hawaii and the Philippines on the morning of 7 December 1941, engineer units that had already been deployed to those islands were called upon to respond a few hours later.

"The skimpy, 1500–man U.S. Army engineer garrison in the Philippines was almost evenly divided between Filipino and American personnel.

"After Japanese forces landed there on 10 December, the engineers destroyed bridges from one end of Luzon to the other to slow the enemy's advance.

"Later, the engineers erected a series of defensive lines on the Bataan Peninsula and fought as infantry in these defenses before succumbing to superior Japanese forces in April and May 1942.

"In the southern Philippines, a number of Army engineers escaped to the mountains of Mindanao, where they worked with Filipino guerrillas and remained active throughout the period of Japanese occupation of the Philippines."

"Inferring that this historical connection between the U.S. Army Corps of Engineers and Mindanao in the Philippines links the Zodiac's concept of collecting slaves for the afterlife?"

"It stands to reason," Bailey confirmed eagerly. "In the Philippines, the 302nd Engineer Combat Battalion, responsible for road maintenance across rice paddies and swamps near Ormoc on Leyte, built or reinforced fifty-two bridges for tank traffic in mid–December 1944, generally working under small–arms and mortar fire, and contributed men and armored bulldozers to flush enemy troops out of their foxholes in the bamboo thicket.

"In northern Luzon and on Mindanao in the Philippines in early 1945 divisional engineer battalions completed essential bridge–building and road projects in difficult mountainous terrain that sometimes rose higher than 4000 feet above sea level.

"The 106th Engineer Combat Battalion on Mindanao constructed a 425–foot infantry support bridge across the Pulangi River and, encountering a gorge 120 feet across and 35 feet deep, blasted out its sides to create in a speedy fashion a crude rock bridge.

"Much of the engineer construction work on Luzon and Mindanao was also interrupted by enemy fire."

"It's a strong connection that makes a lot of sense," Toski conceded, intrigued.

"Let me bounce this off you for a minute," Bailey continued in earnest. "The military construction mission of the Corps of Engineers dates from the early days of World War II.

"Among the major projects in the Pacific area was the air ferry route to the Philippines. To move heavy bombers west across the ocean, the Corps built airfields on a number of Pacific islands. The engineers developed these bases in a matter of a few months."

"After World War II, Army engineer troops were organized primarily into engineer combat and construction battalions, supplemented by topographic battalions and various specialized engineer companies.

"The combat battalions were designed to provide the engineering capabilities required by frontline forces, and their men were trained and equipped to fight as infantry if necessary.

"Engineer construction battalions had heavier equipment suited for the more permanent construction typically required to the rear of combat zones, and its members were not expected to fight as infantry.

"The military's proportion of combat and support forces was frequently termed the tooth–to–tail ratio."

"Inferring that this historic link between the then and now brings us full circle and leads us to our latter–day Zodiac?"

"Do you need me to bust this down for you?" Bailey bantered. "The Corps of Engineers increased its involvement in maintaining and repairing Army housing and other facilities—like at the Presidio in San Francisco!

"In 1968—when the original Zodiac made his deadly

debut—the Army was urged to encourage installation facilities engineers to turn to Corps of Engineers districts and divisions for engineering support by funding a portion of that work.

"The Army agreed to set aside a modest fund for Corps installation support, invited commanders to turn to the Corps for additional maintenance and repair work on a reimbursable basis, and took other actions to strengthen facilities engineering."

"Connecting the dots when nobody else even sees the dots," Toski confessed uneasily, "and when a good many in cop circles don't even want to see if there are any dots is tough sometimes.

"But I take it that maybe we should be looking for our Zodiac of old among the U.S. Army Presidio's facilities engineers?"

"Bravo!" Bailey cheered.

NINETEEN: *KILLING FIELDS*

FRANCISCO RESERVOIR
San Francisco, California

At midnight, beneath a darksome blueblack sky scattered with twinkling stars, the dimly moonlit Francisco Reservoir itself looked like a lurid lunar landscape: a barren, pockmarked, slate–gray waste overspreading a sweeping space at the foot of a rising vegetated hillside overlooking San Francisco Bay.

Over roughly four and a half acres, the steep, woodsy slopes of Russian Hill Park rise from Bay Street below to merge with the lofty, level ledge of tableland buttressing the abandoned, expansive, fence–enclosed reservoir, a sprawling public open space between Hyde and Larkin Streets coveted by avaricious developers.

Higher up above the reservoir, atop a steep flight of crooked cement steps, Francisco Street, rising eastward from Van Ness Avenue far off below, merges with Larkin Street, descending northward from Russian Hill high up above, rounding into a hairpin turn of a curve. From the low–lying roadside retaining wall overlooking the reservoir, the sharply sloping curve commands a panoramic view of Aquatic Park's horseshoe–shaped municipal pier, the glittering waters of the man–made sandy beach lagoon, and the jagged outline of Alcatraz island beyond.

A tilted, crisscrossed signpost stands aslant on the sloping sidewalk bordering the sharply hooked curve of Francisco and Larkin Streets. And Chance Bailey stood as a silent if anxious sentinel, leaning against the signpost, dimly illuminated by dull and shadowed lamplight.

§

Chance Bailey called to mind the telephone call he'd

233

received earlier from Tiffany Mustapha, pleading hysterically.

"You have to help me, Mister Bailey!" she shrieked, her voice frenzied and frightened. "You've got to pick me up and hide me—or else I'm dead! I know everything and they're going to kill me for what I know! They figure if I don't say anything, the police don't got anything! I don't know who else to turn to! Please, Mister Bailey, I'm begging you!"

"Where are you now?"

"I'm on foot close to Chestnut Street in Russian Hill! I'll tell you where you can meet me! Please, Mister Bailey, hurry!"

What Chance Bailey couldn't see was that Tiffany Mustapha was bowed down, stark naked, kneeling at the edge of a regular–sized bed, holed up in some sequestered bedroom hideaway.

Crouched and wriggling into her from behind, his suit trousers unzipped, was police inspector, Derwin Quagmire. Tiffany Mustapha hung up the telephone, bracing both hands at the opposite sidewise edge of the bed.

"That's right, bitch!" crowed Quagmire, swaggering. "Your heart and soul might belong to Mustapha, but right now your tight ass belongs to me! You're in my protective custody!"

Quagmire's rigid palm slapped Tiffany Mustapha's supple bare rump punishingly.

"Now put out the rest of Mustapha's payment and repeat after me!" Quagmire commanded her callously. "I don't know shit! And if I don't say shit, they ain't got shit!"

Penetrating her deeply, Quagmire plowed into her backside, thrusting stiffly and repeatedly, making her squeal aloud.

§

Suddenly two different gleaming black sports cars roared at Bailey from opposite directions—a two–door, two–seater, mid–engine all–wheel drive Audi R8 GT sport coupé shooting up Francisco Street from Van Ness Avenue, together with a two–door, two–seater, Lamborghini Aventador LP 700–4 sports coupé swooping down Larkin from Chestnut Street—grinding to a screeching halt at the breakneck curve in the sloping roadside. Ablaze with the collision of their radiant beams, the retaining wall blacked out once the two facing sports cars promptly doused their headlights. Four tall and burly young black men emerged abruptly from the sports cars—Isaiah and Zechariah from the Audi, Jeremiah and Joshua from the Lamborghini. All four carried Mossberg 590A1 14–inch shotguns. All four moved toward Bailey, closing in upon him in a converging semi–circle with their polished blued barrels firmly leveled. Joshua lugged an extra tool—a 42–inch pair of bolt cutters!

Bailey stopped cold in his tracks, paralyzed with fear, his eyes flitting about anxiously.

"Come here, nigga!" Isaiah barked at Bailey, laying firm hold of one of his arms as Jeremiah tightly clenched his other. On either side of him, the two grabbed and dragged Bailey, ushering him roughly to the top of the nearby flight of crooked cement steps.

"Come on, nigga, keep it moving!" Jeremiah demanded as they hustled him forcefully down the angular zigzag of a lengthy metal–railed stairway, trisected by twin level landings. "We don't have no time for half–stepping."

Bailey flailed in their strong grip and stumbled awkwardly, his shoes scuffing the concrete with their unyielding, wrenching descent.

"Where my dawgs at?" spouted Joseph Mustapha, standing stiffly at the foot of the stairway, cradling in his arms a Stradivarius violin and horsehair bow and nodding at Bailey. "That's my main manz!"

"Do you think you've got enough gorillas here for this meeting, Mustapha?" Bailey remarked glibly.

"You know you have to come with the heat to win," Mustapha responded, gesturing for Joshua to press forward.

Joshua promptly stepped up to the tall chain–link fence gate enshrouded with ivy and hung with the warning sign that read:

NO TRESSPASSING
VIOLATORS WILL BE PROSECUTED
TO THE FULLEST EXTENT OF THE LAW
IN ACCORDANCE WITH CALIFORNIA
PENAL CODE SECTIONS
555, 602, 692. 2, 602.8

Joshua handily snapped the gate's padlock chain clean through with the heavy–duty bolt cutters, flinging the tool aside.

Swinging it open, hinges grinding, they all passed through the narrow gateway. Isaiah and Jeremiah, dragging Bailey bodily, slung him hard to the ground—the sooty, shoreless surface of the reservoir.

"You in the zone!" Mustapha spouted.

"So now what?" Bailey postured, his eyes flitting nervously as the four armed black men surrounded him, their shotguns leveled. Guardedly, Bailey got to his feet again, rocking back and forth on his heels.

"Stop flossing!" Mustapha remarked, dropping back, shrugging and turning his back on Bailey as if dismissing him from his mind.

"It seem a mite airish out here," Mustapha mused aloud, shutting his eyes to Bailey, preoccupied.

"I don't like black reporters who come out here to do a hatchet job on me," Mustapha spouted abruptly after a crisp pause.

236

"You just don't like reporters who ask tough questions," Bailey promptly retorted.

"You a scholar," Mustapha spouted contemptuously. "You got a Ph.D—a player hating degree!"

"I didn't know you were such a player," cracked Bailey, defiant but frightened.

"I'm about to take you to school, scholar," Mustapha said ominously. "You my student. I'm going to drop some science on you and take you back to the essence."

"You think you got all the sense," Bailey said with brash disdain. "You don't know shit from shinola!"

"You think you're jive—slick but you just an educated fool! Let me school you on some things."

"If you think you're qualified."

"You is suspect. You an off–brand oreo who's been perpetrating and working with them peoples."

"Are you going to give me that blacker–than–thou shit just because I don't lace every other word with a foul–mouthed profanity? Or fuck every female in sight? Or jack up anybody I happen to dislike? Is violence and vulgarity the essence of what being black means to you? Between you and me all that shit is pretty see–through."

"When you on top, there's always people out there trying to scandalize your name. You been trying to assassinate my character."

"I think you slipping, Mustapha, being so paranoid," Bailey refuted him. "A mouth can say anything, and you a goffer, because you'll go for anything. I approached you for a profile piece. I approached 'them peoples' for a Zodiac piece. Neither's connected."

"Make it light on yourself. I knew you was up to no good with all that skinning and grinning."

"Catz like me is true to the game. You the one who's suspect, Mustapha."

"I hate to tell you but you going to have to wear this

one. I told you not to dis the program. As long as you were down with the program we was cool. I'm going to make sure you wear this!"

"That won't stop me from dissing your program, Mustapha," Bailey said scrupulously.

"I knew you was a pain freak," Mustapha scoffed, gesturing to the four armed black men bearing down upon Bailey with their leveled weapons. "These are my San Francisco muscle. They the temple's crazy–ass hitters."

"You mean they do all the dirty work you won't soil your own hands with?"

"These young men are soldiers. You cannot fool these young men today. They were born with knowledge."

"Knowledge self, Mustapha," Bailey challenged him. "You know better than that."

Mustapha abruptly stepped up and through his bodily cordon of disciples, kicking Bailey squarely in his groin, doubling him over. Bailey wriggled on the ground in anguish, groaning and groping himself.

"Don't even worry about that, you got that coming!" Mustapha ranted at him.

"You need knowledge of self before you can preach anybody anything, Mustapha!" Bailey bellowed, grimacing and struggling to regain his knees.

"You have that coming, regardless!" Mustapha snapped. "It's my turn now, recognize it!"

"Recognize it, Mustapha!" Bailey cried out, straining the throat. "You hate whites so you call them devils! Then you demonize what you hate and kill what you demonize! Call it what you like, the knowledge you teach is nothing but hate! And you're just an ordinary, garden variety hater!"

"He going to make somebody peel his cap, watch!" Zechariah spoke up, stepping in. "I'm going to put a clapping to you, nigga!"

"When they find you somebody will already had pushed your wig back!" Jeremiah jeered.

"Now I'll finish the job!" Isaiah chimed in impetuously.

"Everybody geared up with their Timbos?" Mustapha stepped in, waving a contrary hand. "We're going to Timberland his ass up!"

"I'm ready for anything!" Zechariah exclaimed. "Let's get ready to rumble!"

"Wait in the cut until they done," Mustapha bid Joshua, holding him back with a restraining hand.

"You is shaking like a pair of Las Vegas crap dice," Mustapha sneered, looking down his nose at Bailey, who curled his lip with bated breath.

"Put some muscle in your hustle!" Mustapha sang out suddenly.

All at once, the four obediently and deliberately pounced upon Bailey—kicking, punching and pounding him with their shotgun stocks—repeatedly and relentlessly.

And then Joseph Mustapha, grinning a ghastly smile, set to playing his melancholy violin—playing for some four minutes an impassioned rendition of the fourth allegro movement to Bach's number two sonata for violin!

In perfect concert, Mustapha's violin played on as Bailey's brutal and sadistic beating went on...and on.

§

Chance Bailey, bloodied, beaten and badly broken from head to foot, lay sprawled on the rough reservoir surface, groaning and thrashing in grinding agony—coming close to rolling over and falling through one of the numerous jagged and yawning holes in the trackless reservoir surface—plunging into the cavernous, pitchy bowels beneath. Joseph Mustapha stopped playing his violin and held up a halting hand. He hovered over Bailey's racked and writhing frame, looking down his nose and running his eyes over him from head to toe.

"When you play you got to pay!" Mustapha spouted at Bailey, spewing a thick wad of spittle on him.

"That's how we do it!" Mustapha, swaggering and gesturing to Joshua, gloated grandiosely. "That's how we get down around here!"

"Tighten up, dawg," Mustapha added as a thundery afterthought. "Now it's your time to shine."

Joshua shrank, looking conspicuously scrupulous and squeamish.

"You gots to be in it to win it!" Mustapha exhorted him.

"Your man is soft jelly!" Zechariah snidely interjected.

"You with this or not?" Mustapha pressed him.

"If I wasn't positively sure," Joshua said grudgingly, "I wouldn't be here."

"I want nothing but soldiers with me!"

"I want to be a good soldier. I want to be a real strong soldier."

"We got to take him out before he slanders us and write bad things about the temple," Mustapha goaded him.

Joshua looked conspicuously perplexed and irresolute.

"I don't think you're a very strong muslim," Mustapha complained, shaking his head dubiously. "You don't hate people enough."

"Dude," interjected Zechariah, exuberant, "you got to do it, man, it's nothing."

"Yeah," Mustapha spurred him, "you got to do it, but you can't miss, man. Get right up on him. Get it tight, point–blank—in the head!"

Reluctantly, Joshua lifted his shotgun to point it toward Bailey's mangled and tortured form. Snappily he slid the pump.

"There you go right there."

"Don't kill me," muttered Bailey, straining every nerve to hold up a pleading hand. "Please don't kill me."

"Shut up, you yelling like a little bitch!" Mustapha snapped at Bailey soullessly. "You keep crying! What the baby going to do?"

"You being tested by God," rasped Mustapha, stooping to egg on Joshua in his ear. "You got to prove your loyalty. Most times people don't realize when they being tested by God. I'm helping you out. I'm telling you, you being tested by God."

Slowly but surely, Joshua raised his shotgun higher to level it at Bailey, drawing a direct bead on his head.

"In the head!" repeated Mustapha, menacing and malevolent, spitefully.

And finally Joshua aimed the weapon's deadly bluish barrel straight at Bailey's lolling head and sluggishly squeezed the trigger.

TWENTY:
INESCAPABLE CAR CHASE

FRANCISCO RESERVOIR
San Francisco, California

**Y**ou the whip!" Mustapha praised Joshua, clapping him heartily on his back. "That was a helluva demonstration! I got to give you stripes for that!"

"He a soldier for that shit!" Zechariah chimed in callously, pointing at Bailey's shotgun–blasted body. "Half his pumpkin's missing!"

Police sirens wailed forlornly in the distant and still dead of night.

"That will teach them to fuck with me!" Mustapha spouted spitefully. "Everything's kick–ass! Now it's time for us to motivate!"

Mustapha hurriedly led the way back to the reservoir's broken gateway, guardedly stepping around gaping openings in the hole–riddled field. He paused abruptly inside the framework where the gate hung open. Enshrouding foliage rustled with the breezy breath of deathlike air blustering throughout the outer footpath.

"You think you can throw me a block?" he asked, confronting Joshua. "You ain't about to put me close to this. There ain't no way this can get connected back to me."

Joshua, looking shaken and shocked, nodded his adverse accord.

"Wait until I'm around the corner!" Mustapha ordered him. "Wait until I'm downstairs, drive off and get around the corner on Bay Street! And then jet off in the Lamborghini!"

Mustapha turned to face his other three disciples.

"Isaiah and Jeremiah take the Audi and jet off in the opposite direction! Zechariah's driving me in the Mercedes!"

Mustapha abruptly gesticulated like a fanatical cheer-leader.

"I love you dudes! Let's tear ass!"

Following on Zechariah's heels, Mustapha hurriedly fled the scene, hustling full–tilt down the slender pro-tracted flight of rusty–railed cement steps, descending the northward woodsy slope extending to the foot of Rus-sian Hill Park, bordering Bay Street where Mustapha's gleaming black Mercedes–Benz S–Class luxury sedan was parked. Promptly they sped off in the easterly direction toward North Beach.

Joshua, treading on Isaiah's and Jeremiah's heels, hur-riedly clambered up the shorter flight of cement steps back up to the sharp, inclined curve in the roadside at Francisco and Larkin Streets, where their sports cars were parked.

"Bust a U–ee!" Jeremiah sang out to Isaiah, who put in gear the 5.2–liter FSI V–10 engine's 6–speed R–tronic transmission of their Audi R8 GT sport coupé, wheeled around and speed down the sloping incline of Francisco Street to Van Ness Avenue below.

Joshua, jumping into the Lamborghini Aventador LP 700–4 sports coupé, put in gear the 6.5 L L539 V–12 en-gine's, 7-speed ISR Automated Manual transmission, and speedily followed the Audi along the steep downgrade to Van Ness Avenue.

At the same instant—like a bolt from the blue—the Ford Taurus Police Interceptor sedan carrying detectives Moretti and Marino cruised across the crest of Chestnut Street high up above and raced down Larkin Street, tear-ing around the sharp crescent curve at Francisco Street in hot pursuit of both sports cars.

At the foot of Francisco Street, both sports cars sheered right onto Van Ness Avenue, shooting north in a charging line for one block toward Bay Street.

"Make a reggie!" howled Jeremiah, and the Audi

sheered right onto Bay Street.

Directly behind, the Lamborghini sheered left, screeching onto Bay Street and speeding in the opposite direction as ordered.

From its passenger window, as the Lamborghini rounded the turn, was flung a charcoal–colored shotgun that clattered noisily into the street gutter.

Directly behind the Lamborghini sped the Ford Taurus Police Interceptor—lights flashing, siren wailing—and the chase was on!

§

Joshua's Lamborghini bowled along by the chalky and lengthy breast–high brick wall fencing in the Golden Gate National Recreation Area(GGNRA)urban park headquarters building in upper Fort Mason.

At Laguna Street, Joshua sheered right, wheeling round a tall, glaring street light at the corner of the great grassy expanse of the Great Meadow, heading headlong for the complex of buildings and wharves situated at lower Fort Mason.

At a low–lying curved cordon of cement posts, Joshua sheered left, merging at a madcap pace onto Marina Boulevard, accelerating swiftly into the lengthy straightaway.

Off to the right side, already in sight of the magnificent, illuminated Golden Gate Bridge a long way off in the dim distance, the sprawling grassy expanse of the 74–acre Marina Green whisked by—together with the sea of teeming and towering masts of sailing yachts, neatly arrayed and crowded afloat into closely packed clusters amid the municipal marina.

At Broderick Street, Joshua flew through the crosswalk, recklessly running the stop sign and dangerously dodging traffic to avoid colliding with intersecting cars—with the Ford Taurus Police Interceptor right on the Lamborghini's flying tail.

To the right, a sidelong grove of towering eucalyptus trees signaled the approaching entrance to the mile–long promenade of Crissy Field. To the left the monumental, 1100–foot, nocturnally lit Beaux–Arts pergola and rotunda of the Palace of Fine Arts hovered high over Marina District mansions.

At Lyon Street, Joshua flew through another crosswalk, running the red light and racing onto Doyle Drive's dilapidated, elevated access through the Presidio by way of the U.S. Route 101 highway—temporarily replaced by the partially constructed structure named Presidio Parkway.

"The fucker's heading for the Golden Gate Bridge!" Moretti spouted disparagingly. "We'll be swerving the whole trip over there!"

Directly to the left the San Francisco National Cemetery presented itself to the view—nine acres of grassy, stone wall–enclosed slopes surrounded by towering eucalyptus trees protruding with the chalky headstones of 26,425 graves. Endless, orderly and unbroken rows of countless gravestones—merging together with the roadway's tall, spaced, vermilion lamp posts— whizzed by in a nightmarishly fleeting and fuzzy blur.

In one charging, careening line the two cars merged abruptly to the right onto the Golden Gate Bridge Freeway. Looming ahead the twin, vermilion, sky–high towers and gracefully curved cables of the Golden Gate Bridge itself soared into full view.

Pursuer and pursued, the two cars tore through one of the outer twelve northbound lanes of the toll bridge plaza and shot onto the suspension bridge's 1.7–mile span, merging into the deck's narrowed six lanes of speeding northbound traffic. Drawing rapidly near, the twin, lofty, 746–foot towers—their four gaping portals massively framing sky, clouds and fog—tapered aloft to pierce the heavens.

Before long, once off the bridge and rapidly approaching the Marin headlands, Joshua sheered right, taking the Alexander Avenue Exit 442 toward Sausalito.

Rapidly downhill, he bowled along a narrow, winding, two–way roadway, turning and twisting through the woodsy foothills of Marin county.

Suddenly a brown road sign cropped up in the Lamborghini's headlights, coming fast and furious at Joshua, who sheered left onto Danes Drive at the direction of the pointing arrow's painted–white heading that read:

Marin Headlands
Tunnel Route

Another road sign cropped up just as abruptly on Bunker Road that read:

MARIN HEADLANDS
GOLDEN GATE

Joshua was then moving meteorically toward the narrow, arched, concrete mouth of the single–lane tunnel cutting the darkened passage through the foot of the headlands.

Clearance for the tight tunnel was just thirteen feet and six inches with a 25 mile–per–hour speed limit. A pair of five–minute red lights overhung the tunnel's vaulted arch. From end to end, slender two–way bike lanes extended along either shoulder of the tunnel's single median car lane—into which Joshua's flying Lamborghini charged at full speed—with the tunnel's twin traffic lights flashing brightly: red, not green!

Inside, the lime–incrusted tunnel was ablaze with a dazzling row of lights outstretched overhead along the arched ceiling. Spangles of shiny, greenish light and shadows flitted eerily across the grim faces of Moretti and Marino as their Ford Taurus Police Interceptor tore through the tunnel after the Lamborghini.

Miraculously, only one compact car entered the opposite outlet as Joshua's Lamborghini rapidly approached the enlarging oval of the tunnel's other end. Bearing down upon each other without letup, the two facing cars braked and swerved automatically to either snug side, sideswiping each other with a clamorous grating and grinding of car metal and concrete.

Joshua floored the Lamborghini, dragging and sliding the other car backwards and sideways, unyieldingly, with a scraping clamor—bursting out of the tunnel to bowl farther along the roadway at a spanking pace. Out of the tunnel's opposite inlet bolted the Ford Taurus Police Interceptor posthaste—still in hot pursuit.

Without warning, a road–shoulder series of three small black–on–yellow, leftward–pointing arrow signs signaled the headlong rush of the oncoming breakneck curve in the roadway. Situated out of sight—right at the hairpin turn in the roadway—were the intersecting dirt–and–asphalt crossroads where oncoming traffic stopped to wait at the tunnel's opposite pair of five–minute red lights.

Joshua spotted the rapidly approaching lights and traffic but far too late!

His Lamborghini broke, swerved and skidded recklessly and violently sideways to the left—overturning, toppling over onto its passenger side and crashing up against a ramshackle, square, cinderblock shack raised at the roadside. Plowing into the Lamborghini's rearmost underside, the braking Ford Taurus Police Interceptor swerved and skidded diagonally to a screeching stop—the one aslant to the other.

Spot–lighting the Lamborghini's upended driver's door, Moretti and Marino burst out of their Ford Taurus Police Interceptor together, crouching in solid stance behind their wide open car doors. Firmly bracing their outstretched arms against the Ford's frontal window frames, they each aimed at the Lamborghini with their firmly gripped Smith & Wesson 627 Model stainless steel revolvers—accurately setting their sights on the capsized sports car.

"If you're able," Moretti called out commandingly, "come out of that vehicle both arms first—where we can see them!"

Creaking on its hinges, the Lamborghini's upended driver's door broke and hung open. Out of the ajar door, Joshua's two upraised arms poked upwards awkwardly. Heaving himself up to his armpits, Joshua clambered sluggishly through the car door and dropped down heavily to the ground, collapsing prostrate. Sprawled at length, Joshua squirmed weakly.

"Freeze!" Moretti ordered him sternly. "Stay on your stomach and don't move!"

Joshua lay flat and still, groaning grievously.

"Place both hands behind your back!"

Feebly, Joshua complied.

Keeping his pistol leveled at Joshua, Marino promptly stepped up and bent the knee to clenchingly handcuff him.

"If you're not too badly hurt, son," Marino said sardonically, "I'll take this opportunity to have the privilege of reading you your rights!"

PART SIX:

PART AND PRESENT COLLIDE

TWENTY ONE:
CROSSING THE LINE

CLIFF HOUSE
1090 Point Lobos Avenue
San Francisco, California

Dave Toski, after having a drink at the closed Zinc Bar, emerged from the double–glass door entrance to the Cliff House—the landmark restaurant and gift shop complex perched high up atop a precipitous rocky outcrop overlooking the Pacific Ocean at San Francisco's westward end. Its restored chalky and blockish neo–classical structure hovers over tumultuous waves crashing against the foot of the steep basalt bluffs sloping down to the seething rock–bound coast far off below.

Instantly smitten by gusty, cutting and wet breaths of blustering air, Toski strode along the inclined sidewalk to the embankment at the building's southward end, pausing to look out on the length and breadth of the Great Highway, cutting its protracted, parallel swath of an asphalt expressway alongside sprawling Ocean Beach for roughly three and a half miles. Pensively he contemplated the frothy crests of the surging swells rolling and spilling uproariously onto the outstretched, moonlit seashore.

Directly Toski slid into his 2008, forest green, full–size, five–door, rear–wheel drive, police–version, Dodge MAGNUM station wagon parked in a slanted curb space at a tall lamp post—just below the sloping hairpin crescent turn in the roadway curving sharply in front of the building. He promptly ignited its V6 engine, put its five–speed transmission into gear and sped off downhill toward the stormy seacoast.

Leaving behind the foot of the lofty Sutro Heights bluffs, rising abruptly from the roadway across from Cliff House, Toski headed for the flat straightaway of the Great Highway, bordered by tall street lights set at spaced intervals, intersected with pedestrian crosswalks and traffic lights. Seaside, expansive parking lots and the sandy, slate beach jaggedly fringe the roadway. Landward, a motely hodgepodge of apartment buildings, condominiums, houses and woodsy foliage are arrayed sporadically at length all along the outstretched roadway—itself sidled by an extended asphalt footpath.

Driving leisurely, Toski's craggy, deeply etched features were fitfully darkened and brightened by the erratic light and shadows spread by the fleeting and dappled lamplight. Brooding upon the road—and his problems— he listened in the calm quiet of his car to its music player, resounding softly with the smooth and sultry voice of soul singer, Roberta Flack, singing the unhappily melancholy song, This Side of Forever.

Preoccupied with pondering the song's lyrics, Toski's private thoughts were rudely intruded upon by the sudden and loud squelch of his police radio.

"Inspector 73," called the police dispatcher's sedate, monotoned voice. "Do you copy?"

"This is Inspector 73," Toski, snapping up his receiver, responded.

"Proceed immediately to the Francisco Reservoir at Francisco and Larkin Streets," the dispatcher directed. "We have somebody you know down on the ground. You know Chance Bailey, right?"

"Yeah, he's probably working his beat."

"He won't be working it anymore."

"Ten—Four," Toski replied with a frown after a crisp pause of deep reflection, "I'm on my way."

Structures become more sparse and sloping, thicket− covered sand dunes more plentiful where the Great Highway dead−ends at twin−lane Skyline Boulevard on the brink of fresh−water Lake Merced's southwestern shoreline.

Wheeling around, Toski doubled back north along Skyline, turning off east onto Sloat Boulevard, crossing the Sunset Boulevard bridge, picking up Portola Drive to steer his course northeast toward downtown—passing by the shaded, hedge–lined St. Francis Wood residential neighborhood—first in sight of Mount Davidson—the city's highest natural point—to the east and then the tri- ple–pronged, 977–foot Sutro Tower antenna to the east. Finally, Toski merged onto the elongated slope of upper Market Street in full view of San Francisco's expansive and sparkling cityscape. He drove the round of Market Street until he turned north on Van Ness Avenue, steering toward the wharf side of San Francisco Bay.

§

FRANCISCO RESERVOIR
San Francisco, California

That restricted area below Larkin and Francisco Streets—ablaze with the daylight brilliance of beaming firetruck floodlights—was cordoned off by the recognized black–lettered yellow tape that read:
Police Line Do Not Cross
Above, an emergency medical services passenger cargo van–type ambulance idled at the curved retaining wall, already aswarm with patrolmen and traffic officers pre- serving the barricaded crime scene for the field forensics criminalists collecting, photographing and processing evi- dence; and keeping bystanders and newsmongers at bay. At the wall was parked a white GMC Savana van display- ing the blue–and–gold insignia: San Francisco Medical Examiner.

Dave Toski came down the short flight of crooked ce- ment steps and came at the slender chain–link gate to the reservoir floor, where he came upon Inspector Derwin Quagmire talking together with a spirited group of pushy news reporters and photographers anxiously asking questions and demanding answers. Toski stood aside, pausing briefly to listen in on their conversation.

"Mister Chance Bailey was killed as a result of a cowardly and senseless act," Quagmire lamented credibly. "It's just another blatant murder that we've all come too familiar with, And his son's just another black kid who'll grow up with only memories of his father."

"Do you know why Mister Bailey was targeted?"

"I have no understanding why anyone would want to hurt Chance Bailey," Quagmire said soberly. "I just don't understand why anyone would want to harm him."

"What do you suspect the motive for this attack on Mister Bailey could possibly be?"

"We have no idea why anyone would do this. With these types of things, we look at all possible motives— family, work–related, money–related. We haven't ruled out anything, including whether it's a personal dispute."

"But Mister Bailey's killing was definitely not indiscriminate?"

"He doesn't appear to be a random attack. It looks like the gunman was definitely looking for him. This was no random act. He was the target of a deliberate murder.

"To me the most shocking aspect about this killing is its callousness. This is the most shocking to me. This shows the killer's ruthlessness and deliberateness in doing this. It was just so brazen."

"Were any threats made against Mister Bailey's life prior to his murder?"

"Chance Bailey didn't portray a persona or live a lifestyle that would suggest this as an ending to his life."

"Can you elaborate on what you mean by that?"

"Chance Bailey was a consummate professional and

a consummate truth–teller. He earned a reputation as a tireless, hard–nosed reporter who lived and breathed newspapers and reporting. He covered the news but he never thought of himself as being the news. His blood was spilled in the streets he covered."

"Did you know Chance Bailey well?"

"Chance Bailey was very well known," Quagmire equivocated. "He was synonymous with San Francisco. In many respects he was the essence of San Francisco. He really loved San Francisco and really loved being a reporter.

"Do I expect an imminent arrest in regards to Mister Bailey's killing? No, I do not. It's an ongoing and sensitive investigation. And I can't comment any further on an on-going investigation. It's an open case."

From the faces in the crowd Quagmire picked out Toski, who was conspicuously taking the measure of him in turn. Recognizing him at once, Quagmire nodded and beckoned him with a wave of his hand. Toski promptly stepped up to the gate and Quagmire—after directing a brawny pair of uniformed police officers to keep out all unauthorized persons—ushered him across the threshold.

"Inspector Toski!" Quagmire held out his hand to press Toski's, introducing himself. "I'm Inspector Quagmire."

"I'm...semi–retired," Toski finally relented.

"It's just awful what's happened to Chance," Quagmire said stoically. "I don't know what happened here tonight but he was a good guy."

"You two were familiar with each other?"

"Me and Bailey's paths crossed many times in the course of our jobs. I've spoken with him several times. I knew him as being a somewhat outspoken type of indi-vidual, assertive in his reporting approach when trying to get at matters at hand.

"Meeting him was always an adventure because he was quite incendiary. Although he liked to stir things up, he had a good heart.

"Even when there were areas of disagreement, we were brothers enough to wrestle through those issues."

"What areas did you disagree on?" Toski asked as they cautiously sidestepped gaping holes in the reservoir floor.

"Chance had this great, infectious personality," Quagmire evaded. "He was a very strong personality, very assured of himself. He was a dynamite guy and sometimes the dynamite went off."

"What do you mean by that?"

"He loved the role of the old–breed reporter, the analyst, the pin that pricked the cushion, the irritant. He relished the role that he played. He lived for that. Some liked him and some not. Some thought he was a crackpot—over this Zodiac thing—and some people liked what he did. He was a great guy who brought great value to the news game."

"You liked him, I take it."

"You either liked him or you didn't," Quagmire evaded again. "But he was very controversial. He wasn't trying to make friends with anybody. People could get caught up in his style. He asked questions that would go down in you. He could bring anger out in people by the questions he would ask and by not backing down. Some people didn't like it. I always admired that in him.

"He had this bulldog tenacity. He was tenacious and wouldn't let people off the hook. He ruffled a lot of feathers because of it.

"He wrote about some pretty controversial topics too. I don't know if he made somebody mad or something."

"Whatever he wrote," Toski said cheerlessly. "he never wrote anything to cause somebody to kill him. He sure as hell didn't deserve to die like this."

"Bailey never missed much. I understand he was investigating some stories about crimes that were committed and the people who could've committed them. He was always diligent in trying to cover such stories."

"Bailey had been looking into the background of this militant muslim organization and the activities of a number of people who are working in the organization, including possible criminal activity."

"Bailey was intense, he was dedicated, he had qualities I admire," said Quagmire, evasively changing the subject. "Then he's killed. It's devastating. It reminds me how dangerous the job is. You have to be fearless and ask the probing, dangerous questions. His death reminds me how important our own job is and how bold we need to be."

Presently they stepped up to the lumpish, sheet–covered corpse sprawled supine on the ground. A Chinese coroner clad in protective white coveralls and gloves got to his feet to greet them.

"Jing, our forensics pathologist," Quagmire curtly introduced them. "Inspector Toski."

"The first officer on the scene checked for a rise and fall of the victim's chest," Jing related sedately, shaking his head, "but there wasn't one.

"He's missing part of his face. A single shotgun blast was fired from close range. The damage to the injury site's devastating. The brain's been reduced to pulp."

With a laconic look, Toski bent his knee without a word.

Quagmire nodded to Jing, who partially stripped the sheet, uncovering the ravaged head of Chance Bailey, whose brain was completely obliterated.

Chance Bailey's skull had been violently exploded— his once cheerful and cherubic face shattered to pieces—a gruesome, misshapen mass of clumpish flesh and jagged bone. His motionless mouth gaped in solemn shock and dismay. Only one darkly discolored and lifeless eye stared starkly—at nothing.

"He was gone just like that," Jing concluded, snapping his finger sharply. "Apparently, after a very bad beating he was just confronted and shot."

"Shot dead as if he were less than an animal," Toski muttered bitterly. "What never ceases to amaze me is how the scum of this city think they can get away with this shit and get off scot–free."

"It never really makes any sense," Quagmire mused aloud. "First it leaves you appalled and then it leaves you angry. It's just madness. Why's the only missing link."

"I think I know who did it," Toski confided, "and I think I know why."

"All I know for sure is," Toski added forebodingly, "somebody will pay for what they did."

"Even catching and killing the culprit never brings the victim back," Quagmire grumbled.

"Everything's come full circle to this place," declared Toski, heaving a heavy sigh of resignation. "You believe in the goddamned system until it lets you down and leaves you complacent about who you can trust and who you can't.

"I think I've looked at my last homicide and stood over my last body."

"But this ain't over," said Quagmire, sounding dubious.

Dave Toski's face was convulsed with simmering fury. His temples throbbed with conspicuously pulsating blood vessels. His irate eyes glazed over, looking worse than wrathful. His infuriated mouth quivered with rage as he glowered, grinding his teeth revengefully.

"Oh, you can bet on that," he swore.

Purposefully, Dave Toski stalked away from the grisly crime scene. Deliberately, forcefully, bodily—he unhesitatingly burst through the police cordon tape!

This time, Dave Toski had most definitely and positively crossed the police line.

TWENTY TWO:
OBLIGATORY INTERROGATION

HALL OF JUSTICE
Interrogation Room
850 Bryant Street
San Francisco, California

"Boy, you're lying!" Moretti snapped at Joshua, sitting across from him at the simple, square table in the bare–walled, box–like, brightly–lit room, fidgeting nervously.

"I'm always going to say I didn't do it," Joshua jeered. "I'm a criminal. You know the old saying, man: in jail everybody's innocent!"

"If you didn't do this crime, would you say that you did it for the temple?"

Joshua hung down his head, staying silent.

"If you didn't do this crime, would you say that you did it?" Moretti repeated perturbedly.

"What?" Joshua asked, posturing. "To you all? Yes. Yes, I would."

"You would?" Marino chimed in. "Okay! Did you do this crime?"

"Yes," Joshua replied positively. "I did."

"And that shotgun you threw out of the car window? Does it belong to you?"

"That's my shotgun," Joshua readily admitted. "I've had that shotgun for a couple of years."

"The shotgun used to kill Chance Bailey is yours," Moretti pressed him pointedly, "and you've had it for a couple of years?"

"It sure ain't no conversation piece," Joshua said smugly.

Homicide Detail
Room 455

"All indications are this was a planned execution,"

Moretti told Dave Toski, who sat across from him at his battered wooden desk.

"That punk should've never been out on the streets," Toski said, seething, "not with the rap sheet he has!"

"He says he knows who killed Bailey but won't tell. If he said who did, he'd have to leave the Bay Area and never come back, and he wouldn't live a long life."

"He's not a stupid punk," Marino offered. "He's not as smart or as slick as he thinks he is either. He's told us several versions of what happened already."

"Oh yeah," Toski scoffed mockingly. "They smart and they stupid."

"He's facing some very serious charges," Moretti stressed, "so it's not surprising that he'd try and find a way to get out of this."

"He's pretty scared," Marino agreed. "I think he's beginning to wake up and realize he's not facing a year in jail for manslaughter."

"Ratchet up the heat on him then!" Toski told them demandingly.

Corridor

"If you ordered him to be truthful," Inspector Quagmire asked Joseph Mustapha, whispering, "would he?"

"He'd better," replied Mustapha, adamant.

"Five minutes, man," Quagmire relented. "Do it!"

"Who can identify me?" Mustapha simpered imperiously. "What can happen now? We good."

"I'm not even going to have you involved with it because it'd make the temple look terrible. If you don't hand this dude over to me, somebody's going to pin it on the temple—that you did it."

Interrogation Room

"Didn't they tell you I was coming?" gently asked Joseph Mustapha, perceiving the conspicuous look of shock flushing Joshua's face.

"They got me for murder!" Joshua cried, raising his voice. "It's my fault because my dumb ass went out and did this thing! My dumb ass is going to sit in jail all over again!"

"Now brother, just calm down," Mustapha placated him. "Don't trip. I'm here now, your best brother. It's going to be better. You an innocent man and God's about to intervene on your behalf."

"Anybody who fucks up loses their life, you once told me. And I fucked up!"

"It's a cause. You got to stay strong. That's why we need brothers like you. We need soldiers like you that's willing to sacrifice for the temple."

"I'm tired of sacrificing, man!"

"The will of God will be transferred to you through me. If you don't hear it from me, that means the work of God isn't ready yet. You have to trust me. I have a lot of enemies out there."

"What am I supposed to do then?"

"All you got to do is say you did it, man, and we'll get you a lawyer and you going to get out and you going to be safe," Mustapha promised him spuriously. "I'm going to get you a kick–ass lawyer and you going to walk.

"Everything's on the line for us and the temple and we're in survival mode. If you take this, you're young, we'll get you an attorney, we'll get you manslaughter, we'll get you probation and a year in county jail.

"You got to act upon your faith. You have to be a strong soldier for the cause and take the fall alone. You must accept that God is testing you, pushing you. If you'll just carry this burden, you'll be home in a year or two and I'll make you rich! You'll get paid big! Stay strong, brother!"

Interrogation Room

"I didn't do it!" Joshua declared in denial.

"This ain't going nowhere," Inspector Quagmire berated him. "You're going to answer to this. Mustapha said you shot him."

"I don't want to talk about brother Mustapha."

"This ain't going away! You're going down for this! Did you get him?"

"Yes, I did it."

"Okay, man, what happened?"

"I shot him. I just shot. I just fired."

"Where did you aim your gun?"

"At his face. I did what I had to do. I shot him."

"Did anybody instruct you or order you to do this?"

"No, sir."

"Did you act alone?"

"I acted alone to be a good soldier for the temple. I wanted to be a real strong muslim soldier and I acted alone."

"Why did you shoot Chance Bailey?"

"I shot him first because I was scared."

"Scared of what?"

"Scared to shoot him."

"But you did shoot him. You killed him."

"I was being a good soldier and killed Bailey because he was working on a story about the temple. I killed him because he was going to write bad things about the temple."

"What kinds of bad things?"

"This guy was going to write bad things about the temple and brother Mustapha. So that's what I did. I considered myself a good soldier when I shot and killed Bailey for writing negative stories about the temple."

"What negative stories?"

"I killed Bailey because he—that reporter—slandered the temple."

"Slandered the temple how?"

Quagmire reached out to lay firm hold of Joshua's knee. Joshua recoiled, scooting back with a woeful wince.

"Brother Mustapha didn't like Bailey much and considered him to have slandered the temple in his reporting!"

Quagmire held fast, clenching Joshua's thigh in a pinching, vice–like grip—tighter and tighter.

"Slandered the temple how?"

"You're squeezing that motherfucker the hell apart!" Joshua squealed. "I don't know!"

"Now let's settle the brotherly history between you and I," Quagmire conciliated for the benefit of the room's recording devices.

"I know you for at least two years," Joshua said scrupulously, "but I seen you around the temple long before that. You always treated me with fairness and respect."

"Have I ever made you any promises that I didn't keep?"

"Not promises, no."

"Beyond that, how would you characterize our relationship?"

"Like I say, you're fair. I know that you're doing the right thing, regardless. You're not one of the corrupt cops that are on the streets of San Francisco.

"I'm willing to talk to you without having a lawyer, without having someone tell me what to say or not to say, because I believe whatever you hear me say, you'll take that and accept that without twisting it around and making it something that it's not."

Corridor

"Did you order anyone to kill Chance Bailey?" Inspector Quagmire asked sedately.

"Of course not," Joseph Mustapha answered in a staid tone of voice.

"Yusuf, did you have anything to do with it? Did you put him up to it at all—Joshua, I mean?"

"Of course not."

"Did you lure Chance Bailey to a place where you knew he would be murdered?"

"No. I never heard about Chance Bailey. I never met him. I never seen him. The first time I heard about Chance Bailey was tonight when I was called down here."

"I am going to ask you, as I asked you before, do you suspect Joshua or anyone else was involved in Mister Bailey's homicide?"

"I don't suspect anything, but from the evidence that I've gotten this morning, the shotgun being thrown out the window of the sports car, it doesn't take a rocket scientist to figure out, to put two and two together, but that's for the court."

"Do you think Joshua's capable of committing this crime?"

"He's just ordinary people. But I guess he misinterpreted our teachings. We don't countenance any bloodshed."

"Did you kill Chance Bailey?"

"No, I did not."

"He says he's going to say who did it at his trial. He said you used his muslim faith to get him to confess."

"He's a good liar for a negro," Mustapha scoffed. "He's got a little finesse to it. The devil's meant to trick and deceive. All his appearances are deceptive.

"Besides, guns aren't allowed on our premises. Period. Based on the fact that I've never allowed guns on the premises. We never had to resort to gun violence since I been at the temple. It's always, you know, face-to-face, it's just unarmed. We'd never be part of any violence unless acting in self-defense."

"Why don't you just give the punk up?" Moretti asked, stepping up to confront Mustapha. "You know he did it on your order."

"Order?" Mustapha mocked. "Order what? All we ever order is some pizza and shit."

"That's enough," said Quagmire, holding up a halting hand. "You can go."

Mustapha turned on his heel to beat a hasty retreat along the corridor.

"Where the hell do you think you're going, Mustapha?" Moretti called out crossly to him.

Quagmire stepped up, palming Moretti's chest with a halting hand. Moretti bristled, swiping Quagmire's hand aside.

"The operations commander's already advised me," Quagmire persisted, cutting Moretti short, "that if Mustapha was completely forthcoming with information—and he has been—we're to release him pending review of the case by the district attorney's office."

"What the hell's this?" Moretti objected strenuously. "What's this shit all about?"

"Mister Mustapha had asked for privacy," Quagmire equivocated, "and it didn't seem unreasonable to me to leave them alone together for a few minutes. I guess you could call it a tactic meant to get the truth."

"Mister Mustapha!" Moretti exclaimed skeptically. "A tactic!"

"I allowed Mustapha to speak to the suspect as part of my investigative strategy."

"Your ploy to let them talk together enabled Mustapha to press his underling to take the fall for this killing."

"To have success, you have to have credibility. People you deal with, they know who you are. If they think everything about you is some sort of trick, you don't have the faith, you don't have the trust."

"We never asked Mustapha to come down to the police department during this investigation.

"This kid's our suspect. Nobody asked you to come

down to the department during this interrogation. Nobody's even spoke to Mustapha."

"Where cops have fallen so often is just dealing with people in a dignified way."

"Bull shit!" Marino challenged him. "What about Mustapha?"

"I don't think he was involved."

"Are you blind?" Marino asked, incredulous. "We don't believe this kid acted alone. We believe Mustapha was involved. I can't believe that all this is new to you."

"It's just a coincidence that a temple person happens to be involved. There's no connection to anything to do with Chance Bailey, the temple, anything like that."

"What you're saying is, I'm not going to look at you, you're not a suspect for whatever reason. You organized this visit. What's your motivation?"

"To get the killer to confess."

"Because Mustapha came in with you," Moretti protested, "we no longer have any control when we're going to have first contact with him—or arrest him if we have to."

"So far as I know, Mustapha's not a suspect."

"Just to put yourself into somebody else's case without their awareness, knowledge or approval, that's a violation of police protocol," Marino reprimanded him. "You just don't do that."

"And a detective who's tight with a murder suspect should have no involvement in the investigation at all," Moretti chastised him commandingly. "Effective immediately, you're to cease all contact with Mustapha—even if we have to get a judge's signed order to that effect."

"You have a problem with black males," Quagmire growled, looking down his nose at the detective. "Don't you?"

"No," Moretti retorted nonchalantly, "I have a problem with obnoxious black males."

"Yeah," Marino chimed in menacingly, "I have the same problem."

"Well," Quagmire snarled, "maybe I'll check you two later so we can resolve your problem."

"Later?" Moretti scoffed satirically, "what do you want—a frigging appointment? What's wrong with right now?"

Quagmire stepped up aggressively, staring Moretti directly in the face, glowering belligerently.

At that same instant, Quagmire reeled bodily across the corridor, staggered, stumbled and fell, collapsing heavily and headlong to the floor in a sprawled, stupefied heap—dead to the world. Moretti had swiftly and unceremoniously slammed Quagmire full force—upside the head—with karate's simple but supremely effective round–house elbow strike!

"I didn't do that!" Moretti cracked to Marino in mock denial. "He must've fallen over something and hurt himself!"

"You two boys sure show a sense of style," said Dave Toski, stepping up and nodding approvingly.

"Dave," said Marino endearingly, "you ain't seen nothing yet!"

Homicide Detail
Room 455

"I really have a doubt in my mind this was an honest confession," Moretti said, unbelieving.

"Mister Joshua's a liar," Marino agreed more bluntly. "He's a liar, that's my opinion—he's an admitted liar."

"He's living in this box, and he can't see out of it. It's like he doesn't know the real world compared to Mosque Mohammed."

"We're sorry we didn't make it to Francisco Reservoir in time, Dave. We knew exactly where he was tonight. We had that tracking device on his car. But we just got the data report too late."

Interrogation Room

"Do you have a lawyer, son?" Dave Toski asked sympathetically.

"They said they going to get a good lawyer for me," answered Joshua, conspicuously suspicious. "He told me he was going to get me a lawyer and whatnot."

"Who told you?"

"Doctor Mustapha. He told me we'll get this down to manslaughter and that I would be sentenced to probation if I confess. He promised me that I could avoid prison time if I would just be a good soldier and confess to the killing."

"They should have brought in the one who sent you," Toski said indignantly.

"They did."

"Mustapha told them that he sent you?"

"No, he told them that I did that on my own will. They brought Mustapha in and he told the police what happened in my face. The person who made the call on the killing told on me to my face."

"The police let Mustapha talk to you in private?"

"Yeah. I saw Doctor Mustapha, he told me to give it up. He told me to tell what happened. He told me to tell the truth, tell them what I told the police. He told me to tell on myself. He said the temple can't go down for this."

"You have to go down for it instead?"

"There was some discussion about who's going to take the fall for this. It ends up that I'm the least important, the lowest on the ladder. The most expendable's selected.

"I was more like a guest overstaying my welcome than a player in Doctor Mustapha's organization."

"As if you were indebted to Mustapha and owed him something?"

"The temple had taken care of me, given me a job and helped me become a man, and that I should repay the temple by confessing to the killing."

"Mustapha instructed you to confess?"

"Doctor Mustapha told me to be a good soldier and take the fall. Yeah, he instructed me to take the fall for the temple because that's what a good soldier does."

"If Mustapha keeps using you as a scapegoat, he's going to be successful if you keep being quiet. What else did Mustapha tell you?"

"Then came that religious shit. He started hitting me with that religious shit."

"What religious shit?"

"He said I was being tested by God. He told me I was being tested by God."

"Do you consider yourself a good soldier?"

"I wanted to be a real strong soldier. I am a good soldier."

"Did Mustapha entice you to kill and confess with anything other than religion?"

"He's like, man, you all do this, man, you all are going to be set for life. He's like you all are going to be set for life."

"Set for life with what?"

"With bank accounts, credit cards, loans, brand–new cars, clothes, houses, real estate. You tempt a man with all that, however he got to get it, he going to be ready to do it, you feel me?"

"Mustapha specifically ordered you to kill Chance Bailey, the reporter?"

"He was like, we got to take him out before he write that story. We got to take him out before he write that story.

"We already understood what he meant by got to take him out. It meant he got to go. He wanted him killed because he was about to write an article. We got to stop him before he write that story, he told me. So he sent me to take Bailey out before he write that story."

"Just like that?"

"Yeah. He wanted, when I got the opportunity, to kill him. He said, take him out when you get the chance."

"Over just a story he might write?"

"Yeah. He wanted me to kill him. He was concerned about what he was writing."

"What makes Mustapha think he's entitled to condemn and sentence somebody to die?"

"The way he makes himself seem. Like he feels it's disrespectful to talk about him. What he's doing, who he is, what he stands for. Killing isn't beyond him."

"What were the precise words he used to tell you to kill Chance Bailey?"

"Take him out. Doctor Mustapha has a hit list—and Chance Bailey's name is on it."

"Why did Mustapha pick you to make the hit?"

"Zechariah works there as a hit man and the go–to guy in the organization. But I guess Mustapha's saving him for bigger and better things."

"You didn't feel that what you did was a big deal?"

"I took it in stride, like okay."

"It's not like you knew the victim. You didn't know him from anyone and that's what makes it so incomprehensible."

"What's this got to do with anything?"

"I mean, that's a person's life. That person has family, children, it's just unreal to me that there's no sense of compassion for someone's life."

"I'm like, okay, I can say I'm a black muslim. It's all a game."

"Why? Why would you let another send you to do something? Why would you let people send you to do something when they haven't done anything for you? Nothing. They did nothing for you."

"I had to do it. I had to."

"No, you didn't. They weren't even doing anything for you. They weren't even taking care of you. So why would you risk yourself for someone else? Why?"

"I don't know."

"You'll be giving the rest of your life to a prison term for those who wouldn't give their lives for you. There's a price for loyalty they're not willing to pay. The friendship you have for them they don't have for you."

"You must've thought something!"

"Man has money. I have nothing. I can do this, this sacrifice. Two years at the most. And I come home and be on easy street. I'm going to have some money. Or I can say no, still be in jail for two years, and come home, struggle again."

"Are you pulling a desperation move with this confession?"

"I'm doing it because I wish I wasn't in this position. I always felt that Doctor Mustapha would never put me through this situation. He never did before. I hate what he did to my life."

"Do you pretend you didn't know what you were getting mixed up in?"

"I didn't know what was going on, and I got all mixed up in it!"

"How did you let Mustapha mess with your mind–state like that? How did you reach the wrong conclusion in thinking that the temple would give you a decent life?"

"It's like this. It's the need for acceptance. I didn't have any personal animosity against whites as a race of people or as a group of people or anything. I was raised to accept people at face value until they showed themselves otherwise.

"It was that strong in me at that time. It was an in-credibly stupid thing to do. I can't make any excuses for myself. I had an incredibly gullible state of mind. I was a black muslim, I believed white people were the devil, the incarnation of evil on earth."

"You took what Joseph Mustapha said to be Islam. It isn't. You didn't really look into Mustapha or his temple. They're a whole different type of muslims. You made the wrong conclusions."

"It was more than that. The bond was strong, like you my dude. But he broke the contract we had. And only then did I figure it was all a lie—that it had been all along.

"Now I want to tell my side of the story, so to speak. I'll get my get–backs. He told on me and now I'm telling on him."

Abruptly, Dave Toski got to his feet to leave the interrogation room.

"Thanks for your time, son," he said appreciatively.

"Hey, man, where are you going?" asked Joshua, looking befuddled.

"Back to work."

"What work? Aren't you my court–appointed lawyer?"

"Me? Oh, no, son. I'm just retired."

"Retired from what?"

"San Francisco Police Department, homicide division."

"What the fuck's this all about, man?"

Dave Toski paused at the open threshold, creasing his cheek with a mirthful smile.

"It was nice chatting with you," he said before heading out the door.

Corridor

Moretti and Marino waited expectantly for Dave Toski, emerging from the interrogation room, to speak.

"He admits to killing Bailey because he was supposedly going to write bad things about the temple," Dave

Toski verified, nodding.

"He spilled his guts about Mustapha?"

"Yeah, he sure does feel betrayed. He's broken up, and he understands that his trust has been taken advantage of and he's been used."

"The question now is whether Mustapha's the not—so—intellectual author of the crime as alleged and whether he'll be held answerable for it."

"Oh, he'll be held answerable for it, all right," said Toski forebodingly. "No question about it."

TWENTY THREE:

IT'S THE BOOTY, NOT THE BEAUTY

Star Security
450 Beach Street
Fisherman's Wharf
San Francisco, California

A lbert Powell's office desktop was cleared enough to bend his curvaceous naked secretary, Aisha Taylor, over it—her discarded garments piled onto the carpet—so that he could worm himself in–between her supple black buttocks. Her plump breasts mashed against the smooth surface, she clutched tight the facing edge of the desk as Powell, his trousers girdling his ankles, deeply impaled her—thrusting repeatedly and roughly.

"Something's got to give," she moaned, "we can't go on like this forever. You be married."

"I'm swept!" he groaned. "You keep my whole body under pressure! You make my love come down!"

Shadowy silhouettes belonging to a trio of tall, burly, darksome figures—together with a solitary fourth of shorter stature—glided gracefully and leisurely through the stilly quiet of the somber outer office—from which the harshly slapped flesh and female outcries echoed lustily.

Unexpectedly, Albert Powell's whole office was brightly illuminated by all the interior lights switching on simultaneously.

Agape, Albert Powell lifted up his startled eyes, slackening the firm hold he'd had on the full feminine hips his hands were grasping. Aisha Taylor squeaked, folding both her arms over her ample bare bosom.

"What the fuck's this?" bellowed Powell, standing bolt upright.

Isaiah, Jeremiah and Zechariah, their snarling lips curled, stepped up, hedging round the front of the desk in a menacing semi–circle. Albert Powell looked aghast at the Mossberg 590A1 14–inch shotguns the three leveled at him.

Strutting up on the trio's heels, the office lamps threw lambent but lurid light upon the imposing face and frame of Joseph Mustapha.

"Yo, dawg!" Mustapha crowed, announcing his own jaunty entrance. "Preacher's in the house!"

"How the fuck did you get in here?" Powell protested.

"Pull up your drawers, dawg," Mustapha bid him with a halting hand and a derisive grin. "It's undignified standing there with a limp dick hanging out with no place to stick it."

"Hold that position, hoochie," Mustapha told the prostrate girl, slapping his palm down hard upon her bare rump, "your coochie ain't done working it yet."

Closing in upon Powell, Isaiah and Jerimiah came at him from either side, shoving him roughly by his shoulders to his knees, driving him to kneel on the carpet.

"Don't even think about pulling any desperation moves," warned Zechariah, bracing himself against the edge of the desk as he rested his shotgun on one knee and leveled it directly at Powell's head, "or your pumpkin will go missing!"

From his coat Mustapha plucked out a Dutch Masters cigar and rolled himself a Philly blunt with a small mixture of marijuana; he promptly lit and smoked it.

"Your man kneeling there looking punch–drunk," Mustapha mocked as he went the round of the room, pulling all the curtains closed.

"I felt the good vibes as soon as we stepped up in here!" he scoffed.

From a nearby liquor cabinet, Mustapha extracted a double–shot glass and a tall bottle of Hennessey Very Special cognac; he poured and sipped it.

"Thick baby got back, ain't she?" Mustapha said appreciatively as he ran his palm smoothly across Aisha Taylor's soft bare bottom. "There ain't nothing in the world like a big bodacious–butt bust down girl. And she be a mad rump–shaker!'"

"We heard you hitting the skins," Mustapha rambled on, snickering sarcastically. "You was trying to knock the walls down. You was really tapping that ass when we came in here. You was hitting it from the back. Was you getting some peanut butter too?"

"What the fuck do you want, Mustapha?" Powell asked unresistingly.

"I came to caution you, dawg," replied Mustapha with a satirical leer. "You shouldn't be playing like that with OOP—other people's pussy. You thought Aisha be your little side joint—and you a family man with kids. Truth be told, you one pussy–whipped motherfucker. You been led—or mis–led—by the head of your dick."

"What the fuck are you talking about?"

"Aisha here's one down–ass chick. She be easy access. She been doing you greasy for months," Mustapha prattled, pausing for emphatic effect. "She been down with me from the start!"

"Let that thought marinate for a minute," he said scurrilously.

Powell made a long wry face, twinging with stupefying shock and dismay.

"Did you do me that dirty?" he asked, directing his bewildered and downcast eyes grudgingly to the girl. "Have you been pulling that cut–throat shit on me?"

Aisha Taylor tossed her head, looked back slowly over her shoulder, sneering and looking down her nose at him.

"You get all sprung talking all that lovey–dovey shit all the time," she derided him facetiously.

"You be vicious!" Powell ejaculated, bursting with bitter, grim–faced rage. "You a straight–out hood rat scank!"

Isaiah and Jeremiah pinched their clinching grip on Powell's shoulders as Zechariah thrust his shotgun barrel into his throat, prodding his head against the wall. Powell flinched with fear and, petrified, ran his eyes over the shotgun barrel, swallowing laboriously.

"Hush!" Mustapha jeered, holding up a halting hand. "It hurts you to your heart, don't it? You got crossed out, dawg. Now you getting your walking papers."

"You a payer," Mustapha gloated boastfully, dousing his blunt and plunking down his cognac glass. "I'm a player!"

Once more Mustapha slapped his palm down hard upon Aisha Taylor's tender backside.

"Aisha be freakalicious, dawg!" he praised her, sniggering. "We came here to get our freak on! This is how we get our recreation."

Mustapha stooped to press his cheek up against her supple rump, looking askance at Powell.

"We're going to run a train on this pussy in the raw," he proclaimed proudly. "Because we pressed for time, we're going to have to be two–minute brothers. Let's wax some ass!"

Mustapha stepped up, taking away Zechariah's shotgun and taking aim at Powell's cringing head.

"Treat yourself," Mustapha admonished Zechariah, "but don't cheat yourself."

Albert Powell hung down his head, looking downcast, and then lifted up his eyes, looking daggers of rage, wrath—and loathing—as the trio of virile young blacks took turns humping and pumping Aisha Taylor's repeatedly slapped rump—rapidly spewing their cream into her over and over again.

"Get busy and get those dicks wet!" Mustapha exhorted Isaiah and Jeremiah by turns. "Beat up that coochie!"

"Now it's my turn to get up in that," Mustapha said

shamelessly, handing over Zechariah's shotgun at the last. Zechariah aimed it at Powell, bowed and held tight.

"Let me slide up in that," he said, looking supremely lewd and lecherous as he positioned himself close behind Aisha Taylor, his pants unzipped, and laid firm hold of her broad, outspread hips, clutching her tightly. "She's as wide as all outside!"

"I'm the mack–daddy with the magic stick!" Mustapha blustered, swaggering and slapping hard her sleek buttocks. "I'm going to put this daddy long–stroke on you!"

"Give up that ass!" he crowed as he burst into her, thrusting deeply and repeatedly, whacking her hard and loud.

"Who yo boss?" he bawled at her.

"You are, Preacher!" she squealed.

"Who yo daddy?"

"You are, Preacher!"

"You can't lose with what I use!"

"I just want to be the one to serve you, Preacher!"

Before long, Mustapha's face flushed and fluttered as he ejaculated, discharging himself deeply inside her. His chest heaving, he panted breathlessly, spent and smiling smugly.

"And you do, my honey–butter dip!" Mustapha puffed. "But we don't want to wear that ass out."

"Blood is thicker than mud," Mustapha smacked his lips, turning on his heel to zip up his pants in front of Albert Powell's face. "Aisha's Tiffany Mustapha's eldest child. She be my blood daughter. I own her body and soul. And I share her with the brothers."

"You're half devil, half snake, Mustapha," muttered Albert Powell, who glared at him disgustedly. "You got great caveman style."

Mustapha lowered himself and lowered his tone to stare Powell down.

"I'm half man, half amazing," he bragged. "And as long as I'm in charge, I'm going to keep my foot on your neck. I told you we're taking over this operation, that's like dot on dice. Now we're about to make our big power move."

"We ought to blast this motherfucker's ass!" Zechariah interjected caustically.

"My daughter would be mad," said Mustapha, shaking his head. "She'd be tripping on it if he was killed. Truth be told, she be sweet on him in spite of everything. Besides, she pounds his typewriter too well!"

"If you were Miss Thang," Mustapha mused with pleasurable malice, "we might ram a hot curling iron up between your pussy lips. But since you a dude, we might just yank out your tongue with a pair of pliers! Or I might just put that steel up and dig off into your nuts with my knife game."

Gradually drawing his hand out of his coat, Mustapha brought forth an extremely thin, stainless steel, single-edged razor blade, which he lifted up to the light pinched between his finger tips. Its keen cutting edge glinted sharply. He ran his eyes over it, inspecting it intently—thoughtfully, watchfully.

"What I think I'd really like to do is chop your ugly grill with this!" said Mustapha finally, turning malevolent.

Mustapha stood up, raising up his chin to signal to Isaiah and Jeremiah to lift Albert Powell to his feet; they jerked him up by his arms.

Suddenly and swiftly, Albert Powell wrenched free from their slackened grip and impulsively made a run for his life. Charging out of the office, he rushed across the hallway, tore through a set of double-glass doors and dashed out onto the rooftop terrace.

Sedately, Mustapha tilted his head, signaling Isaiah

and Jeremiah to chase after him. They sprang in pursuit.

"Help!" Powell screamed, lurching bodily across the low–lying ledge overlooking the noisy, indifferent, nocturnal traffic whizzing by, dizzyingly—back and forth—in both directions along Beach Street below. "Help me!"

Powell caught sight of Isiah and Jeremiah at his heels. Recklessly he dashed full–tilt toward the terrace's eastward end, where a high, chain–link fence barricade penned in the rooftop, separating it from the adjoining building's facing rooftop. He jumped and pounced upon the clanging fence, clutching desperately for finger–and–foot holds on the metal links.

Effortlessly, Isaiah and Jeremiah overtook Powell, catching up to him.

With the butts of their shotguns, the two beat Powell down from the fence, battering him—brutally, relentlessly, mercilessly—until he fell back flat onto the hard and unyielding terrace floor. At one jump, the two bore down upon him and ran mad, furiously lunging and thrusting at him with their shotgun butts, pelting him repeatedly up and down his racked body with unceasingly sadistic blows. Agonized, Powell cried out, squirming in stupefying pain as the two wildly struck his head, kicked his ribs, stomped his crotch—their pitiless attack frenzied and savage.

At the last, Joseph Mustapha, unperturbed, sauntered out onto the rooftop terrace. He stepped up and hovered over Powell ominously. Flushed with smugness, he looked down his nose at Powell's bloodied body, sprawled upon the terrace floor in a mangled and crumpled heap. Nonchalantly, Mustapha bent his knee beside Powell.

"You crippled black motherfucker," Mustapha snarled, looking malicious and triumphant. "I'm going to rip your black ass up!"

Abruptly—with a flashy flourish—Mustapha upraised his hand high over his head—his finger tips still tightly pinching the flashing, perilously sharp razor blade! Then he slashed downward—viciously and hard!

TWENTY FOUR:
FOUR:
TRACKING
ZODIAC

Joseph Mustapha gave a brief interview earlier to a newscaster that was re–broadcast on the late night newscast. In his Russian Hill flat Dave Toski, reclined on his window–facing bed, watched the newscast on his Samsung LED TV 7000.

"For our name to be brought up in such a slanderous, negativity type of way, of course it upsets me," Mustapha deplored, heaving a heavy sigh. "I feel for Chance Bailey and what happened. I've never met him, but I've seen him around. There are homicides in San Francisco every day. We need to clean the streets up. That's one thing we can do, clean the streets up of violence. San Francisco's a magnet for violence. Our job for forty–four years has been to clean the streets up. I hope they get to the bottom of it and solve this problem. Our community's flooded by guns. This has to stop. Somehow as a city, we as human beings have to get a handle on all these guns on the streets and the crazy people who have no sense of the value of a human life."

"There are reports the district attorney's office is looking into allegations that the prime suspect in the Chance Bailey killing has implicated you in the murder," the newscaster suggested.

"Rumors of my possible involvement in the killing make me look like a crazy person to people," Mustapha responded. "They associating my name with something I don't know nothing about. It's harassment."

"Reportedly that suspect claims you were the crime's mastermind."

"I didn't do it," Mustapha objected. "They're out to get me. I enjoy a war, you know. I'm not going in with my head down. I'll be scratching and fighting and putting anything in my hand for a weapon to defend myself. We don't turn no other cheek. We no weak–hearted, turn–the–other–cheek house niggas. I got disciples coming up, and I taught them not to turn the other cheek. They'll fight you until the bitter end!'"

"Why would anybody be out to get you, Doctor Mustapha?"

"I don't know why they got it out for me. We have enemies. We know it's not going to be easy. But that's all right because we got an army. I got brothers on the street with me. I got my righteous family with me. We'll continue to stick together. We'll continue to hire brothers off the street."

"Who are you at war with, Doctor Mustapha?"

"I want you to understand that you ain't playing with no Uncle Tom, no house negro," Mustapha warned threateningly. "I don't turn no damn cheek. I got young men behind me. If I say something, they'll do it. I teach my followers never to be the aggressor. But if somebody aggresses against you, fight like hell. You want to destroy me? I'm going to destroy you!'"

Dave Toski sat upright, his brow deeply furrowed, scowling and glaring at the glowing television screen.

"You fucking hypocrite," he growled to himself. "I'll get you yet you sonofabitch!"

From his nightstand Toski picked up a pile of mail to look through. He was surprised to discover a small manila envelope addressed to him from Chance Bailey. Peeling it open he took out a plain piece of paper he unfolded, reading its hand–printed note:

Dave,
I'm sorry I never told you before,
Chance

From the envelope he plucked out next a shining plastic–wrapped DVD disk which, curious, he promptly inserted it into his DVD player.

Before long Toski was watching a pre–recorded public–access television program called, ***Real Responses,*** broadcast by a black cable TV specialty channel called, *Nu Soul*. Its featured speaker was none other than Joseph Mustapha.

"Anybody out to get Mosque Mohammed or sabotage Mosque Mohammed," Mustapha spouted virulently, "God has plans to go right back against you. This is the reason that, after 44 years, we're still in business. As long as you are doing what God wants you to do, and God is in your favor—excuse my language—the hell with everybody else.

"The prime purpose of the temple is to help the lower class black people who need help—to give them opportunity nobody else is going to give them because of their background, because of where they come from—which is from the streets.

"There should be no reason in the world that they can harass an organization like this and our preacher don't come out and give us a hand and our muslim brothers don't come out and assist us. It's okay. Anything that is weak is wicked, and anything that is wicked, we can't use in this organization. But it's good to know that we have strong brothers here. You give us a little more time, and I guarantee you, you're going to see what we have to offer.

"How in the hell can you pass up Mosque Mohammed? But you'll pass this temple up, all because you don't like Mosque Mohammed, or you don't like what we say in here, you don't like what we do here. You go to the white man's establishment.

"We fight the government, we fight the police, we fight our own families, we fight our own people, and we fight caucasian people daily—just to do right. They use our own people to go against us—people like you or I—to go against a strong organization like Mosque Mohammed. It's going to take strong men to stand up, it's going to take strong soldiers to stand up and do something for ourselves. I don't care how bad it might look, if you really believe in

God, have faith in God and less faith in the damn white man, you'll be a lot better off.

"The government of the United States has failed you. The Christian religion has failed you. You have no justice coming from anyone.

"We don't forgive and we don't forget. When they come for us, though, they got to come with a whole army. As long as the prince of the temple is still alive, everything stands. We ain't no Mafia. But it's all about God. They don't believe in the right one."

"Are you saying blacks and whites can't get along?"

Toski looked aghast, taken aback by the familiar voice he suddenly heard interjecting that question—the voice of San Francisco Chronicle reporter, Chance Bailey!

"Just why do you want to be like the people who have robbed, spoiled, and slain you and your fathers?" Mustapha asked rhetorically, acting incredulous. "How can you go to a lyncher, to a rapist, to a murderer, and turn in your brother? How can you do that? Is it not an act of intelligence and honor to desire to look and be like a member of your own nation speaking the same language and seeking and building the same culture? You're trying to force yourself into white society rather than take the responsibility to build your own society. You're still disgracing yourself in trying to force yourself upon your slave masters' children so that they will continue to support you in the necessities of your existence. In those ways you're telling the world that you're too lazy to go for yourself. God and I want you to be freed of such childish thinking and begin thinking like men and accepting your responsibility. Wait and see, only time will tell if it's genuine."

"So you're saying black people are still enslaved by white people?"

"They have no concern for us. Their job is to go down to the zoo and work eight hours. They're out of touch.

They're not serving us any longer. They're slave masters and overseers. That's a crime. Blacks working for white–owned businesses are modern–day slaves. A slave was brought here for one thing: to get a job, go to work, pick that cotton."

"Respectfully, Doctor Mustapha," Chance Bailey remarked scrupulously, "I'm not acquainted with any black cotton–pickers working in involuntary servitude in the San Francisco Bay Area."

"Why do blacks suffer so much and know so little?" Mustapha retorted, indignant. "Because the white man's more than your oppressor, he's the devil. He is Satan. Why does the devil keep your people illiterate? So he can use them for a tool and also for a slave. He keeps them blind to themselves so he can master them.

"Look what believing in the white man's gotten you. You were in chains cutting his cotton. Now you live here with rats and filth and cold. The devil keeps our people illiterate so he can use them for a tool and a slave."

"All white men are devils?"

"The white man's a no–good bastard. He's not a devil, the white man is the devil. If you say you're white, I'm against you. At one time, I was able to call my mother a mother. We have devils. We have a black devil and a white devil. It's a mentality. A black devil could be a woman with a scarf on with a dark–complexioned face. I know who you are. You reform the devil. And if you're not reformed then I must take your head off. All muslims will murder the devil because he's a snake."

"Then Mosque Mohammed condones violence against whites?"

"Muslims will achieve deliverance by any means necessary."

"Deliverance from what?"

"Hell! Hell for a black person isn't down in the ground.

He'll tell you that hell's right where he he's been catching it. We're all black and we all have the same problems. That's the common denominator. We've got to unite and get out of hell.

"Our babies are used to seeing people get shot in the street every day. Let's kill some white folks in a movie for a change. We got to see some white folks die somewhere. There's a little Hitler in all white folks.

"Kill them all. When you get through killing them all, go to the goddamn graveyard and dig up the grave and kill them a—goddamn—gain because they didn't die hard enough. Anyone of color should be tired of having their black brothers shot down in the street."

"Crime statistics show that more blacks are murdered by their own brothers than by whites."

"It's all just more tricknology, more lies, more deceit. What can one expect from snakes of the grafted type?"

"Then you'll never use non—violent means to achieve deliverance?"

"Anybody can sit. An old woman can sit. It take a man to stand. You might see some negroes who believe in non—violence and mistake us for one of them and put your hands on us thinking that we're going to turn the other cheek—and we'll put you to death just like that. This is how we'll do things."

"So you consider killing those people you call white devils the right thing to do at all times?"

"That's a good thing in my opinion—killing whites believing they're devils. Black muslim brothers who do what they have to do. If you're confronted by chaos, you have to stand up and do what's right."

"Are there any good white people?"

"Not one is good."

"Will there be bloodshed in the days ahead?"

"Desperate times call for desperate measures. When

you don't have options you do desperate acts."

"Aren't you preaching hate?"

"No, I'm not."

"What are you preaching then?"

"Truth. Just truth."

"Truth be told," Mustapha murmured, lowering his voice with a mocking wink. "It's just a racket like any other. I just want to get all the money out of it I can."

§

Abruptly Dave Toski's telephone rang. He snapped up the receiver to his ear.

"Yeah?" he rasped, perturbed.

"Dave," Albert Powell murmured in a harrowed voice at the other end of the line. "This is Al. Could you come meet me at the fort?"

"What's the problem?"

"Mustapha's been up in my spot. He and his gorillas ran up in here. You better get here quick fast in a hurry."

"I thought you minded me being all up in your business."

"Please, Dave," Powell pleaded, "I need you to come do me some justice."

§

Star Security
450 Beach Street
Fisherman's Wharf
San Francisco, California

Dave Toski doused its lights before coasting his police–version Dodge MAGNUM station wagon into the slanted space in the rear parking lot behind the building. Shifting it into park, he got out and shut the driver's door softly without latching it.

From his black–leather shoulder–strapped handgun holster Toski deliberately drew his signature Smith & Wesson Model 29 Fiftieth Anniversary .44–Magnum six–shot, double–action revolver, and held it ready. He stepped up quietly to the canopy–covered, green–framed doorway at the building's westward end, discovering the door slightly ajar. Through the cracked door all Toski could see was pitch darkness. Gradually, he budged the door open to slide through and slip inside, promptly removing his silhouette from the doorway. Guardedly, he made his way up the short flight of carpeted steps to the second floor.

At the top of the second–level landing, Toski peered carefully around the corner of the wall, squinting to acclimate to the darkness. Before his eyes the narrow hushed hallway, reaching afar to the other end of the building, was faintly lit but vacant. From outside, street lamps and neon spread lurid light and shadows flitting across the hallway floor.

By gradual degrees, Toski moved slowly and warily along one side of the hall, sliding snug against the wall, feeling his way. Keenly alert, he peered cautiously into each office doorway he passed until he drew near Albert Powell's outer office, approaching it prudently.

"Al?" Toski whispered audibly, moving to one side of the outer office doorway, readying his revolver.

"Dave!" he heard Powell groan aloud from his office interior. "In here!"

"Are you alone?"

"Yes, they're gone!" he groaned again in a pained voice. "I need help! I'm hurt!"

"All right," Toski forewarned, "I'm coming in."

Instead of barging into the room, Toski's outstretched shooting arm was calmly placed before him, pointing straight toward the office sofa where the only observable movement revealed itself—and the tall dark figure sprawled supine across it.

Albert Powell lolled in pain, clutching his face with a white, blood–soaked cloth.

"Damn, man!" Toski exclaimed, holstering his gun and bending his knee alongside the sofa. "What the hell happened to you?"

"I got a good buck–fifty from Mustapha's blade. I've kept up the pressure to stop the blood."

"Take it easy. I'll get the first aid kit."

§

Albert Powell reclined on his sofa, restful and relaxed, half his face masked by sterile gauze pad dressings and bandages stuck with adhesive tape. Atop the nearby table were scattered discarded, blood–stained antiseptic wipes, antiseptic ointment, cotton swabs and scissors.

"Well, watermelon head," Toski, sitting astride a chair and leaning against its back, chided him, "it looks like you need a check up from the neck up. Now would you mind telling me what happened here?"

"It's Aisha!" Powell sulked. "She's a plant. She's been working me for Mustapha, who's been pimping his own daughter."

"You mean, Mustapha's Aisha's father?" Toski asked, aghast.

Powell nodded ashamedly.

"What've they been hitting you for?"

"Simple extortion shakedown like you thought. Aisha's been giving up all the dope about the company's security details."

"Yeah, that explains how Mustapha's hoods knew which security sites to vandalize—where and when. That's what you get, Al, for not living right."

"Mustapha mentioned making another big power move—whatever the fuck that means. They made off with the company van not to mention some company uniforms."

"It probably means he's planning to attack another of your security sites—this time impersonating security guards. Can you think past go far enough to anticipate which site Mustapha might hit next?"

"I might do. I'll have to look through all the accounts to try and second–guess it."

"Nothing beats a failure but a try."

Powell strained to get to his feet and seat himself behind his desk at his personal computer; he started clicking its keyboard. Toski re–positioned his chair to face him, resting his chin on his crossed arms.

"What I still can't figure out," Toski mused aloud, "is how this Zodiac copycat knew when and where to stalk Mustapha's hoods at two of your security sites—unless he was somehow in with Mustapha's group, which doesn't stand to reason."

Powell paused, lifting up his eyes from his computer.

"Maybe Aisha was feeding information to this Zodiac copycat too," he suggested.

"No," Toski contradicted him, shaking his head, "that doesn't make much sense either."

"I'm glad you're on override, Dave, but fuck Zodiac! What are we going to do about Mustapha?"

"Mustapha's your own fault, Al," Toski chastised him. "When you do dirt you get dirt. Sometimes I don't think you know your ass from your elbow."

"What's that supposed to mean?"

"It means one thing for certain, two things for sure."

"What?" Powell snapped.

"Presuming he was overhearing Aisha giving away information to Mustapha," Toski said solemnly, "there's one and only one way this Zodiac copycat could've been likewise apprised of that information."

"Fuck, Dave, how?"

"By bugging your office, that's how."

"If it's not somebody pimping for Mustapha, then who the fuck could've had access to bug the place?"

"That's the weirdest part of this far—out scenario," Toski mused knowingly. "This Zodiac copycat's got to be somebody inside your own company!"

Powell scowled hard, brooding intently until something conspicuous occurred to him.

"Come to think of it—" he ruminated.

"What?" Toski pressed him.

"Fuck, Dave, not a lot of mental giants work for this company!" Powell bellowed. "But there is one dude who has experience with electronic listening devices and phone tapping. He's an older dude in his late sixties who works as one of our roving relief guards. He's big and rugged. You know who he is! We call him the Cossack because of his South—Russian background. His name's...Viktor Zarkov—Vik for short!"

"You see?" Toski cracked, creasing his cheek with a mirthful smile. "You can learn a lot from a dummy. Where can we find this Viktor Zarkov?"

"He lives in the Richmond district—where lots of Russian immigrants settled in the city."

Excitedly, Toski stood up and slid behind the desk, stooping at Powell's elbow.

"Bring up his employee record," he directed, "and display his address."

In a moment Powell typed frantically.

"Five hundred Ninth Avenue!" Powell announced, ebullient, "Unit Number One!"

"Oh, shit!" Toski exclaimed.

"Do you know it?"

"I'll never forget it," he said seriously. "That's in the inner Richmond. It was the destination of the last dispatch given to cabbie, Paul Lee Stine, at 9:45 on Saturday night the eleventh of October 1969—right before the Zodiac Killer flagged Stine down to pick him up in the theatre district!"

Suddenly a familiar mechanical noise arrested their rapt attention. At the same time the two directed their curious eyes to the outmoded Samsung telephone inkjet fax machine set up atop Powell's desktop. Expectantly, they watched and waited with bated breath as the noisy machine emitted the sound of telephonic transmission. Before long the machine was spitting upwards a sluggishly sputtering piece of printed paper.

Toski abruptly tore the paper from its plastic prop and read aloud its printed note:

This is the Zodiac Speaking

Drop by my place, Inspector Toski, if you want to find out where Mustapha plans to strike tonight!

I'll be watching for you!

Come alone if you expect to catch me!

Catch me if you can!

Only Unsavory Dave Toski can stop Zodiac!

Slowly, Toski stood erect, shuddering with his shoulders.

"I just might pay this Viktor Zarkov a discreet visit," Toski said pensively, pausing to contemplate. "You go home and take care of yourself. It's time both Mustapha and Zodiac were shut down!"

"Don't get careless, Dave," Powell admonished him. "You're not really going alone—are you?"

"When in doubt go without?" Toski asked in response, shaking his head and smiling his classically cheerful, cheek–creasing smile.

"No," he answered sedately with a knowing nod. "I

know a couple of dependable dudes who can go along with me."

EPILOGUE:
CONFRONTING
AND
QUASHING
EVIL

Allen Arms Apartments
500 9th Avenue
Unit 1
Inner Richmond District
San Francisco, California

Hovering high over the southeast corner of 9th Avenue at Anza Street is the grand, beige–colored, triple–story, westward–facing apartment building upraised upon a tall and heavy foundation comprising three garages and four basement–level in–law units. Projecting from the building's face is a twin tier of railed fire escape landings, hanging over the short but steep marbled stairway rising inside of a dimly–lit arched alcove. Crossing Anza Street the familiar unmarked full–size Ford Taurus Police Interceptor sedan swerved abruptly left into the oncoming but narrow traffic lane of 9th Avenue with doused headlights, pulled up beyond the street curb and coasted into the sidewalk space of the building's triple–garage driveway to promptly park.

Out either side of the car eagerly emerged detectives Moretti and Marino—their Smith & Wesson 627 Model stainless steel revolvers already drawn and ready. From the car's rear seat retired Inspector Dave Toski fell out to follow on their heels.

Up the steep stairway the trio hurried—hastily—but staying snug on one side or the other of the wall handrails. Atop the stairway they found the checkered–glass front door trimmed in baby blue slightly ajar. Stepping light–footedly into the carpeted hallway they directly made their way with soft footfalls to unit number one, coming up on either side of its front door. Dave Toski deliberately fell back, bringing up their rear—drawing his signature Smith & Wesson Model 29 Fiftieth Anniversary

.44–Magnum six–shot, double–action revolver, and holding it ready.

Nodding noiselessly to each other their mutual understanding, both Moretti and Marino took up their respective combat shooting positions on either side of the wide open doorway once Moretti heedlessly kicked down the weak wooden door, shattering its door jamb and nearly knocking it clean off its hinges. With both arms stiffly outstretched, their firmly gripped weapons pointed toward the room's interior, the two slid nimbly to either side of the door frame—Marino dropping down to the floor on one knee, Moretti erect, standing and staying bolt upright. Peering into the conspicuously vacant flat, surprised, Marino got promptly to his feet and the pair lowered their guns, leveling them handily at their hips. They stayed parted as Dave Toski stepped up between them, nonchalantly heaving a heavy sigh and nodding knowingly.

"Well," Toski rasped after a crisp pause, "you boys sure show a direct and dramatic sense of style that I like. But I'm not surprised that our coveted quarry has already flown the coop. What I would be surprised about is if he neglected to leave us another taunting note as to his prospective whereabouts. Let's look around!"

"So this is where poor Paul Stine would've wound up had he not been killed by the Zodiac?" Morretti mused aloud.

"Yeah," Toski confirmed, "this was the intended destination of his last dispatch before picking up Zodiac downtown in the theatre district—and then getting side–tracked to Presidio Heights and shot to death at Washington and Cherry Streets."

Toski looked about only briefly before he snapped up from a desktop a piece of plain white paper displaying the familiar, neatly–lettered print, which he read aloud;

This is the Zodiac Speaking

No more games, blue pigs.
I've watched you out looking for me, you are bad.
You will not get Zodiac.
I desperately want to see more people die.
Nothing makes me more ecstatic than killing.
It's great sport for me to kill people.
So be ready for more.
Stupid police, stop me if you can.
I am in control through mastery.
This is the beginning of the final end game.
Look for me off San Pablo Bay
On Ship–Trap Island
AKA
Rodeo San Francisco Refinery

"Frigging fruit!" Toski scoffed scornfully to himself, creasing his cheek with a cynical smile.

Then Toski caught sight of something that stopped him dead in his tracks: placed crosswise upon the same desktop was a rare and elegant hard–bound copy of journalist–writer, Richard Edward Connell Jr.'s famous short story, *The Most Dangerous Game*.

"Jeezus!" Toski exclaimed, snapping up the book and inspecting it intently and muttering knowingly to himself. "Man is the most dangerous animal of all!"

"Clue us in," Moretti prompted him.

"It's something the original Zodiac alluded to in his de–coded cryptogram sent to the Vallejo Times–Herald the 31st of July 1969," Toski explained, "about man being the most dangerous animal to kill. Conventional wisdom has it that Zodiac was inspired by this short story, which recounts how an American big–game hunter becomes a castaway on a Caribbean island—called Ship–Trap Island—where he in turn is hunted as an animal by a Cossack aristocrat named Count Zaroff! Does that ring any bells?"

"This character we're looking for named Zarkov!" Marino quickly concluded. "His name sounds similar enough to Zaroff without being too obvious."

"You're reading my mind," Toski agreed. "It's probably an alias in either case. But this Zodiac copycat's studied his subject well and knows his stuff. And now he's baiting and taunting us to try and hunt him down."

"So where to next, boss?" Moretti asked expectantly.

"Like the letter says," Toski heaved a resigned sigh, "look for him at his idea of Ship–Trap Island, or San Francisco Refinery—which is owned by Conoco–Phillips Company—in Rodeo."

"The East Bay oil refinery?"

"Where Robert Naysmith's primed Zodiac suspect, Arthur Leigh Allen, was once employed as a junior chemist during the summer of 1971. It used to be Union Oil then."

Dave Toski cast his eyes urgently to both city detectives but addressed them in his most taciturn tone of voice.

"And by a convenient coincidence, it just happens to be one of the major and most important security client sites of Al Powell's Star Security company!"

§

**San Francisco Refinery
1380 San Pablo Avenue
Rodeo, California**

Crowded clusters of lofty cylindrical towers soar sky–high, ablaze with countless sparkling lights, and shrouded by colossal, unearthly billowing clouds of fuming steam. A tangled network of convoluted conduits turn and twist into an overlapping labyrinth of distillation, hydro–treater and utility units mingled together with mammoth stor-

316

age tanks. Clouding over everything is a hazy, oily, soot–like mist drizzling down from overhead.

At the oil refinery entrance, the familiar unmarked full–size Ford Taurus Police Interceptor got halted at the security station, where a Star Security guard screened the car's occupants. Detectives Moretti and Marino flashed their S.F.P.D. badges. From the sedan's back seat, Dave Toski identified himself to the guard, who recognized him as the security company's operations director.

They were told by the guard that both the Star Security company van—followed afterwards by Viktor Zarkov, Star Security's roving relief guard, driving his private vehicle—had entered the industrial process plant, bound for the outer site, bordering the bay–frontage shoreline, in close proximity to the oil refinery's Gasoline Blending Pool. Gradually, a chain–link security gate slid aside and the sedan rolled through.

§

Coasting in sight of the parked Star Security company van, irradiated by the Ford Taurus Police Interceptor's beamy headlights, the sedan pulled up slowly from behind. Moretti steered their sedan toward one side of the van's rear end. Marino threw a brilliant spotlight upon the van's back.

Abruptly the van's double rear doors broke open—opening out! Bursting out behind them came Isaiah and Jeremiah, both wielding twin Israeli open–bolt, blow-back–operated sub–machine guns with folding stocks! To the ground the two blacks sprang, stopping stiffly in their tracks to level their weapons at the police sedan, grasping their pistol–grips tightly and retracting their bolts!

"The fuckers have Uzis!" shouted Moretti, sounding the alarm. "Hit the deck, Dave! Get down! Down flat!"

Instinctively Dave Toski ducked down and, lengthwise, rolled bodily onto the sedan's rear floorboards!

Irradiated by the radiant spotlight were the hateful faces of the pair of black hoodlums and their stubbed gun barrels. Squinting, and curling their lips repulsively, they took aim and squeezed their triggers, opening fire!

"Give it the gun!" yelled Marino. "Ram the fuckers!"

Opening up on the sedan, those sub–machine guns repeatedly spewed bullets, peppering the car's front grill and disintegrating its windshield!

Moretti floored his accelerator, holding fast to the steering wheel as he and Marino bowed down their heads behind the dashboard! Screeching forward, the sedan sped, full–tilt, with a jarring lurch—plowing headlong into the two screaming black hoodlums and catapulting their battered and crushed bodies into the back of the security company van! Wrenching the transmission into reverse, Moretti floored the accelerator again, backing up the sedan with a screeching lurch—two bloodied and metal–mangled bodies crumpling up in lifeless lumps to the ground!

"Scratch two murdering mother–fuckers!" Moretti cheered jubilantly, braking jerkily to stop the sedan dead in its tracks!

At one jump, Zechariah had sprung from the collided van's driver's door—brandishing his own Uzi sub–machine gun! He dashed away from the van in a wide, retiring arc—at a discreet diagonal distance from the sedan's driver's side! Then he rushed the idled sedan, opening up on it and pouring an unrelenting broadside of 9X19mm Parabellum bullets into it, firing 600 rounds per minute!

Moretti and Marino flung open their doors, staggering to fall out of the sedan and get to their feet. Both detectives were bombarded by a relentless fusillade of bullets! Moretti, crouching behind the driver's door to take aim, was cut down first, his whole body riddled with bullets.

Swaying, he reeled until his body crumpled up onto the ground in a lumpen heap. Marino, crouching behind the sedan's passenger side to take aim over the car's rooftop, was struck down next—his bullet–riddled body crumpling up in a second lumpen heap.

Throughout that violent onslaught of bullets, Dave Toski cringed and flinched at the startling sound of ricocheting bullets—ringing all around him—as he groped desperately for the rear passenger door handle! Laying firm hold of it, he roughly wrenched it until he broke open the door, shoving and shouldering his way through the open gap—crawling and sliding on his stomach until he hauled himself, heaving, free and clear of the sedan! Sprawled completely prostrate, he kept on crawling headlong along the ground!

Even after felling the two noble detectives, Zechariah kept on shooting at the sedan—back and forth, up and down, from side to side, from end to end—until its fuel tank sparked and exploded convulsively, blowing up the car to bits! Set afire, it blazed in a smoldering glow of feverishly red–hot flames!

Cringing inside the front cab of the security company van, clutching a metallic briefcase tightly to his chest, Joseph Mustapha opened out the passenger door, stepped out and prudently stepped up to the van's rear. Peering carefully around the van's back, Mustapha emerged into the open space—ablaze with fiery heat and light—and apprehensively approached Zechariah.

"Good, dawg!" he commended him shamelessly. "That'll divert attention from us while we take care of business! Come on!"

§

Zechariah stood watchful guard over Joseph Mustapha, crouching to plant and set up the explosive device he drew out of the metallic briefcase he set down on the ground and broke open.

"I've been mapping this shit out for a long time!" puffed Mustapha. "We about to take this to the moon, dawg!"

Without warning a bright, flashing red–and–blue light was thrown upon the pair—taken by surprise by the startling sight and sound of a tall, mechanical, power–driven conveyance bearing down upon them with a loud whirring sound! Riding full tilt against the two was a dark, stocky, costumed figure standing bolt upright on the platform of a rapid–moving, two–wheeled, self–balancing, battery–powered electric vehicle with knobby low–press tires—a Segway PT—personal transporter–patroller!

Before Zechariah or Mustapha could react, thundrous gunshots filled the sooty air as the quickly conveyed figure fired the large–framed, gas–operated, semi-automatic Desert Eagle pistol firmly gripped by the outstretched, black–gloved hand! Before Zechariah could raise and fire the Uzi sub–machine gun he held, he was blasted by three powerful .50 Action Express rounds shattering his right arm and shoulder with tightly patterned precision! He sprang back, groping himself, and toppled over, screaming and squirming in racking pain. His Uzi clattered noisily to the ground.

Hopping off the Segway patroller's platform, the dark figure stood directly in front of Mustapha to confront him with the large, six–inch, titanium gold handgun!

"Now take it easy, Mustapha," rasped the costumed attacker. "There's absolutely nothing to worry about. Make no sudden moves—or there's four more big bullets reserved just for you."

"Who are you, freak?" spouted Mustapha. "What the fuck do you want?"

Illuminated by lurid, shadowed light the barrel–

320

chested attacker wore a ceremonial midnight–black executioner's hood, stitched perfectly square on top, its four corners like an upside–down paper sack. Draped over his stocky shoulders, the sleeveless hood's front and back flaps reached almost to the waist of his blueblack nylon, parka–type windbreaker.

Emblazoned across his chest was stitched–in–white that distinctive three–inch square cross superimposed upon a circle—its tips protruding past its ring. Into the cloth were cut slits for the eyes and mouth over which he wore a pair of clip–on sunglasses.

He had on baggy, pleated pants tucked into half–boots. At his left waist hung a foot–long, bayonet–type knife sheathed in a scabbard with brass rivets. At his right waist hung a black, open–flapped holster.

"First I want you to lose that Glock pistol tucked in your waistband," he answered sedately, "and drop it like it's hot—using just your thumb and fore–finger."

Mustapha passively complied, dropping the gun to the ground.

Leisurely the gun–toting stranger exposed to view a looped coil of white hollow–core plastic clothesline.

"Now I want you to tie up your accomplice–in–crime there," the stranger directed, "hands behind his back."

"I'm shot!" Zechariah groaned aloud. "Get me a doctor!"

"You should've thought of that before playing with grown–up guns you can't handle," the stranger scoffed mockingly. "Tie up that porch monkey, I said—and good!"

Once more Mustapha complied, tying Zechariah's hands behind his back, knotting the clothesline tightly.

"Now I want you to lay your black ass face–down on the ground!" the stranger ordered.

Mustapha hesitated, glaring defiantly.

"I told you to get your black ass down—hands behind

your back!" the stranger repeated emphatically, aiming his formidable gun directly at Mustapha's head at almost point–blank range.

Once Mustapha laid down on the ground, prone, the stranger roughly kicked his legs apart to a wide spread–eagled position. Crouching between Mustapha's legs, the stranger brought out another looped coil of clothesline with one hand, jamming his gun muzzle into Mustapha's crotch with the other.

"Just don't start playing hero on me!" the stranger admonished Mustapha ominously. "Or I just might blow your balls off!"

Deftly, the stranger looped Mustapha's crossed wrists with the coiled clothesline and proceeded to tightly hog–tie his wrists and ankles. Another coil of clothesline the stranger looped around Mustapha's neck, tying it tightly to the ankle coil, compelling Mustapha to arch his back to prevent strangling himself.

"You're choking me!" spouted Mustapha, retching. "Motherfucker!"

"No worries, Mustapha," scoffed the stranger stoically. "I'll put you out of your misery. In the case of your worthless life, I'm a big believer in mercy killing!"

Holstering his gun, the stranger suddenly drew out from his scabbard his long, gleaming bayonet–like knife—upraising it snappily, preparing to plunge it downward and deeply into Mustapha's back!

At that same exact instant, Dave Toski stood a long way off, his shooting arm stiffly outstretched as he took painstaking aim with his Smith & Wesson Model 29 .44–Magnum six–shot, double–action revolver—drawing a bead on the knife–wielding attacker's back and firing!

Struck hard in the back, the attacker toppled over, sprawling prostrate—the bayonet clattering across the ground. Reacting, the attacker rolled over into an erect sitting position, hurriedly drawing his Desert Eagle pistol! Bracing his elbows on his knees, he gripped his gun firmly with both hands, pointing it straight toward Toski and rapidly shooting his last four rounds before it clicked empty!

Dave Toski flinched, cringing behind a mesh of metal, ringing with ricocheting bullets!

At one jump, the attacker got hastily to his feet, pounced onto his Segway patroller's platform and sped off, fading with its whirring sound into a nearby dark and shadowed tunnel of mazy metal–work!

Before long, Dave Toski stepped up to the prostrate shapes of Mustapha and Zechariah, nodding nonchalantly.

"It couldn't have happened to a nicer couple," Toski scoffed with a sarcastic crease to his cheek.

"Help us, motherfucker!" Mustapha rasped, retching. "Zechariah's shot!"

"First things first," Toski scoffed, "I've got to go try and find his assailant then—and maybe thank him for it. At least the right one got shot for a change."

"Toski!" rasped Mustapha, straining strenuously against the taut clothesline. "You're a fucking cop! You have to help us!"

Retiring from sight, Toski stopped cold in his tracks, looking back coldly over his shoulder and shaking his head.

"Tisk, tisk," he muttered indifferently. "I'm retired!"

Into the tortuous tunnel Dave Toski stepped prudently, his gun held ready.

It was a labyrinthine concrete–and–metal maze Toski entered with caution—a snaky network of square concrete columns shoring up solid gridiron, tubular ducts and pipes—both thick and thin—together with discolored and rusted metal lattice–and–trellis–work and wheels, winding all around on all sides. Underfoot Toski's shoes scuffed across metal gratings embedded in solid asphalt and putrid puddles of mottled water. Everything was heavily enveloped in murky and reeking mists of piping–hot steam.

On some shadowy and smoky gantry overhead, Toski overheard footsteps scuttling along the metal. He stopped cold in his tracks, lifting up his flitting eyes, squinting to inspect the gantry intently for movement.

"Toski!" the stranger called out to him. "If you're within the sound of my voice, as I presume you are, I must congratulate you on a nice shot! You did well. Not many men can shoot that good. But I'm still a beast at bay! Better luck next time, Toski!"

"Yeah," Toski rasped in response. "Too bad you're vested up with that bullet–proof armor."

"Heads up, Toski!"

Toski side–stepped just as a conditioned, hard–plate, reinforced, bullet—proof vest plumped down heavily at his feet from high up above!

"I'm not anymore! That's just to prove to you my competitive spirit!"

"It's a shame you weren't so sporting with the rest of your victims."

"It's survival of the fittest, Toski!" rambled the stranger. "Life's for the strong to be lived by the strong—and, if needs must, to be taken by the strong! I'm strong so I hunt! I lust after the hunt because it gives me pleasure! The weak of the world were put here to give the strong pleasure! So why shouldn't I use my skill and hunt? We're very much alike, Toski, we both hunt down the scum of the earth!"

"If I hunt it's in the name of the law—not to get my rocks off."

"What about justice?"

"What about it?"

"Justice isn't always legal! Even you must admit: I

picked the right prey to target this time!"

"I won't fault you there. So what?"

"I was created to be a hunter! I was born for the hunt! My hands were made for the kill! My life's passion is the hunt! So my whole life's been one prolonged hunt!"

"You're a born killer whose hands were made to murder, more like."

"Come now, Toski, hunting's the world's greatest sport!"

"For the hunter, maybe, not the hunted."

"Be real, Toski, the world's made up of two classes—the hunters and the hunted! Fortunately, you and I are hunters! We live on the edge. We live for danger—real danger! We enjoy the challenge of the chase! And we've had some excellent hunting together—you and I—haven't we? After all, we've hunted only the biggest and most dangerous game! And man's the most dangerous big game of all!"

"The victims you murdered were hardly ever dangerous. Not to mention all the pain and misery you've caused."

"They were never any match for a hunter with my skills, I must admit. That's always been a bitter disappointment. Sometimes hunting's a big bore because I always catch my quarry! It's always been too easy. So far I've never lost! And there's no greater bore than winning all the time!"

"You haven't won all the time. Some of your victims survived."

"That's why I baited and taunted you to chase after me! Somehow I had to make the hunt more of a sporting proposition. Suddenly I was struck by a brilliant inspiration: I became your quarry so we could match wits with one another! The pleasure such a hunt provides is beyond compare! So long as you live, I'll never be bored, because you've proved to be the ideal rival!"

"You won't be bored if you're dead."

"That's the spirit! With such high stakes, our cat–and–mouse game of outdoor chess has been one worth playing—your wits against mine!"

"What about the innocent people you've killed?"

"How mighty trite and self–righteous you are? I can't believe you're so puritanical that you entertain such sentimental beliefs—that you harbor such silly scruples—about the value of human life!"

"It looks like you've underestimated me."

"Maybe." the stranger said. "I'm going now. But I'll be back...I'll be back."

Suddenly, Toski heard hurried scrambling across that gantry overhead.

"Are you the real fucking Zodiac?" he called out.

"That, my dear Toski, I'm afraid you'll never know!" the stranger's voice echoed eerily, fading in the distance.

Screwing up his eyes, peering upwards, Toski could see nothing except obscure, darksome shapes and shadows clouded over in a smoky haze of misty fog and steam.

Out of sight—and out of reach—this latter–day Zodiac killer was scampering to escape! Far off, he was climbing down a gantry ladder to abscond again!

Hurriedly, Toski pressed forward, threading his way through to the facing end of the mazy, metallic and misty tunnel enveloping him. Bursting out of its opposite mouth, he was taken abruptly aback by the startling sight of the Zodiac killer's satiny and shiny midnight–black executioner's hood and costume—emblazoned with that notorious, white–circled crosshairs—swooping down upon him like some stupendous airborne bird of prey!

Momentarily blinded by the dazzling, red–and–blue light of the erratically–shifting thing pouncing upon him—with its unworldly whirring sound—Toski reflexively aimed straight at it and shot his .44–Magnum revolver, firing all five remaining rounds in rapid, deathly accurate succession! Into a concrete column crashed hard the aimless Segway machine, toppling over onto the ground together with the black hooded costume draping the patroller's upright handle–bar!

In the offing, Toski heard only maniacal laughter reverberating eerily throughout the hazy dead of night as he watched his Zodiac quarry retire from sight—driving and riding a second, back–up Segway patroller! And at that remote, secluded spot situated along the flat, bay–frontage service road, the second Segway conveyance was abandoned and traded for this latter–day Zodiac's modern getaway vehicle: his shiny black Holden WM Chevrolet Caprice full–size luxury car—speedily skidding off into the looming, unlighted distance.

§

"You must've been born with a rabbit's foot stuck up your ass, Toski," Mustapha snarled, curling his lip repulsively once Unsavory Dave Toski returned to hover over them menacingly. Flipping open his gun-chamber, he stuck his left fingers through its breach, speed–loading a fresh six rounds.

"Turn us loose, Toski!" Zechariah screamed in anguish, straining every nerve, his head–and–neck blood vessels bursting. "I'm still dying to break necks, punch out eyes and bust hearts because whites have castrated, killed and stomped our babies!"

"You must be stuck on stupid, boy" Toski told him bluntly, "because you won't be doing any injury to anybody—anymore."

"The brother tells the truth!" spouted Mustapha. "I didn't make him come! I don't tell him to lie! He wouldn't do it, anyway! He's a strong black man! He's just like his preacher! He's got his soul!"

"Why do you agitate these fanatic punks to hate and kill?" asked Toski.

"Somebody teach you the truth, you say he's teaching hate. Who taught you that? Who taught you that the preacher's teaching is hate–teaching? The white hater!"

"All the wrong you've seen is justification for all the harm and all the wrong you've done?"

"White folks look at black people and they hold their purse, thinking black folks are going to steal. Black folks look at white folks and hold their brain, thinking they going to steal their mind!"

"If you had a mind, you'd clean up your act and stop acting like hoods and thugs in general, then maybe white folks might look at you differently and wouldn't have reason to hold their purse."

"I'm Joseph Mustapha's number one soldier!" proclaimed Zechariah, directing his idolizing eyes to Mustapha. "I'm your number one soldier! There's nothing I wouldn't do for you!"

"Soldiers are made for dying as much as they're made for killing, boy," Toski told him.

"I'm a black muslim warrior!" cried Zechariah. "The temple's still a beautiful place! It brought truth to our people! It'll always live on in my heart! Brother Mustapha'll always live on in my heart!"

"Your people? So you discard everybody else? You picked up black bigotry mighty good," said Toski, adding ominously. "Your heart may belong to Mustapha, but right now your ass belongs to me."

"Look at you, Toski, a fucking cop who's supposed to uphold the law, standing there like he's judge, jury and executioner!"

"Exterminator!" Toski snapped. "When vermin overrun the streets, they have to be removed!"

"If we're vermin then what does that make you, Toski?"

"It makes me the Scum Control, punk!"

"I wish you'd just put a bullet in me because I want to be a martyr for Mustapha!"

"Where did you put a bullet into Chance Bailey at?"

"Right in the head!" Zechariah scoffed cockily. "Pow, pow, poof! So what are you going to do about it? Ask me if I feel lucky?"

"No, because I'd say you're shit out of luck. In fact, I'd say you're up shit creek!"

"And I'd say you're out of options, Toski!"

"Well, this is the forty–four magnum, the most powerful handgun in the world," Toski said coolly, making a showy display of brandishing the gun. "And it's going to blow your head clean off!"

Decisively, unshakably—his mouth grimly compressed—Unsavory Dave Toski took casual aim and fired point–blank before Zechariah could even gape and gasp! Blood splattered Toski's firm and unflinching arm.

"You filthy, cock–sucking mother–fucker!" Mustapha spouted rabidly.

"The black tail's never going to wag the white dog!" he said defiantly. "But as long we live in the belly of the beast, we going to cause a fucking bellyache!"

"That's what douchebags are for, Mustapha," Toski scoffed with a facetious crease to his cheek. "Douching."

"The devils keep fucking with me to the end!"

Nonchalantly, Unsavory Dave Toski holstered his pistol and crouched to cursorily rummage Mustapha's open metallic briefcase.

"All the playthings any cult–terrorist toy–kit ought to be equipped with," Toski remarked, taking inventory out loud. "Blasting caps…timer fuses…wire…a couple pound packages of TNT…a stick of gelatin dynamite…a pipe bomb...and what's this?"

Toski held up a spherical steel object up to the dirty, lackluster light, fingering it approvingly.

"An M67 fragmentation grenade," Toski observed with an admiring nod. "We have a perfect place to stick that, haven't we, Mustapha? It's just too bad it's not up your ass!"

Toski hooked up the clip of the grenade's safety spoon tightly to the coiled clothesline gagging Mustapha's mouth! Overwhelmed with petrifying, trembling terror, his horrified eyes bursting from their sockets, Mustapha strained his throat shrieking through his teeth!

"No, Toski, don't! Please, don't, Please!"

"Make your peace, Mustapha," Toski told him unaffectedly. "You've got about four to five seconds to get to hell!"

Mustapha shrieked harder and louder, thrashing about wildly.

"Just remember what Chance Bailey once told me," Toski said vindictively through gritted teeth. "Stay strong in the storm!"

Sharply pulling the pin, Unsavory Dave Toski stepped lively, rushing behind a remote row of upright concrete columns, pressing up his cheek flush with the cold, stark, stony surface. He cringed, flinching with the powerful, rumbling reverberation of the convulsive, explosive outburst!

Once his despicable, deplorable deed was done, Unsavory Dave Toski emerged from his fortified, unbending barrier, nodding and muttering knowingly to himself as he trudged, plodding, away from the fiery, smoky and smelly human carnage and wreckage.

"Stay strong in the storm, Quagmire," he snarled. "I'm coming to see you next."

Stay strong in the storm!

OTHER BOOKS BY JOSEPH COVINO JR
FICTION:
Francesco Ferrari Explores Chinatown
Francesco Ferrari Mines The Mission, A Homage To Vertigo
Francesco Ferrari Combs North Beach
Francesco Ferrari Navigates Fisherman's Wharf
Edgar Allan Poe's San Francisco: Terror Tales of the City
Frankenstein Resurrected
Arabian Nights Lost: Celestial Verses I
Arabian Nights Lost: Celestial Verses II
NONFICTION:
...And War For All: The Pledge of Subjection
...And Peace For All: The Pledge of Survival
Berkeley Bashed: Victim's Guide to the Backward, Barbaric, Butt–Ugly Bog
Elenore Sylvie Jeanne: My French Cookie
Impotent Cops: And Their Wee Willy Complex
Lab Animal Abuse: Vivisection Exposed!
Sexcapades by the Decades: The Twenties
Sexcapades by the Decades: The Thirties
Stay Fit(And Hot)For Life
UWF: University of West(Worst)Florida Exposed!
Yet Another Way The Federal Government Loots Its Citizens

www.ingramcontent.com/pod-product-compliance
Lightning Source LLC
Chambersburg PA
CBHW032241010726
47494CB00002B/574